"I pray you will understand how sincerely I feel your kindness," Alicia said.

With difficulty she raised her head and met Nigel's gaze. In spite of the buzz of conversation around them, she felt very much alone with him, aware only of the warmth in his smile, the keenness of his eyes, the strength of his presence.

"If it were possible, I would welcome you at the court routinely, Lady Coombs. It is scarcely satisfactory for me to speak with you only in the shop." He ignored her distracted flush and continued, "You are busy, I realize, but you must arrange to visit the court while Lady Gorham is here. It is you she has come to see."

"I do intend to make time to see Lady Gorham," she murmured, unable to still the tumult his words had raised in her breast. It was nonsense of course to place too much significance on them. His observance was flattering, to be sure, but very confusing to her. Doubtless she was responding to his authority and capability, having had to rely on her own wits for so long. And there was no denying that he was a handsome man with a thoughtfulness rare in her experience. He meant nothing more than to put her at ease because she was a shopkeeper, though gently born.

Or did he?

Also by Laura Matthews

Published by
WARNER BOOKS

ALICIA

by
Laura Matthews
writing as Elizabeth Walker

WARNER BOOKS

A Warner Communications Company

WARNER BOOKS EDITION

Published by arrangement with the author.

Warner Books, Inc.
666 Fifth Avenue
New York, N.Y. 10103

 A Warner Communications Company

Printed in the United States of America

First Warner Books Printing: January, 1985

10 9 8 7 6 5 4 3 2 1

For Paul, with love

CHAPTER ONE

Jane Newton looked up from the letter she was reading with a concerned frown creasing her brow. "Stephen." There was no response from the handsome man seated opposite across the mahogany breakfast table; his attention was completely absorbed by the paper he was reading. "Stephen."

Mr. Newton had spent many years instilling in his wife the virtue of not disturbing him at his breakfast. Since she had apparently accepted this lesson, her interruption of his attention was noteworthy enough for him to set aside the paper and offer her a slightly quizzing countenance.

"Yes, my love?"

"I have had the most distressing letter from your sister, Alicia."

"I should have thought she would be more comfortable now that Sir Frederick is dead, in spite of the circumstances," he remarked coldheartedly, never having had much respect for his brother-in-law.

"Stephen, he has left half of his property to his mistress."

"Good God! You cannot be serious!"

"There is no doubt of it. Alicia has had to sell Katterly Grange so that the proceeds could be shared with that woman." A tear escaped her eye and dropped onto her plate. "Poor Alicia. Seventeen years married to that rag-mannered loose-pin and now this."

"I should have gone to her when he died," her husband muttered contritely. "But I made sure she would not be grieving and with several of the boys down with the whooping cough I felt I could not leave you."

"I know. I felt horridly selfish, but there was nothing for it. She does not reproach us. But, Stephen, what will she and Felicia do? Where will they go? She says very little, except that they are now staying with Lady Gorham until they can relocate. And her intention seems to be to move as far from Scarborough as she is able."

"Well, of course she shall come to us," Stephen said, determination and anxiety written clearly on his countenance.

Jane dropped her eyes to the letter. She loved her sister-in-law and would welcome the opportunity to assist her, but their own residence was bursting at the seams with the five boys, the youngest barely out of leading strings. "Oh, Stephen, she knows we have not the room for them. She has said as much in her letter."

"She could take a cottage nearby then," he replied stubbornly.

"Yes, that would be perfect!" Jane perused the final lines of the letter once more and sighed. "But I think she has not the least intention of doing so. Here, you read it."

Stephen accepted the letter from his wife, the frown on his brow deepening as he concluded his reading. "Nonsense! She cannot be serious. Surely Lady Gorham could dissuade her from such a scheme."

"Alicia has spent many years looking out for herself, all but deserted by that . . . Well, he deserves to be called what he was, but one tries not to speak ill of the dead. How humiliating for her! I should die of the shame."

"Alicia is hardly like to do so," he retorted dryly. "But I cannot countenance this idea of purchasing a shop."

"She has very reasonably pointed out, though, that with a daughter of sixteen she can hardly go as a governess. Is it possible that Sir Frederick could have left her that badly off?"

"I have heard rumors for some time that his gambling debts were like to sink him and that the property was mortgaged. No doubt all would have been well enough had Alicia inherited the whole of the estate. Curse the man! He has not paid her the least attention since that woman gave him a son. And what good an illegitimate son would do him only heaven knows." Stephen pounded the table in frustration. "Alicia might have provided him with a son had he stayed by her."

"He was besotted of that woman, as well you know. I have never seen a man make such a fool of himself. And to set up house with her in the most open way, where all London knew of it. Poor Alicia has managed his estate for some sixteen years. Sixteen years! And now to have it wrested from her to provide for his mistress and son." More tears were forming now and Jane laid her head down on her arm in a gesture of despair.

Stephen hastened to her side and comforted her awkwardly. His wife was not given to tears in the ordinary way. She was cheerful even in the midst of the chaos of their crowded, demanding brood. But her sympathy for her sister-in-law, her realization of the pain Alicia must be going through, the confusion for dear Felicia, overcame her. "You must go to her at once, Stephen," she sobbed.

"And so I shall. But, Jane, you must not let yourself be so cast down by this. You know that Alicia will not give in to such discouragement. When I get there she will be smiling and Felicia will be up to some romp. You know that. Dry your tears, love. We will do all we can."

Jane's tears subsided gradually as her husband held her and patted ineffectually at her face with his handkerchief. "Bring her here if you can. Somehow we will manage," she gulped.

He gave a snort. "There is little chance she will attend to me." He accepted her reproving look and continued, "Yes, yes. I shall see what I can manage. Do look in on the boys, and I shall come to you before I leave."

When Stephen Newton arrived at Peshre Abbey, he found that Lady Gorham and his sister, Alicia, were expected back from Scarborough shortly. He gladly accepted the offer to rid himself of his travel stains in the guest room which Lady Gorham kept continually ready. He was only slightly acquainted with Lady Gorham and did not wish to disgrace his sister before her hostess. His travels had occupied the better part of two days from his home in Oxford, and it was with relief that he changed into clean buff-colored, knitted pantaloons which extended to his calf, a frilled shirt, and an embroidered waistcoat with a plum-colored coat. He had taken to wearing his own hair without powder over the last year, and felt more comfortable that way.

From the window of his room he heard a carriage draw up to the door of the abbey and he saw his sister, smiling as he had predicted, seated beside an older woman. His niece sat opposite them with another young woman, possibly one of Lady Gorham's daughters. The barouche was old but elegant; a bewigged footman put down the steps for the ladies, who stepped leisurely out into the warm September sunlight and strolled into the house. Stephen quit his room and was coming down the stairs into the main hall when his sister saw him.

"Stephen! What are you doing here?" Then she turned to her hostess with a mischievous grin and said, "I told you a letter would only upset him, Lady Gorham. I should have presented him with the accomplished fact."

Stephen was presented to Lady Gorham and her daughter Cassandra, and set upon by his niece, who hugged him fervently. He stood back from her in amazement—even the black of her mourning outfit could not conceal the fact that she had become an enchanting beauty since he had seen her three years previously. She was developed beyond her sixteen years, but friendly as a puppy, and obviously delighted to see her uncle.

"How are my aunt and my five cousins? How I long to see them!" Felicia cried. "You have not brought them?"

"Not this trip. Jane wished me to make all possible speed, something which does not happen when the whole family travels." Stephen turned to Alicia and said, "I do not wish to impose on Lady Gorham, my dear, so I would beg a word with you now."

Lady Gorham interposed to urge that he plan to spend several days with them, as he had not seen his sister in so long. Although he thanked her kindly, he remained determined to settle matters as soon as possible, and took his sister out into the garden for a private discussion.

"I hope you know how sorry I am about this pass you have come to, Alicia," he said as he seated her on a bench in the sunlight. "You know I never liked Sir Frederick above half, but this latest information you have sent is truly shocking."

Alicia touched the black mourning gown with its pleated bodice and full skirt distastefully. "I know, Stephen. Do you realize that I had not seen Sir Frederick for two years before his death?" she mused. "I only heard from him when he was in need of money and urged me to increase the tenants' rents or sell another horse. There was not a great deal left when he died."

"But to will half of that to his mistress!" he exclaimed, the muscle in his jaw tightening. "It is hardly credible. But then he never seemed to mind in the least creating a scandal," he remarked bitterly, his eyes intent on his sister's face.

Alicia gave him a perfunctory smile. "You must understand that he was very happy with Andrea Carson. She gave him the son I had not."

"You could have given him a son."

"Yes, probably, but I could never forgive his unreasonable anger on the day of Felicia's birth. I remember him coming into my room. . . . Never mind. When he returned to London, he met Miss Carson and from then on I did not exist for him, not as a wife, not as a person. It has been a very strange life for Felicia and me, and now I have a chance to start again." Alicia allowed her gaze to wander over the distant pond and trees on the horizon. "I wish only to provide for her as best I can."

"Jane and I want you to come back with me."

"Oh, Stephen, that is a great deal too good of you, but I am aware of your situation and would not for the world impose myself and my daughter on you. Do you know I am actually looking forward to having something of my own to do? Not that I did not enjoy running the estate, but the constant demands Sir Frederick made on it seemed to make all my effort for naught. Lord, I sound mawkish. You must not think I am resentful any longer. It is six months now, and I have grown accustomed to my new situation. It took several months to find a buyer for Katterly Grange and to vacate, and I am reconciled."

"Why did you not write me of this before now? Jane and I assumed that the property came to you and that you would be reasonably comfortable there."

"I had not intended to write at all until I had established myself somewhere, but Lady Gorham kept pestering me until I wrote." She smiled suddenly at him. "She is the dearest woman and has had us on her hands for two months now. I cannot stay longer. Since I wrote you, I have been advised that there is a shop for sale in Tetterton. Not quite so far away as I should like, but it might do. I am to see it tomorrow. Would you like to come along?"

"Alicia, you must see that it is not the thing for a gentlewoman such as yourself to do any such thing." Her brother regarded her sternly, tapping his gloves against his leg.

"Stephen, I really have no other choice. I have enough to buy a business from which to earn a living. Or I could buy a modest cottage and run through the money I have in the space of two years. Prices are not like to come down with the troubles in France. I see no other option. If you can see one which is realistic, I pray you will tell me."

Stephen had considered a variety of matters on the journey to Scarborough. His sister should come to live with him, but everyone involved knew that it was not feasible. There was not room enough; there was not money enough. He was silent for some time.

Alicia finally spoke again. "It is not such a bad plan, you know. I think I would enjoy such a venture. I cannot look for a governess's position or to be a companion because of Felicia. I would that I could provide her with an unassailed position of gentility as she has known until now . . . for the most part." She sighed and her full mouth twisted into a comic grimace. "Not that we were not the gossip of the neighborhood for several years, but after everyone had discussed the shocking state of affairs, they grew to accept us again. I cannot wish to stay here, though. I feel it would be better to be out of reach of these goodhearted people who wish to do what they can for us. We are an embarrassment to most of them. Not to Lady Gorham, of course. She is so independently minded that it seems not to shock her in the least that Sir Frederick could have left half his property to his mistress. In fact," she confided, her voice bubbling with laughter, "we sometimes make up the most preposterous stories about him, you know. How he secretly instigated the overthrow of the Bastille last year and left half his money to the revolutionary cause."

Stephen regarded her perplexedly, and caught her

hand in his. "And does that help to ease the pain?"

"Yes. We have all but dissolved it away now, Stephen, please believe me. Lady Gorham is most remarkable. I shall miss her."

Stephen paced about the garden for a while, disturbed by his sister's revelations. He knew her strength of character to have grown considerably over the years, what with the burdens she had had to bear. She had been married to Sir Frederick at seventeen, against her better judgment, but their parents had insisted. The Newtons had been desperately in need of money at the time and Sir Frederick had seemed the answer to their prayers. He was twenty years older than their daughter and a gauche, self-consequential man, but he was rich. They had squeezed what they could from him in the way of a marriage settlement, attended the wedding, and then left for the New World without a word to their daughter. Stephen himself had been horrified at their plans but had been unable to convince them of their folly. After selling their daughter and abandoning their son with only an encumbered property and few prospects of improving it, they had sailed away and were never heard from again. Stephen with his wife and their first child still a baby had had to struggle to make ends meet. Alicia had been abandoned to her fate.

Stephen remembered what a happy girl Alicia had been. But there had always been a streak of sensitivity that had kept her innermost self to herself. He pictured her now making light of her fate with Lady Gorham and shuddered. "You are determined to have a business?"

"I think it would be my wisest choice, yes. You do understand?"

"Oh, I understand," he replied with suppressed anger. "If your misbegotten husband were still alive, I think I would choke him to death myself."

"Well, fortunately Francis Tackar has saved you the trouble."

"Do you know that?" he demanded. "Do you know that it was with Tackar that he dueled?"

"I know it. I can feel it. Stephen . . . there is something more I must tell you." Alicia bit her lip and hesitated, while her brother stopped his pacing to stand before her. "I believe you met Francis Tackar when you stayed with me at the grange some years ago." Her brother nodded encouragement when she paused. "He has a very handsome property of his own not far from the grange but he was intent on buying it. I refused to sell to him, but the solicitor insisted that the property had to be sold to divide Sir Frederick's estate. It took me some time, but I found a buyer willing to better Tackar's price and the lawyer agreed that it had been prudent to wait. At the last moment Tackar overbid the new buyer and he now owns the grange." Alicia's eyes held a smoldering anger and her hands agitatedly plucked at her skirt. "He informed me," she said, her voice choking, "that he had purchased the grange for me and that I might stay on there if I . . . received him when he chose to come to me."

"By God, I shall kill him!" her brother rasped.

"No, you shall not," Alicia said firmly. "You must understand, Stephen, that Sir Frederick's . . . behavior toward me gave rise to some strange speculation in the neighborhood. I have told no one of Tackar's proposition. I tell you now only as a safeguard for the future. My purpose in leaving the area is to be rid of him. He is disgusting, and disgustingly persistent. No one here shall know where I go except Lady Gorham, under promise to disclose my direction to no one. I wish you to abide by this also. Oh, Stephen," she cried, alarmed by the anger which flared in his eyes, "it is not worth taking note of such scum. He could buy and sell you and me twenty times, a hundred times over. I will not have you tangle with him. He is a dangerous, unprincipled villain. Promise me, Stephen."

"I cannot. I will not stand for such an insult to you."

"Promise me, Stephen." Alicia's eyes snapped with determination. "I have quite enough to bear without such an added responsibility. He would kill you, you know. Oh, I know you do not lack the courage to face him, but I should never be able to face my dearest Jane. Promise me, Stephen."

"I cannot," he said stubbornly.

"You must. I shall have your promise now, or I shall never speak to you again. I mean it, Stephen. Promise me."

Stephen's lips compressed into a tight line. "I promise you."

"Thank you, Stephen. I understand that it goes against the grain with you but I have had misery enough without adding you to it. Dear brother, I would not have told you except . . . well, someone else should know. And should I need your help, I will not have to go into explanations in a letter. Now," Alicia shrugged off the concern and bestowed a cheerful smile on him, "let me tell you what I know of this shop I am to see tomorrow. Tetterton is rather midway between York and Hull and the shop does a sizable business in dry goods—cotton twills, stuffs, bombazines, sarsnets, satins, millinery, pelisses, dresses, and so forth. It is by way of being a linen drapers, too, and a plumassier." At Stephen's blank look she explained, "You know, ostrich and fancy feathers and artificial flowers for hats and bonnets. They carry ribbons and lace and fancy trimmings as well as tippets and muffs and such. I shall so enjoy being surrounded by such a selection of goods, and no doubt shall fit Felicia up in style. There is a young man who could stay on with the business, but the owner is ill and wishes to sell. So I would have someone with experience as my assistant."

Stephen was horrified at the very sound of such an endeavor but restrained himself by asking only, "Do you not think that people will hesitate to patronize a shop owned by a young woman?"

Alicia gave a gasp of laughter. "No doubt. I had thought to powder my hair and wear a cap which would make me appear quite elderly." She pulled a handkerchief from her reticule, tucked it over her auburn curls, and pursed her mouth. "Surely I shall pass for fifty," she grinned, her eyes sparkling in the late morning sun.

"Indeed," her brother retorted, as he snatched the handkerchief off her head. "I'll be bound you will attract customers just to see such a performance. I daresay you will make a go of it, Alicia, but you are to remember that Jane and I will provide you and Felicia with a home if you ever need it."

"That I will never forget. It shall be my port in a storm, I promise you." Alicia rose and shook hands with her brother. "We are agreed, then. You cannot like the scheme, I know, but I am delighted that you are willing to accept it. Thank you, Stephen. Now tell me of Jane and the boys."

CHAPTER TWO

In spite of an early start it was afternoon before Alicia and her brother and daughter reached the town of Tetterton. The main street was wide and boasted a green between two secondary lanes which diverged from it. The row of shops was handsome, some with slightly bowed windows and sparkling small panes of glass. Alicia noted that the inn, the Feather and Flask, was an old brick building with numerous gables. A glistening red ivy covered most of its surface. The inn chimneys dotted the skyline and welcoming smoke drifted forth to proclaim that the establishment was well used. A glimpse of the stables behind showed a modest amount of activity going forth. Next there was a bookseller's shop, obviously given over to prints and paintings as well. The pastry cook's front was narrow and somewhat dark, but more than made up for by the tantalizing aroma of freshly baked breads which issued forth.

Alicia's eye next fell on an older sign, Joseph Dean, Linen Draper and Haberdasher, Established 1775. She gave a sigh of contentment and smiled at Stephen. "Here it is. Shall we have Lady Gorham's barouche taken to the inn? No doubt you are both sharp set, but I cannot wait to see the shop."

Stephen and Felicia agreed to postpone their meal, as both were only slightly less interested than Alicia herself in ascertaining the condition of her proposed purchase. Stephen appraised the double-fronted building with its three fan windows skeptically, but noted that it would take little more than a coat of trim paint to make it look very attractive. The room into which they entered was enormous. Shelves on either side were stacked with rolls of fabric and reached at least twelve feet to the ceiling. There were tables, counters, chairs, and ladders in the first room, with a smaller room behind where ready-made items were displayed. Mr. Dean himself came to assist them; he looked sallow and shrunken and Alicia had a strong desire to recommend that he seat himself. She did not wish to embarrass or upset him, so she quelled her desire and allowed him to explain to her the workings of his shop. His assistant, Gregory Allerton, quietly and efficiently assisted the customers who wandered in during their tour of inspection. These customers were of as much interest to Alicia as the inventory Mr. Dean rattled off of Irish poplins, French gloves, Indian muslins, brocades, and a staggering variety of other items. The shop was obviously patronized by a wide range of country society, including men, women, and children of almost every class.

Mr. Allerton treated them each respectfully, and he surprised Alicia by showing great deference to an eccentrically dressed elderly woman who tended to snap at him.

"You need not tell me these will wear well, young man, for I have the evidence of my own eyes to disprove it. Did I not buy a similar pair of gloves not two years past? Look at them now—a bundle of rags," she stormed, waving the offending items in his face. "There is not an item carried in this shop which can hold up to a bit of use."

"Perhaps if you were to consider these kid gloves rather than the satin, my lady," the young man suggested deferentially.

"Kid gloves? Why, they cost the earth!" she protested with a glare.

"They justify the extra expense by how well they

wear, I assure you. And our price for them is quite reasonable."

"Reasonable! I should not consider two guineas reasonable. Why, in my youth they were to be had in London for under a guinea." The old woman's eyes glazed reminiscently. "I had a pair of lavender kid gloves for ten years. Now that is something you cannot provide nowadays—a pair of gloves which will wear for ten years! Ten days, more like."

Mr. Allerton, uncomfortable under this attack before Alicia and her party, cast a worried glance at Mr. Dean, who hastily excused himself from them and trotted over to the recalcitrant customer.

"Good day, my lady. Is there some problem? Perhaps I can personally assist you to find what you need."

Her ladyship bent a disparaging eye on him. "I doubt it, Mr. Dean. You cannot produce what you do not carry, which is quality merchandise."

"If your ladyship wishes to have me order something from York or London . . ." he suggested tentatively.

"And pay for the service? I should think not. My son can bring me anything I need, I thank you."

At this point Mr. Allerton re-entered the conversation. "Perhaps you would care to consider these white satin mitts for the time being, Lady Stronbert. They might serve until the marquis makes a journey to town." He laid the mitts carefully on the counter and murmured, after a questioning glance at Mr. Dean, a reduced price for the item.

Alicia watched appreciatively as the old woman's stubbornly set face relaxed somewhat in her belief that the battle was won. Not that her ladyship immediately agreed to the purchase; she examined the mitts minutely and, unable to find any fault with them, grudgingly said, "You may put them on my account." Mr. Dean voiced his appreciation and excused himself while his assistant wrapped the tiny package. Wiping his forehead, he returned to Alicia muttering apologetically of the dowager marchioness of Stronbert before he resumed his discussion of the shop. Just as they entered the rear cubicle that served as an office, Alicia saw the customer depart with a swish of her incredible orange-striped puce walking dress over old-fashioned panniers.

"I fear I have not been up to keeping ahead of the paper work this last half year," Mr. Dean remarked with a wave at the disorderly piles, "but you will find that everything is paid for immediately." He began to cough discreetly, and turned aside from them when he was unable to contain the racking gasps which overtook him. Alicia quickly pulled up a chair for him and Stephen gently seated him in it. It was several minutes before he was able to recover himself to speak further with them.

"I beg your pardon," he finally managed. He turned red-rimmed eyes to Alicia and explained, "I am anxious to sell the property and the business, as you can see, due to my health. I should like to show you the cottage myself, but I fear I need to rest for a moment." He handed a ring of large keys to Stephen and explained that the cottage was right behind the shop, facing on Fetter Lane and could be reached through the rear of the shop or by going back to the entrance and turning down the lane. "I wish you will understand that the cottage is very small and not in the best order at this moment," he apologized. "I have not taken care of it as I should since my wife died several years ago."

Alicia chose to exit through the rear of the office and found a small L-shaped, overgrown garden with a well-traversed path leading to the small white cottage. There was not a great deal of space in the kitchen or the maid's room, and the dining room and sitting room beyond were only of moderate size. But the wood wainscoting was attractive. Somehow it reminded Alicia in miniature of the home of a friend she had

had as a girl. The entry hall had stairs leading directly up to the floor above, where two bedrooms came off either side. These rooms were dusty and dark, and Alicia hurried to open the dark and fading draperies. When the autumn sun shone into the rooms, dust drops dancing in its beams, there was an indefinable change in the atmosphere. Alicia and her daughter smiled at one another suddenly and a decision was made. "We shall have it," Alicia announced.

Stephen turned an alarmed countenance on his sister. "But you have not even seen it from the front yet. And what about the shop? Mr. Dean is obviously months behind in his bookkeeping and . . ."

"Now, Stephen, you know that matters not the very least. If you are willing, I would have you negotiate the price with him. But do not take advantage of his illness. I can afford to pay a fair price since the cottage will be adequate for us."

"But, Alicia, it is tiny!" he protested.

"Yes, but it is also charming and we shall easily make do. And Stephen, make sure that the assistant, Mr. Allerton, is willing to work for a woman. Also, find out how soon I may take possession. I want things settled as quickly as possible. My solicitor is in Scarborough, and the funds from the sale of Katterly Grange, my share of them, are immediately available."

Stephen could not accept this rash decision without demur. He was used to handling all the business for his family and found it difficult to see his sister invest her modest financial worth in such an endeavor on the basis of a few minutes' inspection. His voice was tinged with sarcasm as he asked, "Would you not rather prefer to handle the transaction yourself?"

Alicia bent a quizzing look on him. "You, too, Stephen? I have managed an estate for something like sixteen years, and I have had a rather successful time of it, you know. It was difficult, not to say impossible, at the start to convince those I dealt with that I took the position seriously. I am no less serious about this endeavor, and I have seen several businesses in the last two months. This shop is ideal for me. Yes, I should like to handle the transaction, but Mr. Dean will feel more comfortable if you do so. However, if you object . . ." Her eyes held his steadily, bringing a flush to his cheeks.

"I shall be happy to assist you," he admitted grudgingly. "Lord, Alicia, when you stare me down that way I wonder that I should ever question your judgment. But one is not used to having a woman make such a large decision, and on such a brief inspection."

"Few women are called on to do so. I could dither and worry and consider all the drawbacks, of course. But then I should probably lose the shop. Shall we go out the front way to see the facade of this gem?" she asked her companions laughingly.

They were all delighted with the twin-gabled appearance of the cottage from the lane. The half-timbered structure had latticed windows on the ground floor and in each of the bedrooms above which gave it an appealing symmetry and simplicity. Felicia pointed out the autumnal cyclamen and blue cornflowers interspersed with golden arnica that grew around the cottage and added their colors to the scene. There were trees along the lane and it was but a few steps to the main street with its green across from Mr. Dean's shop.

"Stephen, if Mr. Dean is willing, I should be interested in purchasing the furniture with the house," Alicia commented as her daughter skipped ahead of them down the lane.

"You might be able to afford something better, my dear," he suggested.

"No doubt, but I shall not have the time, I fear."

"As you wish."

Mr. Dean was delighted to rid himself of the whole. He was planning to let a furnished cottage in Cornwall and had no intention of carting his furniture to such a remote locale. He and Stephen quickly came to an agreement on a price for the whole which Alicia feared was below its worth. She held her tongue, however, as her brother imperceptibly shook his head at her when she would have protested. Over a late luncheon at the Feather and Flask he explained, "Mr. Dean had set the price a trifle high so that we might bargain. I assure you that he is perfectly satisfied with the conclusion. He is aware that he is leaving the business in a state of chaos which will absorb a great deal of time for you. And he is in a hurry to be rid of the business, which will always cost a seller, as I am sure you know. We have not taken advantage of his illness, I assure you. He will be out of the cottage within the month, but his suggestion that you might stay here, at the Feather and Flask, for a few weeks ahead of time to acquaint yourself with the workings before he leaves is a wise one. I feel sure Mr. Allerton was sincere in his assertion that he would be pleased to work for you, and give you the benefit of what experience he has. You know, Alicia, I am tempted to believe that this whole endeavor of yours is like to prosper," he remarked with a cheerful grin.

"There is one thing," Felicia began hesitantly.

"Yes, love?" her mother prompted her.

"I shall miss riding dreadfully," she admitted.

"Yes, and I. I dare say we can work it out, though. Wait until we are settled here and I have the time to look about us for a solution, can you?"

"Of course, Mama." Felicia sipped at her cider thoughtfully. "I shall enjoy it here, I think. I saw several young ladies strolling along the street as we came out."

Alicia sighed and her forehead creased in an anxious frown. "You must realize, my dear, that in taking the shop I have lowered our social standing. It may not be possible for you to associate with all of the young women you would choose." Alicia's troubled eyes sought her brother's. "That is, of course, the worst of it. I could work my fingers to the bone on the estate and yet maintain our standing because it was not obvious. I shall hate to see Felicia snubbed because of this." She returned her gaze to her daughter and reached out a hand to clasp the girl's firmly. "It is not easy to accept one's reduced circumstances, ever. You shall have to be brave, my love. I could not think of a better solution to our problems than a shop, but things will not be as they were before."

"Oh, Mama, do not think me such a gudgeon! What do I care for those who will snub us?" Felicia cried. She could not bear to see her mother troubled on her account after watching her work for years only to be tossed about in such a manner. "I shall have more than enough to do with you in the shop. There will not be so much time for visits and teas and rides."

For the first time since Stephen had arrived he saw Alicia's eyes overbright with the suspicion of tears. His sister could obviously bear any burden for herself, but she could not so easily see her daughter suffer for their situation. He wanted nothing more than to pack the two of them off with him to his home and protect them from their fate, but he was realistic enough to accept that it could not be so. "I think perhaps Felicia should not spend much time in the shop," he suggested in a gruff voice.

"No, of course not. I have no intention of allowing such a thing," Alicia retorted, as she had managed to gain control over her emotions again.

"Not help in the shop!" Felicia wailed. "If I am to have no friends, and no rides, what else am I to do?" she asked mulishly, knowing that she had phrased the question so as to hurt her mother but upset enough not to care.

Surprisingly, Alicia was not in the least put out by this behavior. "My dear girl, you may not have noticed that the cottage we are to occupy is in need of a great deal of work. Your uncle feels, as I do, that if you stay out of the shop some of the taint of it will not rub off on you. But I assure you that I have plenty for you to do. And," she added helpfully, "we will have merchandise enough no doubt to squander a little on your clothes. You would not believe, Stephen, how clever she is with a needle. She has made most of her own clothes for the last two years with only some ideas from the fashion magazines. Should our endeavor fail, I have every intention of sending her out for a seamstress!"

Felicia giggled and her uncle looked puzzled at this jesting acceptance of their penury. Could his dear Jane be so calm in the face of such a fate? Could he? "We should be returning to Lady Gorham's. It will be dark before we arrive, even now," he said. Stephen picked up his cane and gloves and assisted his sister and niece with their belongings. As they left their private parlor Alicia caught a glimpse of the spacious kitchen hung about with copper and tin utensils which shone; hams, tongues, and flitches of bacon suspended from the ceiling. She caught a glimpse of Lady Gorham's coachman seated at a scoured deal table on a high-backed oaken settle with a foaming tankard of ale in his hand. How comfortable it looks, she thought. "Stephen, before we leave I should like to arrange to stay here in two weeks' time. Felicia, you may choose to come then, or when we may occupy the cottage."

Felicia had long since repented her outburst and declared, "I should like to come when you do, Mama, if you please."

The landlord showed them the modest accommodation they sought, an oak-paneled room with a deep bow window facing onto the High Street. The women were delighted with the room and settled that they would take it for a week or two when they returned. "For I have a suspicion," Alicia confided to her brother, "that Mr. Dean will be more than ready to leave when the transaction is completed. and I do not believe that will take the whole of a month."

Stephen shook his head helplessly. "You are rushing things, my dear. Heaven knows these solicitors always manage to slosh about for unmerciful lengths of time."

But in the end Alicia was proved right. Stephen left the morning after their visit to Tetterton, and Alicia drove in to Scarborough to set her solicitor in motion. Mr. Crew had a fondness for his young (to a sixty-two year old man thirty-four was young) client, and, once he saw that her mind was made up, worked with all possible speed to complete the arrangements. Lady Gorham regretted their early departure but promised to visit them once they were settled. "And do not press me to stay at your cottage," she said forcefully. "You have described it to admiration and I shall be delighted to see it, but if you have an inch to spare for a guest I shall be most surprised. No, I shall stay at the inn you mentioned—the Flashing Feather, was it?"

"No," Alicia laughed, "the Feather and Flask, but we can make room for you in the cottage."

"Nonsense. Not another word on the matter. Indeed, I believe I have an acquaintance in the neighborhood of Tetterton. Though I dare say she would not be all that excited to see me. Quite an eccentric she is," proclaimed Lady Gorham, who often appeared to have pretensions in that direction herself.

Alicia accepted this decision easily enough, but remarked, "I want nothing more than to have you visit, Lady Gorham, but there is no blinking the fact that I am becoming a shopkeeper. It will change our station, and I cannot expect you to show me such kind observance as has been your habit."

"Disabuse your mind of the fear that I shall cut you, my dear. I am proud of the way you have taken hold after such a shock and have nothing but admiration for you. I shall bring Cassandra with me. Felicia may lack for company for a while," she said thoughtfully.

"Yes, I fear that is so. You have been much too

good to us, Lady Gorham, and I only hope that one day we shall be able to return your kindness."

Alicia and her daughter were sent off in a flood of tears and hugs in a post-chaise Alicia insisted on hiring, much against Lady Gorham's wishes. Their trunks were strapped to the carriage; a carter had been hired to bring forward the remainder of their possessions in two weeks' time. Felicia gave a last forlorn wave at the diminishing figures and sat silent beside her mother for a while.

At sixteen Felicia had had a most unusual upbringing, since she had seen her father rarely more often than once a year when he came to Katterly Grange to assure himself that everything possible was being done to produce the maximum rents from his tenants and the minimum expenditure in the household. He had paid no attention to Felicia at all on these visits, and had verbally abused her mother during the entire length of his stays. There had been neighbors who had refused to include Felicia in their amusements because of the strange situation at the grange. But there were also those kindhearted people who accepted the laughing, spirited girl on her own merit. And these last few years the resistance of even the most hardnosed had been broken down as their youthful offspring (frequently male) had insisted that Felicia be a part of their activities. She was fiercely loyal to her mother; over the years she had heard comments enough which had sparked a strong protectiveness in her toward Alicia. But she was only sixteen and occasionally a stubborn streak of selfishness asserted itself, as was only natural. She was ashamed when she hurt her mother, because she was more aware than most young women of her age just how much her mother had done for her, and how much Alicia had had to bear through no fault of her own.

Now Felicia tried to imagine the life she would lead in Tetterton and it frightened her. She would know absolutely no one there, and she would not be accepted by those young women of family that she was used to associating with. Felicia unconsciously lifted her chin, but her stiff upper lip quivered slightly.

Alicia leaned over and hugged her daughter tightly to her. She was not unaware of the girl's feelings on this occasion and they laid an almost unbearable burden on her. The need to reassure her daughter helped to distract her from her own misgivings. "You know, my dear, when first I came to the grange I knew not a soul in the area. It was not so very long, though, before I called it home. And now we have such friends as Lady Gorham and Cassandra to come and visit us in our new home. You will be surprised at how quickly you adjust. I think what I shall like best is that there are just the two of us to make a go of it. There will be no interference and no pressure but for ourselves." Alicia pinched her daughter's cheek affectionately. "You were never one to be without friends, even when some in the neighborhood were set against us."

"But, Mama, how shall I know how to go on? What I mean is, I am so used to being on easy terms with people of quality that I fear I shall appear encroaching to those in Tetterton."

"I am persuaded that we shall just have to take our cue from those we meet, love. How one can change the habits of a lifetime I do not know. I own it has been troubling me. We shall both of us have to cultivate a bit more reserve, I cannot doubt. How does any poor relation become a companion? How does one act the role of a governess? It cannot be easy for anyone of reduced circumstances to reshape her life, but it is obviously done all the time. You must prepare yourself for snubs and slights until you hit on the behavior expected of you. Frankly, Felicia, I would hate to see you any different than you are now."

"What will happen if some accept me and others do not? You know that Jack Miller convinced his mother to have me to Luella's ball. What if something of that nature should happen again?"

Alicia regarded the lovely face turned up to her. It would happen again, she had not the least doubt. "We shall deal with events as they arise, my dear. I can make no pronouncements without knowing the circumstances. Just do not be disappointed if it seems wisest to refuse some treat you would dearly love to take part in." Good God, what was she saying? You could not tell a girl of this age not to be disappointed. There was bound to be disappointment, and heartache, and sorrow beyond measure for such a child. She would make it as easy as she could for Felicia, she promised herself, but her heart sank at the prospect.

Felicia steadily regarded her mother with her uncompromising blue eyes. "Mama, you must not think that I intend to mope about this. I do not blame you. Why, we should be in the suds in no time if we did not go into . . . trade."

"Yes, Felicia, but I am sorrier than I can ever say that you should be brought to such a pass."

"Well, I hope you will not say so again," Felicia retorted. "It is not your fault but Papa's."

"We will not go into that," Alicia replied firmly. "Look, we are joining the Bridlington Road now. I am relieved that we do not pass the grange. One parting is enough."

They were silent for some time when Alicia remarked, "Some of the hats Mr. Dean sells appeared a bit frumpy to me. Do you think you could do something for them, with the resources we will have?"

"Oh, I should dearly love to get my hands on that straw bonnet with the high crown and small brim. The crown should be ribboned with a blue velvet band. It would make all the difference. And the lavender helmet would be all the better for a trimming of white lace. You mean I may work on them?" she asked eagerly.

"Why, of course, my angel. But not in the shop. You shall have what you need in the cottage. Not that I intend you shall spend all your time working, mind you. You will want to get to know the town. And I shall need to make some provision for a horse for you. Perhaps the Feather and Flask would make an arrangement with us."

CHAPTER THREE

As the post-chaise came out of the forest, they caught sight of the inn almost immediately. Even though the day was gray, the brick building looked welcoming. The green across from the row of shops was now occupied by the stalls and booths of a country fair and Felicia squealed with delight.

"Oh, what a crowd. There is a Punch and Judy show! May we go, Mama? Please say we may." Felicia sounded like the child she should have been, if the harsh realities of life had not forced themselves on her. Alicia nodded her amused agreement, but insisted that they claim their room first. When they presented themselves to the landlord, however, he was apologetic and harassed.

"Oh, my lady, I saved your room for you just as I promised, but I cannot get the gentleman out of it! He came last night and I said as how he could have the room for one night, but it was spoken for from today. He agreed to such an arrangement, but he will not budge now. Him be out to the fair and left his man in the room. What with all the activity, I have not another bed in the house, not a shakedown or sofa not occupied."

Alicia regarded him quizzingly. "Surely a man of your size should be able to move a gentleman's valet from a room. My daughter and I have been promised a room and I assure you that we intend to have it, since we must. Would you prefer that I route this interloper?"

The landlord smiled reluctantly at her. "No, my lady. I can handle it better'n you. Would you care to rest yourselves in the parlor for a moment?"

Alicia agreed to do so, and led Felicia into the oak-paneled parlor, where they seated themselves comfortably on the two winged chairs provided there. They grinned at each other when they heard a disturbance on the floor above them and it was some time before the landlord arrived to announce, "Your room is ready, Lady Coombs. My wife has set things to order and I will show you there myself. Your trunks will be sent up directly."

"Thank you, Mr. Harper. We appreciate your . . . efforts," Alicia remarked, a wide grin bringing out her dimples. "I hope we have not lost you any important custom."

"I assure you I never set eyes on the young man before in my life," he proclaimed.

When Alicia and her daughter had refreshed themselves and bestowed those belongings they would need immediately from their trunks, they descended again to the ground floor, assured the landlord that everything was to their liking, and emerged into the cloudy afternoon to view the fair. There were a myriad of delights to fascinate Felicia—marionette performances, a ropewalker, a trained monkey, the Punch and Judy show, a skittle alley, and a gambling booth. There was even a small roundabout and a fiddler. Felicia watched a sword swallower with amazement and bought a sweet from the bellowing vendor. She ate this treat while she watched a young man at the shooting gallery miss his target each time, amidst the goodnatured disparagements of his companions.

Alicia delighted in her daughter's enjoyment of the festivities and laughingly suggested that it would be wisest not to buy a ballad from the young man hawking them, as they were like to bring a blush to her face. Felicia wandered on and eventually settled before the Punch and Judy show, her countenance reflecting the vicissitudes of that age-old entertainment. Alicia was more interested in the people about her and surveyed the crowds of laughing people carefully. They had discovered that this was the last day of the fair, and there was an undercurrent of reckless abandon about the partakers. Mr. Dean made his way through the viewers of the Punch and Judy show and bowed to Alicia.

"I am delighted to see you, Lady Coombs. The fair brings more business than usual to town, so we have been busy, but I saw you a moment ago when I looked over and wished to come and welcome you to Tetterton." Mr. Dean looked, if possible, worse than he had two weeks previously.

"I cannot think it is wise for you to be out in this unruly crowd," she murmured solicitously. "But we appreciate your welcome. I intend to come round first thing in the morning to start learning the business. Mr. Allerton is still agreeable to staying on?"

"Indeed, yes. You will find him a most admirable young man. He has been with me for two years now and knows the business as well as I do. I wonder . . ." He hesitated, his body resting heavily on his cane.

"Please do not hesitate to speak your mind, Mr. Dean."

"I have not been quite up to pluck these last weeks and wonder if you would mind if I left next week when the papers will be signed. I had intended to stay on a bit to assist you, but I fear in my present condition I shall not be of much use."

"I would have you do just as is best for you. Mr. Allerton can assist me in my learning, and Felicia and I look forward to moving into your charming cottage."

Mr. Dean sighed with relief. "As soon as the papers are signed then I shall plan to leave. I appreciate your consideration, Lady Coombs."

"Not a bit. Things are like to work out just as well for all of us this way. Now I hope you will not let me keep you standing here in this press. I shall see you in the morning."

When Mr. Dean had wandered off, Alicia's attention was caught by an altercation taking place to the rear of her. She was about to turn to see the speaker, but the angry words froze her.

"The damn fellow has put me out of my room! Griggs, my valet, you know, just came to tell me. I left him there to hold it for me, and he has let himself be forcefully put out, along with all my belongings," the whining voice persisted.

"To hold it for you? Why should you need to leave him to hold it for you?" a lazy voice queried.

"Stupid oaf of a landlord said it was reserved for . . . You won't believe this, Stronbert . . . said it was reserved for Lady Coombs. You remember Sir Frederick," the speaker sniggered.

"Sir Frederick's widow? There could be another Lady Coombs."

"Doubt it. I asked the fellow if she was in mourning and he assented." The speaker obviously found this very amusing. "Wonder what brings her to such a godforsaken place. Got too hot for her at the grange, no doubt."

Alicia could feel the anger and humiliation swell within her. She checked to see that Felicia was engrossed in the show and sighed with relief. The voices at her back continued.

"Really, Parker, you have the most vivid imagination, and it is so seldom based on fact that one wearies of your tongue," the second speaker drawled.

"Little you know!" Parker snapped. "I had it from Westerly himself that it was Tackar who killed Sir Frederick in the duel, though I have never seen any such affair so well cloaked in secrecy."

"That's enough," the second speaker rapped out, his voice of steel.

His companion paid no attention to him, though his

tone of command had almost made Alicia jump. "And Westerly knows Tackar, who comes, you might note, from the neighborhood of the grange. You've met Tackar. Me thinks there is some hanky-panky between the neglected Lady Coombs and him."

This was really too much for Alicia, who had gone ramrod straight as these delightful bits of gossip were spread. She spun on his concluding words and lashed her hand across his face with all the fury of her pent-up anger and mortification. His astonishment more perhaps than the pain led him to utter the bellow that followed. Even in the din of the fair this attracted a goodly amount of attention, but Alicia merely turned away from his spluttering, took Felicia's arm firmly, and walked away from the scene.

"Whatever happened, Mama? Why is that man so red in the face and jibbering like a monkey? Could I not see the end of the show?"

"No, dear, for I slapped him and I think we had best depart the area," Alicia informed her calmly.

Felicia stopped abruptly. "You slapped him? Who is he? Why did you do it?"

"I do not know who he is precisely—Parker, was it? No matter. He insulted me."

"He spoke to you?"

"Not precisely."

"Then how did he insult you?" Felicia asked curiously, as she obeyed the tug at her sleeve and continued to walk toward the inn.

"He was speaking about me, my dear, and I fear I took offense. Not such a promising start in Tetterton after all. I should have ignored him," Alicia remarked sadly, "but somehow I could not."

"Never mind. Hopefully it will help him to mind his tongue in the future," Felicia suggested.

"Unfortunately it will probably start more tongues wagging. I should have ignored him," she said again.

* * *

When the two women had left the scene Mr. Parker was still muttering in his astonishment and rage. His companion regarded him contemptuously and said, "I tried to warn you, Parker, you fool."

"Warn me! How in the hell could you know that she was there? You've never met her, have you?"

"No, but it did not take a vast amount of intelligence to recognize her, Parker. There is no one else at the fair in mourning clothes." He awarded his companion a meaningful glance. "I should take it amiss, Parker, were I to hear you had spoken on the matter again."

Parker assumed a sullen expression and flicked a particle of dust from his immaculate coat. "Can't see what difference it makes to you."

"Let us merely say that I do not wish to be painted further with your brush, Parker. You have provided me with enough entertainment for one day, and enough distress for a lifetime."

Parker retorted sarcastically, "Well, she has caused me distress, too. She took my room. Where am I to stay?"

"From your description of the circumstances I should say that you attempted to take her room. You may stay at the court for the night."

Parker did not seem to appreciate this coolly offered invitation. "Your mother in residence?" he asked.

"Yes."

"Rather not, then. Makes me nervous, your mother. No offense, of course."

"Of course. In that case I shall wish you a pleasant journey. You go to Bridlington, I believe."

"I had no intention of leaving until tomorrow," Parker snapped. He recognized the determination in his companion's gaze and muttered, "Might as well leave now, though, since there's not a room to be had here. And nothing worth staying around for," he concluded rebelliously.

"As you say." The two men bowed, Parker somewhat stiffly, and parted company.

Alicia tossed her bonnet on the four-poster and smoothed her auburn curls carelessly. She caught sight of her reflection in the mirror next to her daughter's. They shared the auburn curls and blue eyes, and Felicia would probably attain her medium height when grown, but there the resemblance ended. Alicia was an attractive woman, and looked younger than her thirty-four years. But her daughter, with an oval face and creamy skin, was truly beautiful. Her blue eyes held a beguiling innocence in spite of the problems she had shared with her mother. Alicia said suddenly, "It is more than six months now since your father died. I think it is time you changed to some more colorful clothes."

Felicia smiled impishly and retorted, "Only if you do, Mama."

"I must admit that I have begun to tire of black," Alicia responded with great understatement. "Since we are not likely to offend anyone here by the lack of observance I think a change is in order. What do you say to gray?"

"Pooh! You shall wear your dark blue and your forest green, or I shall not budge from my black."

Alicia shrugged with mock despair. "What am I to do with you? So be it. Dark blue for the shop tomorrow. I spoke with Mr. Dean and he expects to be out of the cottage in about a week." Alicia walked over to the window and twitched back the draperies to obtain a view of the fair on the green. This did not afford her the pleasure it might have and she paced restlessly about the room, touching the solid mahogany furniture now and again. "Do you wish to dine in the parlor or here in the room?"

Felicia frowned quizzically. "You are not still upset about that man, are you, Mama? Surely if you do not know him, what he said can make not the least difference to you." She lifted a puzzled face to her mother.

"It is not that so much," Alicia admitted as she seated herself beside her daughter on the bed. "What vexes me beyond bearing is that I should have made such a pea-goose of myself. We will have a different sort of position to maintain here in Tetterton, but it hardly includes showing such a temper as I did. I vow I am ashamed to show my face in the dining parlor."

"You could not be so poor spirited! When you have no one to protect you from insults, you must protect yourself. Or I shall!" Felicia declared fiercely.

A gurgling laugh escaped Alicia. "Please spare me, my love. I shall endeavor to mind my manners in future if you will allow me to fend for myself. Shall we go down to dinner now?"

Mr. Parker made the majority of his journey to Bridlington in a snit. Really, Stronbert was too high-handed by half. And his mother was crazy as a loon, Parker sniggered to himself. He remembered the occasion several years previously when the dowager marchioness was in London on a visit to the Stronbert town house. Parker had come round to settle a gambling debt with the marquis and had arrived just as the dowager was descending from her carriage. He had watched with fascinated horror as several eels started to wriggle out of her cloak pocket. She had purchased these on an impulse as she had passed a market and stuffed their inert forms carelessly into her pocket. But her body warmth had revived them and Parker watched in amazement as she discovered their attempted escape and casually thrust them in her reticule to be delivered forthwith to the cook.

There had also been the occasion at Ranelagh when the old woman had been pacing along the side of the colossal gilded amphitheater past the alcoves with their tables laid ready for those desiring coffee and tea when she had stopped abruptly and declared that the famous orchestra was playing out of tune. She had charged past the huge fireplace ornamented with lamps and descended on the musicians. One hapless viol de gamba player had been singled out as the offender and soundly berated by the dowager, to the astonishment of the assembled crowd. Parker remembered that the marquis, with his intolerable calm, had waited patiently while his mother completed her diatribe and then led her off to some friends, without the slightest sign of discomposure.

Parker had other memories of the dowager, however, which were not so soothing to his lacerated sensibilities. The old woman had taken a severe dislike to him and managed to put him to the blush whenever they met which, fortunately, was not often. He had not the least desire to spend the night at Stronbert Court.

Edward Westerly's family home was located several miles west of Bridlington and Parker arrived there when the evening was well advanced. Mr. Westerly had not expected him until the next day and was in the process of entertaining Francis Tackar for the evening. They were seated in the library over a game of piquet when Parker was announced.

Westerly rose eagerly at his friend's advent and his companion in a more leisurely manner. Westerly was a short, red-haired man approaching his twenty-fifth year, where Mr. Tackar had certainly reached his mid-thirties. Tackar wore a single-breasted bottle green coat cut square at the waist with a very high collar and large revers. The tight-fitting sleeves and the coattail to his calf set off his athletic figure. There were four buttons at the sides of his extremely tight breeches, which covered his knees, and his frilled shirt peeked out from beneath a striped waistcoat.

Parker betrayed his admiration of this outfit by inquiring of Tackar who his tailor was, but turned almost immediately to his host to explain his unexpected arrival. "I had thought to spend another night on the road, my dear fellow. There was a fair in Tetterton with the usual trappings," he explained, with a smirk. Remembering his grievance he frowned. "Stronbert invited me to spend the night at his seat but you know what his mother is! Had to give up my room at the inn to a widow and her daughter," he declared virtuously.

Westerly laughed. "Turned out, were you? I shall see the day you play the gallant when your own comfort is in question."

Parker had accepted a glass of brandy and downed it quickly. His host refilled it. It had been an uncomfortable day for Parker, all told, and the brandy loosened his incorrigibly wayward tongue. "Indeed, I had no intention of giving up the room but my oaf of a valet allowed the landlord to forcefully eject him when I was out." Parker eyed his auditors belligerently, daring them to believe that it would have happened had *he* been there. When no comment was made, but he could detect the cynical gleam in Tackar's eyes, he decided to change his tack. "You will hardly credit who the widow was," he offered provocatively.

"Someone we know?" Westerly asked curiously.

"I dare say you have never met her, but you knew her husband!" Parker asserted, his eyes straying to Tackar.

Francis Tackar found his boredom diminishing. He would not give Parker the satisfaction of asking, but he awaited, with hooded eyes, the name which he was sure would not long be withheld.

Westerly, too, began to have some idea of where the conversation was headed and he surreptitiously regarded Tackar's blank face. It would perhaps be wise to make a turn in the conversation. After all, Tackar had dueled with Sir Frederick. Westerly ran his fingers inside his collar and asked hopefully, "Would you like me to order you some supper, Parker? You probably have not had time to bait."

Parker refused to be turned aside from his purpose. He indicated his acceptance of the offered meal and proceeded to inform his audience, "It was Lady Coombs! Sir Frederick's widow." He sipped at his brandy and smugly settled back in his chair. The reactions which his announcement produced did not live up to his expectations—Westerly eyed the cards on the game table and Tackar's expression did not change. But Parker was not altogether disappointed; he could feel the suppressed excitement that exuded from Tackar in spite of the disinterested countenance and lounging attitude of the older man. Parker was well satisfied with his work, and he congratulated himself hazily that he had said nothing to which Lord Stronbert could take exception.

Far from being hazy himself, Tackar rubbed a finger caressingly back and forth over his brandy glass and took no part in the discussion that followed. He had spent the previous week on his estate, dull as that had been, in an effort to glean information on the whereabouts of the delectable Lady Coombs. That she had departed, bag and baggage, from Katterly Grange was a well-known fact in the neighborhood, but it had taken him several days to ascertain that she had gone to Lady Gorham. Tackar had no intention of laying siege to that stronghold! Although he had been acquainted with Lady Gorham for many years, there was no love lost between the two of them, and he did not doubt that he would be handled roughly if he tried to approach the fair Alicia at Peshre Abbey.

No, he had determined to wait until his quarry made a move, as he had been sure she would. Alicia, proud Alicia, would not quarter herself for long, even with her dear friend. And the stupid Parker had provided him with just the information he needed. There was the possibility, of course, that Lady Coombs and her daughter were merely passing through the market town, but even if that were the case, Tackar did not doubt his ability to track them from there. Alicia had become an obsession with him. After purchasing the grange specifically to install her as his mistress, she had spurned his offer, and fired his desire. One would have thought a lady reduced to her circumstances would have welcomed such an opportunity.

Had he not seduced every wife, widow, and maiden who had previously caught his eye? Of course, he had the intelligence to hunt on the fringes of society, where his wealth and looks, coupled with his social position, carried more weight than they did with the *ton*. Only his wealth gained him admission to decent circles, and there were those, the starchiest of the matrons, who disparaged his acquaintance.

And who was Alicia to scorn him? A woman deserted by her husband, barely able to hold her head up in country society, and now a widow with so few resources that she could not even hold on to the grange. Tackar would like to see that head bowed. Seldom did he make a gamble that served no purpose, and there was the grange—an expensive toy, and her home for years—now empty and useless. Alicia could have stayed there in luxury, not the scraping, scrimping life she had known for more than a dozen years. Was he not ready to lavish baubles on her? There could be no thought of marrying her; his life would not be enhanced by the addition of a wife. And the girl. No, really, it would be too much to think of marrying Alicia, when she brought with her a child of Sir Frederick's.

Tackar raised the brandy glass to sip meditatively at its contents. Besotted as he was with Alicia, he had not taken into consideration her natural concern for the child. It had been foolish of him to attempt to set her up in a neighborhood where she was known, where her daughter had a social position to maintain. At the time the idea had seemed logical—the grange was near enough to his estate to necessitate little inconvenience for himself, and it was Alicia's home, where he assumed she would wish to stay if it were possible. Given the strange position she had sustained for many years, it had not occurred to him that the subtle difference between a deserted wife and an acknowledged mistress would be enough to sway her decision. Tackar was willing to concede that he had erred in his judgment. No matter, he would profit by his mistake. The grange could be sold again, if at something of a loss. Alicia could pay for that by services rendered, he thought with a cold smile.

CHAPTER FOUR

Before leaving for the shop in the morning, Alicia discussed with the landlord the possibility of hiring a horse for Felicia's use during the day. The landlord offered to introduce Felicia to the ostler, who would help her choose a suitable mount. Alicia left her daughter in high spirits discussing the points of the various hacks in the inn stables.

Alicia was greeted by Mr. Allerton and was informed that Mr. Dean would be along presently. She made a more thorough tour of the shop this time, turning over bolts of fabric and opening drawers to examine the skeins of thread in their blue paper. There was every kind of thread from that made of flax to the delicate lisle for darning muslin. Mr. Allerton, a serious young man with curly blond hair and intent brown eyes, proved to know the inventory exceedingly well. They had covered the larger room of the shop when Mr. Dean appeared.

"My solicitor has informed me that all the necessary papers are ready to sign, Lady Coombs. He will be by with them this afternoon, and has assured me that your solicitor has found everything in order. So the exchange may be made within the next few days."

Alicia regarded his pallid skin with concern but merely said cheerfully, "That is good news indeed. I hope you will plan to leave as soon as you wish, then. If it will be convenient, I should like for you to explain your record-keeping to me. Since Mr. Allerton is well acquainted with the shop, I should like to spend my time bringing the records up to date while he handles the customers, if that would suit you."

Alicia's head was awhirl with figures and manufacturers' names and customers' accounts when she left the shop to join her daughter at the inn for luncheon.

"Mama, it is the prettiest town! And there are forests and fields all about, and the most beautiful country lanes. Hodges, the ostler, put me on the sweetest little mare. She reminded me of Girandole. I saw gardens full of china asters and chrysanthemums. There are cottages dotted all over the neighborhood and another row of shops on either side of the green for a ways. I rode west of town and swung back toward the south. There is a huge estate there, though of course I did not go through the gates. The carriageway is so long that I could not even see the house. But there were two children riding there, a boy and a girl, having a race, I think," she laughed. "Did you bring the hats for me to work on?"

"No, indeed! There is no need for you to put your hand to that yet."

"But, Mama, I have been looking forward to it. Could I not come back with you to the shop and bring some hats and ribbons and such here with me?"

"I suppose you could, but there is no *need* to do so as yet. I shall be working in the little office at the back most of the afternoon. Do you not wish to ride again this afternoon?"

"It's coming on to mizzle and I would rather sit before the fire and try my hand at those hats, honestly."

The two women arrived at the shop simultaneously with the old woman they had seen on their first inspection of the place. She wore her hair powdered and again wore the puce panniered gown with the orange stripes. She was attended on this occasion by a maid and two children. Alicia allowed the party to pass into the shop before them and Felicia whispered that she recognized the children from her morning's ride. The boy was perhaps twelve and the girl slightly younger. Their faces wore the eager expressions of those being indulged in a treat, but Alicia saw them share a rather nervous grin as well.

Mr. Allerton and Mr. Dean both welcomed the old woman, addressing her as Lady Stronbert. She was unimpressed with their greeting and announced in stentorian tones that she had come for a bonnet for her granddaughter and some handkerchiefs for her grandson, not that she expected to find what she wanted in *this* shop, heaven knew. Felicia's lips twitched, but the children shared a glance and they adopted the pretense of really not being with this crotchety old woman at all.

Mr. Dean assured her ladyship that they would indeed find just what they might require, and could not Mr. Allerton perhaps help Master Matthew while he looked to Miss Helen's needs. Alicia mentally considered the bonnets the shop had to offer for a child and frankly admitted to herself that Lady Stronbert was probably correct in assuming she would not find what she wanted. She whispered to Felicia, "Go with them and see what you can do, love."

Felicia awarded her mother a triumphant smile, which was ruefully acknowledged with a sigh. The young woman joined Mr. Dean and, catching his eye, was introduced to Lady Stronbert as the daughter of the woman who was taking over the shop soon. Felicia made a small curtsy to the old woman, who eyed her skeptically and nodded ungraciously. Miss Helen, however, recognized the young woman and piped up, "I saw you this morning when Matthew and I were riding."

"Yes," Felicia agreed, "and I have been longing to know who won."

Miss Helen smiled suddenly and giggled, "Well, I did, you know. But only because Matthew's horse stumbled," she confided.

"Good for you," Felicia responded. "I have been

thinking that this bonnet needs a very large red ribbon to do it justice. What do you think?" she asked, as she lifted a child's bonnet down from the shelf and exhibited it for the girl.

"I am not so very good at picturing things," Miss Helen admitted doubtfully. She looked at her grandmother rather apprehensively, as that woman commented disparagingly on each of the bonnets Mr. Dean produced for her inspection.

"Yes, it is especially difficult when there are so many items about," Felicia agreed, to recapture the girl's attention. "Let me show you what I have in mind." She walked purposefully to a counter strewn with ribbons of all colors and widths and selected a rose-red of two-inch width. She gathered up a scissors as well and returned to the little group, aware that the old woman's piercing eyes were now on her. Felicia grasped the bonnet firmly and wound the ribbon round the base of the crown and arranged a large double bow on the left. She snipped the ends so that they trailed well below the bonnet and stood back, her head to one side considering her creation. "Yes, that is more what I had in mind," she mused.

Miss Helen was contemplating the bonnet rapturously and her hands twitched in their desire to reach for it. Felicia asked, "Shall we try it on you?" Without waiting for the girl's response and ignoring the old woman's deprecating snort, she placed the bonnet on the dark brown curls. She tied the ends carefully under Miss Helen's chin, nodded her approval, and took the girl to a large mirror to see the charming picture she made. "The bonnet matches your dress admirably. Have you others it would be well with?"

"Oh, yes, for this rose-red is my favorite color. I do love the bonnet!" She turned beseechingly to her grandmother and asked prettily, "May I have it, Grandmother? It is excessively pretty."

Lady Stronbert grudgingly admitted that the bonnet was becoming, but she seemed to hesitate over buying it. Miss Helen did not cozen or cajole her, but waited patiently for her decision.

Felicia remarked, "It will only take me a moment to tack down the ribbon. Shall I do that while you make your decision?" She untied the ribbon under the girl's chin and lifted the bonnet carefully from her curls. Miss Helen watched the bonnet being removed in the mirror and schooled her countenance to accept what she feared must be inevitable. Her grandmother had the most awkward habit of refusing to purchase even those items she wanted, just out of perversity.

"Young lady, there is no need to tack down the ribbon. We will not be purchasing the bonnet," Lady Stronbert called after Felicia.

Felicia turned calmly to the speaker and said kindly, "Oh, I had intended to decorate it with a ribbon in any case, Lady Stronbert. As well now as another time. Surely the next young woman to come looking for a bonnet will find it more interesting for the bit of color." She noticed the suspicion of a tear in Miss Helen's eye and minutely shook her head, at which the girl blinked her eyes and raised her chin firmly. Felicia rewarded her with a smile.

Lady Stronbert was disconcerted by Felicia's reply. She had really wanted to make the purchase, but her uncertain temper had been aroused by the ease with which Felicia had changed the plain bonnet into a delightful confection. She was herself totally unable to understand the niceties of fashion; she could see an item worn and feel that it was elegant, but she was unable to duplicate the exercise in her own clothes. She knew that people thought she dressed ridiculously, and she did. Lady Stronbert was accordingly jealous of those with the facility to accomplish what she could not. She turned now to find her grandson, who had chosen some handkerchiefs under Mr. Allerton's direction. Although her temper was even higher because she realized she had disappointed her granddaughter, she made no demur at the selection and had the parcel wrapped and given to the maid. Felicia had not returned with the bonnet, and Lady Stronbert quickly shepherded her party out the door as she promised to buy them a special tea. Miss Helen gave a last, lingering look toward the rear of the shop where Felicia had disappeared and followed in her grandmother's wake.

Mr. Dean sighed and Mr. Allerton wiped his brow. Alicia could not help but note these signs and asked, "Does Lady Stronbert always cause such a commotion when she shops?"

"Yes, it is ever the same," Mr. Dean remarked. "I would not have you think that it is only this shop she seems to hold in aversion. It is the same everywhere she goes. Poor Miss Helen. Your daughter is adept at decorating the bonnets, Lady Coombs. I myself have long passed the point where I can understand what is in fashion."

"Yes, Felicia has a certain knack and had already agreed to work on some of them for me. I had not intended . . . well, never mind. Shall we continue with the books?"

Felicia arrived then with the finished bonnet and set it carefully on the shelf. An inspection of the other bonnets there showed a half dozen she felt could stand improvement, and she lifted them down. Each one was then taken to the ribbons and laces and she selected those items she would need for her work. Before she left the shop she poked her head into the doorway of the office to inform her mother that she would be at the inn. Her mother smiled her appreciation and returned to her work.

An hour later Mr. Dean was obviously too fatigued to continue and she urged him to return to the cottage. As she could not continue the work without his assistance, she wandered into the shop and explored the smaller room while Mr. Allerton waited on some customers in the front. She was surprised to see Miss Helen enter again, this time accompanied by a man who looked vaguely familiar, perhaps because the girl resembled him somewhat. As Alicia approached them, the girl burst into speech, "We have come back to purchase the bonnet! Papa said over tea that it would be a shame if someone else were to have it, when it was fixed especially for me." Her countenance glowed with her delight.

"Lady Coombs?" The man spoke lazily and Alicia immediately recognized his voice. And that was why he had looked familiar; she had caught a hurried glimpse of him as she had slapped Mr. Parker. She felt a flush rise to her cheeks.

"Yes. Lord Stronbert? I am pleased to meet you. Come, Miss Helen, you shall put on the bonnet for your father and see if he approves of it." She led the girl to the shelf and lifted down the bonnet with steady hands, but inwardly she was quaking. The shame she had felt at her behavior at the fair had not left her. She arranged the bonnet on the brown curls and tied the ribbon in a bow under the girl's chin.

Miss Helen did a little dance step and smiled beguilingly up at her father, who had positioned himself a short distance away. "Well, Papa, shall I have it?" she asked mischievously.

"Certainly, imp. It is enchanting." His eyes sought Alicia. "I understand you added the ribbon."

"No, no, Papa. It was Lady Coombs's daughter. Am I right, ma'am? She is your daughter, is she not?" Miss Helen asked anxiously.

"Indeed she is."

Lord Stronbert regarded her with a puzzled frown. "You are perhaps purchasing the shop from Mr. Dean?"

Alicia occupied herself untying the bonnet as she replied, "Yes. The purchase is almost completed, and Mr. Dean is teaching me the workings. He intends to leave shortly for Cornwall."

"Shall you live in his cottage?" Miss Helen asked curiously.

"Yes, we have bought the cottage as well," Alicia replied. She took the bonnet over to the counter and began to wrap it, then paused to ask, "Would you rather wear this one and have me wrap yours?"

"Yes, please. You would not mind, would you, Papa?"

"Certainly not." His clear brown eyes watched Alicia as she made the exchange and continued the wrapping. Whatever could have induced this young woman to purchase a shop, he wondered. Surely Sir Frederick could not have left her that badly off. "You did not choose to stay at the grange?" he asked abruptly.

Alicia raised snapping eyes to his. "I had no choice, though it can certainly be of no interest to you." She noticed that she had discomfited the girl by her sharp response and turned to her to say with a smile, "Felicia did not tell me who won the race."

"I did," Miss Helen replied proudly, "though Matthew's horse stumbled."

"Well, that is fair enough. I think he must be older than you are."

"He is twelve and I am but turned ten."

"So old," Alicia laughed. "Do you have your own horse?"

"Oh, yes, Papa gave her to me on my eighth birthday. I hope you can see her one day. She has the most perfect manners," Miss Helen confided.

"I hope I shall. And I hope you will be happy with your bonnet," Alicia said by way of farewell.

Lord Stronbert turned to his daughter and said, "Run along and catch up Miss Carson, imp. I shall be along in a moment." He watched her as she obediently danced out of the shop, a tender expression on his face. His own countenance had adopted a certain gravity when he spoke to Alicia. "I wish to apologize, Lady Coombs. It was rude of me to question you on your private life." A slow smile spread over his features. "And I should not like to suffer Parker's fate at your hands."

"Your friend was insulting, Lord Stronbert. But I am ashamed that I should have acted so violently." Alicia could not share his obvious amusement. "I had hoped that in leaving the Scarborough area we might start fresh, but I suppose there will always be those Parkers around to see that it is not possible." She did not meet his eyes during this comment but played instead with the wedding ring on her finger.

"I pray you will acquit me of friendship with Mr. Parker. I am no more than the merest acquaintance," he replied lightly. "May I wish you success in your venture, Lady Coombs?"

Alicia raised her face then, a firm smile imprinted on it. "Thank you, sir. I hope we may continue to serve you."

"I am sure of it," he drawled. "Though my mother is difficult to please, even she has found no substitute for Mr. Dean's. Good day, Lady Coombs."

"Good day, Lord Stronbert." He bowed to her gravely and walked off with a careless grace. Alicia sighed and moved over to Mr. Allerton. "I think we should discuss your wages, Mr. Allerton. Much more will be required of you under my management, I fear, and I should like to compensate you proportionately."

"Mr. Dean makes me a very handsome wage, Lady Coombs," he replied, embarrassed.

"It may have been adequate for what you have been doing, but my inexperience will lay a burden on you which I intend to recompense. And, Mr. Allerton, I had thought to keep Felicia out of the shop as much as possible. She is not used to this kind of life and will have matters enough to handle, I cannot doubt."

Alicia was beginning to feel the strain of her first day in the shop. "I think I should like to leave now, Mr. Allerton. You will not mind finishing alone and locking up, will you?"

"Not at all, Lady Coombs. I do it often," he reassured her.

As she wandered down the street to the inn, Alicia was so engrossed in her own thoughts that she did not notice the gentleman approaching her. A firm hand on her elbow stayed her and she looked up, startled. There was no one she less wanted to see than Francis Tackar with his arrogant, cold brown eyes, his carefully tended curly brown hair, and his determined jaw. Although not much above her own height, he was powerfully built and the sight of him made her shiver. She struck his hand from her elbow and eyed him frigidly.

"The elusive Lady Coombs comes to light and in the guise of a shopkeeper, I hear at the inn," he remarked insolently.

"I have nothing to say to you, sir," Alicia stated flatly and made to pass on.

"But I have something to say to you, dear lady." His eyes wandered insinuatingly over her body. "Coming out of mourning, I see. Tsk. Tsk. That hardly shows the proper respect for Sir Frederick."

Alicia had a maddening desire to slap his smugly handsome face but remembered yesterday's occurrence too vividly. Instead she walked away from him toward the inn. He followed her and spoke confidently. "It had not occurred to me, I must admit, that you might not desire the arrangement I suggested in the neighborhood where you had friends. No matter. I can as well provide an arrangement for you here under the same terms."

Alicia stopped and glared at him. "Mr. Tackar, it has obviously not occurred to you that I do not intend to accept your 'arrangement' at any time or place or on any terms. I detest you. You insult me by your very presence. Just stay away from me."

"Alicia, Alicia, you are overwrought! You cannot have thought of the advantages I can provide for you. Sir Frederick did not leave you very well off, I know.

I was one of the few who knew how he had left matters in his will because he foolishly bragged of it in his cups one night."

"And so you killed him!" Alicia's voice was rigid with contempt.

"It was a duel," he snapped, "and a fair fight."

"You killed him," she repeated.

"He was not so very handy with a pistol," he rejoined smugly. "Why should you care? He did nothing but disgrace and impoverish you."

"I was not impoverished until his death."

"But I assure you that you need be no longer."

Alicia fled from him then, into the inn and straight up to her room. She found her daughter at the window. Felicia turned with a troubled frown and said, "Did Mr. Tackar upset you again, Mama? What does he want? Why has he followed us here?"

Alicia dropped into a chair and tossed her hat on the bed. "Lord, child, if I could explain that. Mr. Tackar is a detestable man and I hope you will avoid him always."

"But he bought Katterly Grange for more than it was worth," her daughter protested.

"Nevertheless he did it only to make us beholden to him. I refuse to be so." Alicia did not wish to pursue the subject and said more calmly, "You will be pleased to hear that Miss Helen returned to the shop, this time with her father, and purchased the bonnet."

"I am glad. Her grandmother is a harridan, is she not?"

"Yes, rather," Alicia said with a grin. "Show me what you have been doing."

Felicia brought over the two hats she had finished, and illustrated for her mother how she intended to liven up the others. "It will take no time at all, and I think they will be much more likely to sell when they are finished."

"There can be no doubt of it, love. I should not

have set you to work this afternoon, and especially not in the shop."

"I enjoyed it enormously."

"I might have known you would," Alicia said with a helpless shrug.

CHAPTER FIVE

When Lord Stronbert left the shop he assured himself that his daughter had been reunited with her governess, and waved them off on their way back to the court, his mother and son having already departed. He had left his horse at the Feather and Flask but was not as yet ready to leave town. The carriage maker was located a short distance from the center of Tetterton and he walked there to consult on the progress of the carriage he had ordered. He was well known in the town and frequently stopped to speak with acquaintances as he made his unhurried way along the street.

His task accomplished, he was returning to the Feather and Flask when he witnessed Lady Coombs accosted by Mr. Tackar. He was unable to see her expression but he saw her reject the man's touch on her arm. He could not hear their words, but the tone of them drifted to him, hers contemptuous and his sneering. Lord Stronbert was tempted to intervene in the confrontation, but Lady Coombs had rushed into the inn by that point and there seemed no further need. Tackar shrugged elaborately to the empty air and went into the inn more slowly.

Lord Stronbert went round to the stables and called for his horse. He passed the time of day with Hodges while he waited. "Is Mr. Tackar staying here?"

"Yes, milord. Said it might be for a night or two, possibly more. Flashy sort of fellow, ain't he?" Hodges asked companionably.

"Yes," Stronbert agreed with a frown. "I hope he

does not stay long." He mounted his horse then, waved to the ostler and rode to his home. A row of poplars led on either side from the entrance gate for half a mile before the carriage drive swung around to face the mansion. The court was a fifteenth-century stone building with twin castellated towers and parapet. Including the gabled west wing there were close to a dozen imposing oak-paneled reception rooms, an extensive library, several offices, thirty bedrooms, a solarium, and various domestic areas and storerooms. Lord Stronbert, in addition to his immediate family of his mother and two children, housed within the ancient pile of stones half a dozen impecunious relatives, a governess, a tutor, scores of servants, and an army of cats and dogs. He had lost his wife, Marcia, two years before to consumption. She had been a distant relation of his mother's and a saintly, meek woman. He had married her because she fell in love with him, and because she was kind to everyone and he respected her. The children had been greatly distressed by her death, but Lord Stronbert had half expected it, as her constitution had never been strong. He had left the court very little during that first year after her death when the children were bewildered and frightened. Now he journeyed to London more frequently and visited friends in other parts of the country, but he was seldom away for more than a month at a time.

The butler, Williams, greeted his arrival quietly as he took coat and gloves from his employer. "The dowager marchioness asked that you wait on her in the minor parlor, milord."

"Thank you, Williams. I will go to her now."

He found his mother still dressed in the puce gown with its hideous orange stripes, although the dinner hour was approaching. She was sitting, straight backed, on a Windsor chair, and she was scowling.

"You sent for me, Mother?" Stronbert asked, as he bent to place a salute on her cheek.

"Nigel, you spoil that child," she declared emphatically.

"Which one?"

"Both of them! But I am speaking of Helen. You should not have taken her back to purchase that bonnet."

"Why not?" he asked with a quizzing look at her under his sleepy eyelids.

"You will spoil her."

"But, Mother, it was my understanding when you left the house today that you had promised to purchase a bonnet for her."

"And so I did. But not that bonnet."

"Oh?" He raised his eyebrows slightly and swung one leg over the other. "I thought it enchanting."

"But I had refused to purchase it," she retorted querulously.

"So I understand. Why was that, Mother?"

"Because that little chit just threw it together," she pronounced, her temper starting to flare again.

"Well, I have not met the little chit yet, but if she can throw together a bonnet like that, I shall look forward to doing so."

"Was she not there when you made the purchase?"

"No, her mother finalized the transaction."

"The girl is a beauty," his mother sniffed. "Has no right to be waiting on one in a shop."

"If their circumstances warrant the action, Mother, I can only find it admirable that they have the spunk to do it."

"I shall shop there no longer," she pronounced flatly.

The note of steel entered Stronbert's voice. "Yes, you shall, Mother. And you will do so with a better grace than is your wont."

The dowager marchioness toyed with a fan in her lap. "It cannot be any concern of yours."

"If you refuse to patronize Lady Coombs's shop, others in the neighborhood will take their cue from you. I will not have the woman ruined for a passing fancy of yours. She is like to have hard work of it as it is. Do you agree?"

"You think me a crotchety old woman," she declaimed plantively.

Stronbert's mouth twisted in a rueful smile. "And so you are at times, my dear. I will have your promise."

"Oh, very well," she grumbled. "Agatha is in bed with the migraine and will not be down to dinner. And the general has ridden over to his friend in Dastor."

"You remind me that I should be changing. Until dinner, Mother."

Alicia and her daughter were seated before an array of veal cutlets, pigeons, asparagus, lamb, salad, apple pie, and tarts when Mr. Tackar entered the dining parlor. She had been enjoying the warmth of the fire near the table, and the spotless table linen and good plated cutlery, as well as the delicious food. But all this was changed when he entered; her appetite was on the moment destroyed and she wished nothing more than to be in her room above. Felicia glanced up as Tackar seated himself at the table without asking leave. Tackar murmured to Alicia, "You would not wish to make a scene, Lady Coombs," as he watched her eyes flare.

"You are wrong, Mr. Tackar. If you do not reseat yourself elsewhere I shall be more than happy to make a scene. Or leave. You have destroyed my appetite."

His suggestive eyes traveled slowly over her body and he replied, "And you have whetted mine."

"Are you going to leave our table?"

"No."

Alicia rose and Felicia rose with her. Without a backward glance they left the room. Alicia stopped in the hall to speak with the landlord. "Is Mr. Tackar staying at the inn?"

"Yes, my lady. Perhaps for a night, perhaps longer. He could not be more specific, he said."

"Thank you."

When Alicia and Felicia reached their room the older woman closed the door and barred it. Felicia's puckered face showed her confusion and fear. "What does he want, Mama?"

Alicia regarded her daughter thoughtfully. "Oh, lamb, it is so difficult to explain."

"But I must know," Felicia responded stubbornly.

"Yes, I feel you must. I have explained to you about your courses and what they signify. You have seen animals mate on the estate. Do you understand that this is how children are produced? That men and women mate in somewhat the same way?"

Felicia dropped her eyes to her hands and whispered, "I had not thought about it."

"No, when one is young and shielded from certain realities, one does not. When a man and a woman wed they mate so as to have offspring. My mother did not speak to me of this, and I had not thought much on it either. All children are conceived by mating, my dear. It is a fact of life. A woman may at any time conceive a child through bedding with a man. Men sometimes conceive a . . . desire to bed a woman. I am not sure if this happens with women also; I have not experienced such a desire. That does not mean that it does not exist, though."

"Are you trying to tell me that Mr. Tackar has conceived such a desire for you?" Felicia asked incredulously.

Alicia choked back the laugh that bubbled up in her, an almost hysterical laugh. "Yes, my love, that is what I am trying to tell you."

"But you are not wed to him!"

"Well, you see, that does not preclude such a desire developing. An honorable man would not pursue an honest woman in such a situation. Mr. Tackar is not an honorable man."

"Does he not wish to wed you?"

"No, he wishes only to bed me. And he has offered me insulting inducements to effect just that. I have, of course, refused him, but he is not willing to accept my rejection." Alicia passed a weary hand through her auburn curls. "I had hoped that our presence here would not become known to him. I have no doubt that that odious Mr. Parker could not wait to blab it about. He insinuated, in my hearing, that there was some sort of illicit arrangement between Mr. Tackar and myself."

"No wonder you slapped him!" Felicia exclaimed. "How could anyone believe such a thing?"

"There are some women, my dear, who out of a financial need, or perhaps a desire," Alicia shook her head wonderingly, "or it might simply be out of a weak moral character, do just that. I should think for the most part that young maidens do so out of ignorance, and with their ruin have nowhere else to turn. There have been fatherless children born at the grange and I have done what I could for their mothers and themselves, often enduring the censure of the vicar and the village. It is why young women of your station are so carefully chaperoned."

"What will Mr. Tackar do?" Felicia asked anxiously.

"I do not know. Perhaps he will leave me alone, perhaps he will persist. I am sorry I had to tell you this," Alicia admitted sadly, her eyes on Felicia's drawn face. "But he is an unprincipled man and if he should . . . Men have been known to force their attentions on women, who are weaker physically. I have told your uncle of Mr. Tackar's suggestions and made him promise that he would take no action. You know that you can always go to your uncle, do you not, Felicia?"

The girl was sobbing now, her head buried in a pillow on the bed. "Do not speak so, Mama, I beg you," her muffled voice came. Alicia sat on the bed beside her and stroked the glowing hair, whispering comforting words.

"Do not weep, my poppet. Mr. Tackar is unlikely to take any drastic measure, I assure you. But we are alone, you and I, and unprotected, so you must be made aware of the dangers. Avoid him. It is unfortunate that he knows where I am, but what is done is done. We live in a civilized time and nothing is like to happen to me. Dry your tears. I shall help you with the hats."

Morning brought a sparkling fall day, but Alicia's face was drawn and her daughter looked peaked. There was an unspoken agreement to discuss Mr. Tackar no more. "Come with me to the shop today," Alicia offered. "You shall choose some material for a new gown."

Felicia pretended to enter into the project with enthusiasm, but her heart was heavy. Her mother had burdens enough without the added one of Mr. Tackar. She blushed at the remembrance of her mother's explanation of mating. If one had to do that when they were wed, she wondered that so many people married! Still, since almost everyone did, perhaps it was not that bad after all. Felicia had never seen a naked man and her face prickled with heat at the thought of it. She had not, in fact, paid a great deal of attention to her own body, though it had held a certain fascination as her breasts had developed. She had been cautioned by nurse and governess to keep herself well covered at all times. It occurred to her that she had never seen anyone else naked. Not even her mother. It must be frightfully embarrassing to be naked before someone else, especially a man.

Felicia chose a deep green crepe, explaining to her mother that she would be able to embroider flowers on it when their mourning period was over, and in the meantime could have a little cream-colored lace at the wrists and neck. She sorted through the vast array of laces before deciding on just the right one for the dress she had in mind. When she had collected everything she needed and was about to depart, Alicia said, "Do not coop yourself up in the inn all day. Mr. Harper has assured me that there is almost always a horse available for you. I should not like for you to miss such a glorious day for a ride."

"Perhaps after luncheon, Mama. I am anxious to be started with the dress. Shall I see you for your meal?"

"Yes, dear. Enjoy your morning."

Felicia wandered out into the sunlight, her parcel under her arm. The leaves on the trees were turning colors now and there was the smell of woodsmoke on the air. She breathed deeply and reveled in the crispness brought into her. Autumn and spring were seasons full of anticipation, of promises of things to come. Felicia felt an eagerness within her which made her eyes sparkle and her lips draw into a merry smile. A young man passing by doffed his hat at sight of such an enchanting creature. Felicia smiled shyly at him and went on her way to the inn.

Before ascending to her room, she asked the round, bustling Mrs. Harper if Mr. Tackar had left yet and was told that he had. In her relief she danced up the stairs and into the room where she flung the parcel on the bed. She then hesitated momentarily before returning to the door and barring it. Felicia placed herself before the large rectangular horse glass on its trestle feet which could be tilted to any angle. She studied her reflection, starting with her hair and face, and allowing her eyes to descend to her shoulders, breasts, waist, hips, and feet. With an embarrassed toss of her head she began to disrobe in front of the glass. First the long, tight, pleated bodice, with its large fichu, and long sleeves ending at ruching at the wrist; then the full skirt with ruching at the hem. She intended to make her new dress in the one-piece style. Her chemise, gathered at the neck with a drawstring, and her petticoat were discarded in a heap at her feet. Finally her black tights were removed and she stood before the glass naked.

She closed her eyes for a moment, hesitating, before she opened them wide and surveyed her body minutely. Her collarbones were prominent and her shoulders slight. Her arms were thin and sparsely freckled, ending in narrow, shapely hands. She was most interested, however, in her breasts, which swelled out gracefully and ended in the buttons of her nipples. The waist was narrow and the legs long and sturdy, with well-trimmed ankles and shapely feet. Felicia's eyes ascended again to the curled auburn hair at the beginning of her legs. She felt a flush spread over her cheeks and refused to meet her own eyes in the glass.

Tentatively she reached one hand up to touch the swell of her breast, firm and soft at the same time. She touched a finger gently to the nipple and felt a strange sensation run through her body. Fascinated by the unusual feeling, she experimented further with her breasts, aware that an aching developed lower down in her body. She met her eyes in the glass; they were shining and rather moist. The blush had not altogether faded, but she was no longer concerned with it. Her breathing was coming more rapidly now, and it frightened her a little, but she felt elated somehow and did not wish to don her clothing until she had satisfied her curiosity.

Instead she laid down on the bed until her breathing became a bit calmer, though she retained a feeling of urgency. Cautiously she rubbed her breasts again and then moved one hand to the site of the aching between her legs. The motion of her fingers there intensified the aching until it reached such a pitch that she could no longer choose to continue, she *had* to. And then her body acted on its own, rhythmically lifting and gripping, as she moaned. Amazing how light and beautiful she felt.

She lay on the bed for some time experiencing the unique sense of release. Then she rose and walked in her nudity to the basin on the stand. It was while she washed her hands that the shame stole over her. One was not supposed to touch one's body. Felicia wondered rebelliously why not, when one's body could provide such exquisite pleasure. She began to gather up her clothes and redress herself carefully. It was some time before the thought occurred to her. Like a stallion with a mare, that was where a man with a woman . . . But then would not the woman receive such pleasure with a man? It was difficult, and Felicia eventually gave up the distressing effort, to visualize a man with her mother. It was unthinkable! It was no less unthinkable to visualize a man with herself. Her body was private, a special thing of her own. There was no man she would think of allowing to touch it!

But children were born every day. Then every day men were touching women. Men like Mr. Tackar with his insolent gaze resting on her mother's fully clothed body. Felicia's skin crawled at the thought of such a man touching her body. Even Mr. Harper, the landlord, pleasant as he was; it would be disgusting. She found, though, that if she wove a cozy fantasy about the young man she had passed in the street on her way back to the inn that she could almost imagine it. Not quite, of course, but almost. Someone you cared about, and who knew your dreams and you knew theirs. Almost then she could picture allowing him to touch her breasts, with her clothes on, of course. She saw herself in a sunny dale, lying amidst the violets . . .

"Felicia, are you all right?" Her mother's voice came through the door.

"Yes, Mama," Felicia answered absently.

"You might let me in then," Alicia suggested with some asperity.

Felicia sprang to the door and unbarred it hurriedly. Her face was stained with a ridiculous blush, and her mother surveyed her anxiously as she entered the room. "Are you sure you are feeling quite the thing?"

"Oh, yes, Mama. I . . . I was just sitting thinking."

"Are you ready for something to eat?"

"Yes. Well, no, not just yet, Mama. I . . . I should like to talk to you for a moment."

Alicia seated herself with relief and drew off her gloves. She waited patiently for Felicia to speak, but the girl merely studied the closed door. "Has something happened? You did not see Mr. Tackar, did you?"

"No, no. Mrs. Harper says he has left. I felt relieved."

Alicia sighed. "Yes, that is good news. Now it seems so silly to have burdened you with my problems."

"You had to, Mama. I had to know." Felicia stopped speaking again and tried to meet her mother's eyes but could not. She unwrapped her parcel and gently stroked the material.

"Something is the matter. Can you not tell me?" Alicia asked softly.

"I . . . thought about what you explained to me last night."

"About men and women? Did that distress you?"

"It was strange to think of, but it interested me," Felicia admitted.

"I see."

"Well, when I left the shop this morning it was so beautiful and I felt very happy. And then I thought about it some more."

"And . . ."

"When I got here I barred the door," Felicia said with a heightening of her blush, "and I took off my clothes in front of the glass, and I . . . touched myself."

Alicia regarded the bent head affectionately, a tiny smile on her lips. "And did you feel anything?"

"Everything," Felicia responded simply.

Alicia gave a gurgle of laughter and her daughter raised surprised eyes to her face. "Had you never done so before?"

"Oh, no. I had never thought to do so," Felicia answered, eyeing her mother warily.

"Obviously I have been remiss in your education," her mother replied, unable now to contain her mirth.

"But, Mama, is it not wrong?" Felicia asked incredulously.

"So they say," Alicia admitted between gulps of laughter, "but I have always found it immensely comforting."

Felicia ran to her mother and hugged her as the two women enjoyed their laughter, Felicia's of relief, her mother's of genuine amusement. Eventually Felicia drew a little away, a frown gathered on her forehead. "And does that not happen with a man?"

"It should, I suppose," Alicia admitted. "But I have not experienced it. Perhaps you will. Perhaps you will have a kind husband who will be gentle and understanding. Certainly I hope you will have a fond regard for him, and that should make you at ease. But you see, my dear, we are all reared to think of our bodies as very private, to be hidden and ignored. I remember not understanding what my mother was talking about when she spoke of her duty as a wife. She sent me into marriage unprepared. It might have been different otherwise; I cannot know."

Felicia received a good deal more information from this speech than her mother would have liked her to. Alicia had been hesitant always to speak with her daughter about such matters, for she felt wholly negative on the subject and did not wish to taint her daughter with her own judgments. Lord, what a job was raising a daughter when one had to hide so much. The previous evening Alicia had had to mind her tongue carefully so that she would not let slip that Mr. Tackar had killed her husband in a duel. There was little she could say about these intimate matters between men and women which would not reflect her own sorrows.

"Mama, what I did this morning . . . it is what the vicar calls self-abuse, is it not?"

"Yes, dear, but then I should not let that bother me overmuch. The vicar has disagreeable names for almost everything, and is a most un-Christian sort of person to boot. I can see no harm in it, but you shall have to decide for yourself. I forget sometimes that you are nearly grown up now. In another two years you will be thinking of marriage yourself. Pooh! This is altogether too serious a discussion for such a beautiful day. Shall we have luncheon and ride together for an hour? We can talk more then if you would like to."

CHAPTER SIX

After luncheon Felicia proudly presented to her mother the little mare she had ridden the previous day, but Alicia insisted on choosing a different hack. She was an experienced horsewoman and chose a spirited mount while the ostler eyed her skeptically. "I promise not to bring him to grief," she assured Hodges as she brought the horse's frisking under control.

They rode north this time through a stretch of forest and on past the hedgerows and fields. The lane was empty and they determined to race to the copse ahead. For all the little mare's endeavor Felicia was not able to win, but she had rosy cheeks and sparkling eyes from the ride. "Lord, how I have missed that," Alicia sighed.

"Lady Gorham urged you to make free with her stable, Mama. Why didn't you?"

"Because she does not like to ride and I wished to spend my time with her. I do enjoy her company and these last weeks I knew we would be leaving soon. She has promised to visit us, you know, but I rather hope she will think better of it. Not that I should not love to see her and Cassandra, but I should hate to be an embarrassment to them."

"You could never be that, Mama. I cannot believe Lady Gorham has a stuffy bone in her body!"

"Perhaps not. In any case, it is lovely to have a gallop again. I should not be gone too long, though, for poor Mr. Allerton must bear the load alone." Alicia directed her horse back to Tetterton and asked over her shoulder, "Did you wish to speak further of what we discussed?"

"There was just one thing. Do other women . . . touch themselves?"

"Truly, Felicia, I could not say. It is not the sort of thing one discusses over tea." The very thought of it sent them both into the whoops, and that is how the Stronbert Court party found them when they entered the lane from Mr. Tooker's farm.

Lord Stronbert had his son and daughter with him for the call he had paid on an elderly former tenant. The sound of laughter made him turn his head just as the Coombs ladies rounded the bend behind them.

"Look, Papa, it is Lady Coombs and her daughter. Shall we wait for them?" Miss Helen asked.

"Certainly," he replied easily as he watched Lady Coombs acknowledge their presence and attempt to stifle her mirth. Her daughter was not so successful and was still chuckling when the two parties joined.

Alicia, a smile lurking at the corners of her mouth, spoke first, "Good day, Lord Stronbert, Miss Helen, Master Matthew. I do not believe you have met my daughter, Felicia. Felicia, Lord Stronbert. You will remember his mother, the dowager marchioness."

Felicia, who very nearly had her laughter under control, dropped her eyes at this mischievous gambit of her mother's and was barely able to utter a greeting.

"Unfair, Lady Coombs," Stronbert retorted. "We are indebted to you, Miss Coombs, for Helen's enchanting bonnet. You may have noticed that she is unable to part with it."

Miss Helen was indeed wearing the bonnet, the ribbon beneath her chin tied jauntily under her right ear. "And she has already made an improvement in it," Felicia said with a grin.

"I knew you would think so," Miss Helen said proudly. "Grandmother was fit to be tied when she saw what I had done, but I like it."

"Such language, young lady," Stronbert cautioned

his offspring with a mild but meaningful glance. He turned then to Alicia, as carelessly graceful on horseback as on foot. "You are headed back to town?"

"Yes, I have deserted my post for far too long, but I could not resist a ride on such a day."

"You certainly seemed to be enjoying it," he commented.

"I was," she replied, then caught the gleam in his eye and added, "and I still am."

They rode off, Lord Stronbert and Alicia in the lead, Felicia and the children close behind. Alicia could hear her daughter chattering with them about the town and about the shop and about the grange with its marvelous rides. "My mother said your daughter was a beauty. She did not understate the case," Stronbert remarked indolently.

"Thank you."

"How old is she?"

"Sixteen."

"You must have been wed from the cradle."

"Very nearly," she replied tartly.

"Oh, dear, now I have said something personal again." His contrite countenance and bowed head were belied by the twitch of his mouth. "Can you forgive me?"

"Not when you do not wish to be," she said, her voice mournful.

Stronbert regarded her closely and a note of concern crept into his speech. "I did not intend to . . ." This time he did not miss the laughter lurking in her eyes. "It could be frightfully difficult to carry on a conversation with you," he said ruefully.

But Alicia had recollected that this was a stranger, a thing which she had somehow momentarily forgotten. He was a marquis and she a shopkeeper and she could hardly carry on a bantering conversation with him such as she might have with the men in the neighborhood of the grange. She had not done much of that, either, after she had met Mr. Tackar. Men had begun to seem very dangerous game to her. "Mr. Allerton mentioned to me yesterday that there are several standing orders from the court. They appeared to be from a bewildering variety of people. Do you suppose they would wish them continued under my management?" she asked a trifle stiffly.

"What sort of orders?" he inquired curiously.

"The dowager marchioness has required a half dozen linens every three months, but Mr. Allerton says they are usually sent back anyhow."

Stronbert could not tell this time if she was mocking him. He waited for her to continue. "A Miss Agatha Cummings has the shop send a new parasol each month, whatever is just arrived."

"Good Lord. I wondered where they all came from," he muttered.

She ignored him and continued, "A Miss Carson has us order chalk and notebooks regularly. A general Granat has a standing order for military hairbrushes every four months. A . . ."

"Please spare me," he begged. "I am sure there will be no change in the standing orders."

"As you wish. You might just mention to these people about the change in ownership, and they could let me know if they wish any alteration to be made."

"I said there would be no change." There was an undeniable firmness about his voice.

"I beg your pardon. I did not mean to contradict you." Alicia felt and sounded mortified.

Stronbert gave an exasperated sigh. "You will find, Lady Coombs, if you have not already, that the charges for all those at the court are sent to me for payment. Therefore I am in a position to assure you that there need be no change. I did not mean to snap at you."

Alicia kept her eyes straight forward and she spoke hesitantly, "Except the dowager marchioness's."

Stronbert swung around in his saddle and said sharply, "My mother is billed separately? Why?"

"Presumably because she requested it so."

Stronbert's lips became a firm line. "And is she current with her charges?"

"No, my lord."

"Just how uncurrent is she, Lady Coombs?"

"I cannot be exact, my lord, but I should say that she has not paid for her purchases in the last year and a half. The total she owes Mr. Dean must be upwards of five hundred pounds."

"Dear God! I will speak with her this afternoon and the matter will be settled tomorrow to your satisfaction, Lady Coombs."

"They are Mr. Dean's charges, Lord Stronbert. I think he had intended to write them off. The shop does not pass into my hands for another two days."

"Nonetheless, I should have been advised," he said grimly. "I wonder if there are others in Tetterton with the same problem."

"I should think it likely, sir, from things Mr. Dean has let drop."

Stronbert cast his eyes heavenward. "I do not look forward to my interview with my mother. I hope you will convey my apologies to Mr. Dean and assure him of my ignorance of the situation. I cannot imagine why he did not advise me."

"Can you not?"

He regarded her quizzingly and remarked, "You did not hesitate."

"Well, I cannot like to see him suffer. He is ill and holds the country gentry in great deference."

Stronbert gave a choke of laughter. "Well, I am sure the gentry will not pose the same problem for you."

"It will pose an even greater problem for me," Alicia responded quietly.

"Yes," he said thoughtfully, "I can see that it might."

They rode on in silence for a while, the sound of laughter and happy chatter behind them. As they neared the Feather and Flask, Lord Stronbert commented, "Your daughter seems to have a way with youngsters. My children are not usually so at ease with a stranger."

"Many of Felicia's friends at the grange had younger brothers and sisters, so she is used to the company of younger children."

"I have a niece and nephew staying at the court for a few months while their mother recovers from a bad bout of influenza. Perhaps Miss Coombs would care to call on them."

"That is kind of you, Lord Stronbert. I will mention it to Felicia." Her voice held little promise of an acceptance of his offer.

"You do not intend to keep the girl away from her own kind, do you, Lady Coombs?" he asked coldly.

"What have I to do with it?" she asked angrily. "Soon enough she will have to accept it. Not that she does not understand. We have discussed the problems and Felicia has been most forbearing."

"Nonsense. She is young and will need the companionship of others of her age."

"I am aware of that, Lord Stronbert," Alicia retorted. "And I have no doubt she will find them. But not amongst the gentry, which will naturally reject her for her mother's being in trade."

"I have invited her to the court."

"Where your mother will no doubt accept her with open arms! And what will your wife have to say?"

"My wife has been dead for two years, so I doubt she will have anything to say," he replied with some heat.

They were in the inn yard now, and Lord Stronbert had dismounted to assist her down. She could not bear to meet his flashing eyes, but he remained standing there with his hand outstretched. "I am so sorry. No one had mentioned that you were a widower. Please forgive my stupid tongue." She raised sad, penitent eyes and the anger in his died.

"How should you know? Come, I am waiting to assist you."

Alicia allowed him to lift her down, and then her daughter. There was a moment's awkward silence before he turned to Alicia and said, "Perhaps we can expect Miss Coombs at the court tomorrow for tea."

Felicia bowed her head to hide the eagerness in her eyes, but Alicia knew how she must be feeling. The girl asked diffidently, "Do you think that would be possible, Mama? Miss Helen mentioned that she has a cousin there but a year older than I."

Alicia was torn by conflicting emotions and surveyed Lord Stronbert's languid countenance. There was something there which she could not define but which was firm and insistent that she accept. "Yes, my love, you may go to tea at the court."

Stronbert turned to Felicia and said, "Fine. We will expect you at three then. I am sure my niece and nephew will be pleased to make your acquaintance. Lady Coombs, Miss Coombs." He bowed to them, remounted, and rode off with his children.

"How kind he was to invite me, Mama. Truly you do not mind if I go?" Felicia asked anxiously.

"I don't know. I fear the dowager marchioness will not make things pleasant for you, my dear. And I would not have your hopes raised that others will accept you," Alicia admitted.

"I see. Did you know the children's mother died some years ago?"

"Unfortunately, I did not know and made a miserable *faux pas* just now. Lord Stronbert corrected me, and none too gently. But there, I did not deserve less. I must rush to the shop now. Poor Mr. Allerton has no doubt expected me this last hour. Did you plan to work on your new dress now?"

"Yes, for a chill is coming on and I shall relish sitting by the fire. Or I could come with you," she suggested impishly.

"Go work on your dress, miss."

* * *

Together with Mr. Allerton and Mr. Dean Alicia spent the rest of the afternoon learning the organization of the shop and familiarizing herself with the books. She found that the dowager marchioness's charges came much closer to six hundred pounds, and hoped that the marquis would discover the full extent of them before coming to settle the account. She did not inform Mr. Dean of her conversation with Lord Stronbert as she had no desire to upset him and his comments had led her to believe, as she had suspected, that he did not intend to press for payment of the account.

Felicia had determined that she would finish the green dress in time to wear it to tea the following day. Since she had not begun, this required a supreme effort on her part and she set to work with a will. She was an expert needlewoman and knew exactly what she wanted, even without the latest edition of the fashion magazine before her. Within the hour she had cut the material and pinned it. She sent down for a pot of tea and worked steadily on the dress until her mother arrived after the shop closed. Alicia realized immediately what her daughter intended and after a hasty meal set out to assist her. When she left for the shop in the morning she knew that the dress would be ready in time, and that it was bound to be totally charming.

Mid-morning brought Lord Stronbert, who greeted Alicia amiably and then closeted himself with Mr. Dean in the back office for half an hour. Alicia spent this time waiting on customers and setting out some goods which had arrived at dawn. When the two men re-emerged from the rear, Mr. Dean looked overwhelmed and Lord Stronbert grimly satisfied. Stronbert took Alicia aside, lifted a bolt of fabric to examine it and said, "I hope in future you will send my mother's bills directly to me. You cannot imagine the state of chaos she showed me in her dun drawer. I shall be the rest of the morning settling her accounts.

I appreciate your informing me of the situation."

"It was my pleasure, sir," Alicia confessed with a grin.

Stronbert waved an acknowledging hand indolently. "This fabric, what is it?"

"A French brocade."

"Would it make into a reasonable mantua with a petticoat for my mother?"

"Not reasonable in price, my lord, but," Alicia considered it carefully, "it would become her, if the style chosen was suitable."

"Which does not seem to be one of her most dramatic achievements," he said dryly. "How many yards would it take?"

"That would depend on the style, of course, but I should think at least twenty-five to thirty."

"Good heaven. And what would that cost?"

"Perhaps eighty, eight-five pounds."

"A bargain," he commented negligently, a grin curving his wide mouth.

"Does your mother use a particular seamstress?"

"We appear to have one living at the court."

"Truly?" Alicia asked with some astonishment. "And she makes your mother's clothes?"

"I fear so."

"Then I would not use her if you wish to have the brocade made into a stylish gown," Alicia commented, straightfaced.

"She is a very biddable woman, as I recall," he mused.

"Then take the brocade to her and have Felicia speak with her when she comes to tea," Alicia suggested.

"Your daughter has not been invited to tea to consult on dressmaking," he said with some annoyance.

"Then you must find a solution of your own," she responded impatiently. "Felicia would not mind in the least; in fact, she would thoroughly enjoy it, if I know my daughter."

"And perhaps I should pay her a fee for her services when she leaves," he retorted.

"No, I will bill you," Alicia flashed, her eyes snapping.

Stronbert threw up his hand in a gesture of defeat. "I do not wish to quarrel with you," he said gravely. "Put the matter to Miss Coombs if you like and I will abide by her decision. In any case I will take the fabric."

"As you wish, my lord," Alicia bowed her head in acquiescence and attempted to lift the enormous bolt of fabric. She was unable to do so and turned to beckon Mr. Allerton, but he was occupied with a customer. Lord Stronbert ignored her gesture of protest and carried the bolt to an empty counter. "How many yards would you like?"

"I believe you mentioned thirty."

"At the most. I could give you twenty-five and set the material aside should you need additional."

"No, I think it best to have the thirty now."

Alicia did not look at him again but began to measure the material carefully, aware the while that his eyes were on her. She refused to lose count, but his continued gaze disconcerted her and she was hard pressed to keep her hands steady. Eventually she snipped the material and folded it carefully, then wrapped it into a parcel for him. "You will wish it put on your account, no doubt."

"Certainly. Lady Coombs?" He refused to speak further until she at length lifted her eyes to his. "I am persuaded you refine too much on this new role of shopkeeper. No, let me speak, if you please. You and your daughter are gently born no matter what mischance has placed you in your present situation. I assure you the court is full of gentlefolk come on harder times. For all her outrageous behavior, you will find that my mother does not treat any of them as socially inferior. Some come determined to make themselves useful, like our seamstress, and where their pride dictates such a position, they are accommodated. But nightly we dine together—the governess, the tutor, the seamstress, the general, my mother. And I warrant it would be very dull without all of them, with their multitude of interests and personalities. Sometimes I tire of the stimulation," he remarked ruefully, "but then I can always dine in my room, as they can."

"And do your neighbors accept all these impecunious relations as equals?" Alicia asked softly.

"Some do, some do not. What difference can it make? They have a home where they are comfortable and where they *are* accepted. The neighbors have learned," he chuckled, "that if they snub members of my household, they are like to receive treatment in kind from my mother. My mother was not perverse with your daughter out of snobbery, but out of jealousy. Mother has always had a secret desire to dress to the nines, you know, but somehow she always muffs it. It was unbearable for her to see such a young woman, a girl, in fact, create so enchanting a confection before her very eyes."

"Then she will not like it if Felicia designs a gown for her."

"By your leave, and your daughter's, I would rather she did not know. Though she may guess," he said wryly. "However, my hope is that she will enjoy the gown enough that such a matter will not overly concern her."

"I pray you are right, sir."

Stronbert shrugged. "It is not even decided that Miss Coombs will wish to take part in my plot. I must finish my errands. Good day, Lady Coombs."

"Good day, Lord Stronbert." Alicia handed him the parcel, careful not to touch him as she did so. He noted this with a mixture of amusement and perplexity, bowed, and was gone.

When Alicia joined her daughter at the inn for luncheon Felicia had almost completed the green dress. Over a light meal Alicia explained the purchase of the

French brocade and her suggestion that Felicia might advise the seamstress on the style of gown to be made for the dowager marchioness. "I did not mean to spoil your social call, but the brocade is really sumptuous, and I could not bear to think of the dowager having something hideous done with it! Lord Stronbert took exception to my suggestion but allowed that I might put it to you. I told him I would bill him for your services," she remarked defiantly.

"Oh, Mama, you should not be so stuffy with him! He seems a nice man, not the least top-lofty. But I should like to design something for his mother," she confessed. "That orange striped gown is beyond anything. Do you suppose most of her clothes are so ridiculous?"

"From what Lord Stronbert said, I have not the least doubt of it. And I should tell you, my love, that the court appears to house a goodly number of impecunious relations which his lordship assures me are not treated to any snobbishness by the dowager marchioness. He was trying to tell me, I take it, that you would not be frowned upon there, for all your mother is become a shopkeeper."

"There, you see? He is a most accommodating gentleman."

"Hmm. Perhaps, but there is something about him which I think will brook no argument when his mind is set, all the same. No matter. I have no doubt you shall enjoy your afternoon. I will go back to the shop now, to make up for being away so long yesterday. You should have just enough time to finish your dress. You will hire a gig to take you, please."

"Of course, Mama. I have already spoken with Hodges."

CHAPTER SEVEN

But there was no need to hire the gig when the time came. Lord Stronbert had spent more hours relieving his mother's debt than he had expected. Because he also had called for his new carriage, he found himself unable to set out for the court until shortly before three. He therefore thoughtfully called at the inn and offered to take Felicia up with him, assuring her that his nephew would welcome the opportunity to drive her back in his uncle's new phaeton, as he was forever itching to get his hands on the ribbons. "You will not be alarmed by the height, will you?" he asked as he ushered his passenger to the carriage.

Felicia regarded the splendid vehicle, which had two iron cranes with bends in them under which the front wheels could turn, making the vehicle more wieldy. The marquis's crest was on the side of the black-painted body. "I have never seen anything like it," she breathed with awe.

"It is an indulgence of mine," he admitted somewhat sheepishly. "I have just gotten it from the coachmakers and the horses may be a trifle skittish for a while, but I am not like to overset us."

Felicia allowed herself to be handed up and discovered that his last comment was an understatement. She had seldom seen anyone exert the graceful control over his horses that Stronbert did. And the horses! She would not have been surprised to hear that they could do sixteen miles in an hour without being touched in the wind. They were young chestnuts with splendid shoulders and a glorious matched step that made her feel as though she were floating. Her eyes sparkled with enjoyment.

"Do you drive?" Stronbert asked as they approached the gates of the court.

"I have driven a gig, yes, but nothing like this. Two horses must be much more difficult to control than one."

"A little, but when they are well schooled it is not a difficult matter. Would you like to try? The carriage-way is straight here."

Felicia gulped down the nervous lump in her throat and nodded, as she was not able to speak. Stronbert showed her how to position the ribbons and the whip so that she might have use of both. The horses broke step at the unfamiliar hand on the reins and Stronbert held his own over Felicia's until they regained their stride. As they approached the bend in the drive Felicia asked, "Do you wish to take them round the bend yourself, sir?"

"Not if you think you can handle it. The curve is gentle to the left and the horses are used to it."

Felicia took one quick look at his confident countenance and settled down to the task before her. She thought he murmured, "Good girl," but she could not be sure and her attention was soon directed to the magnificent building before her. "Best stop in front. I see Rowland is eager to try his hand."

Felicia exerted a gentle but firm pressure on the ribbons and the chestnuts came to a standstill beside the young man she had seen in town the previous day. His eyes were all for the phaeton and did not seem to take her in at all. "I say, Uncle Nigel, it's a bang-up rig! May I take it to the stables?" the young man asked enthusiastically as he ran to the chestnuts' heads.

Lord Stronbert handed Felicia to the ground and said distinctly to her, "You will have to forgive my nephew. He sometimes forgets his manners and he has hardly been able to wait for the carriage to be ready."

Rowland flushed a deep crimson and mumbled a hasty apology to Felicia. Lord Stronbert introduced them formally and Rowland bowed and said, "Your servant, Miss Coombs." Felicia returned the greeting with a demure curtsy, but she had not missed the recognition in his eyes.

"You let her drive it, Uncle Nigel?" Rowland asked suspiciously.

"Yes, and for a first time with two in hand she did remarkably well."

"May I drive it round to the stables?" Rowland asked again.

"So long as you do not reach them by way of Tetterton," his uncle admonished. "Your grandmother will be expecting you for tea."

"Oh, thank you, sir. If you will excuse me for a moment, Miss Coombs?" he remembered to ask.

Felicia assured him that she would and watched as he sprang up onto the high seat. He grasped the whip and ribbons with an enthusiast's eagerness and gave the horses the office.

"You are very trusting, Lord Stronbert," she murmured as his lordship turned his back on the carriage and his nephew, and offered her his arm.

"Yes," he sighed, "but there is nothing for it. He will have to try it out sooner or later. Shall you be afraid to have him drive you back to the inn?"

Felicia half turned to see the young man round the corner of the west wing carefully and responded, "I think not," just as the massive front doors were opened by the elderly but extremely distinguished-looking butler, Williams. Stronbert nodded and led Felicia himself up the grand staircase to the gold parlor where his mother was seated with perhaps a dozen other people. Felicia was overwhelmed by the dimensions of the room, its elegant Adams fireplace and its beautiful Turkish carpet in the center of the room. There was a handsome harpsichord to one side, a table in the center, and several dozen chairs placed about the room in groups. Facing the window were a fauteuil sofa and two armchairs. From these two latter Matthew and Helen erupted at sight of Felicia and bounded across the room, tugging a young woman behind them.

"Oh, I am so pleased that you have come," Miss Helen cried. "I have been waiting to introduce you to my cousin Dorothy."

"Children," Stronbert said firmly, "you must allow me to present Miss Coombs to your grandmother first." The young people, looking somewhat abashed, stepped back while their father led Felicia to his mother and said, "I believe you have met Miss Coombs, Mother. I beg you to introduce her to everyone while I make myself presentable."

The dowager marchioness eyed Felicia's new dress suspiciously, but was unfailingly polite as she presented the other occupants of the room. The bewildering number of names and faces frightened Felicia somewhat, but she relaxed when the young people finally drew her over to their side of the room. "Dorothy has a brother who is twenty, but he has not come in for tea yet," Miss Helen explained.

"Yes, I met him outside. He cozened his uncle into allowing him to drive the new phaeton round to the stables."

Matthew was indignant. "Now is that not just like my cousin Rowland. And I have not yet even had a ride in it."

"You will, young man," his father, who had just re-entered the room, announced placatingly. "In fact, I have a mind to teach you to drive it. Miss Coombs tried her hand on the way here."

"Did you?" Matthew turned to ask Felicia. When she nodded, he regarded her wonderingly.

"But only for a short while. The horses took exception to my hand on the ribbons," she confessed.

"Never say they bolted with you!" he exclaimed incredulously.

"No, no, for your father steadied them for me. And then they were very well behaved."

Rowland joined their group then and expressed once again his admiration for the new phaeton. "May I drive it again soon, sir?"

"I have in mind that you will take Miss Coombs back to the inn when she is ready to leave. Why do you not all show her about the grounds now? I cannot believe that you wish to stay in here." He gave a deprecating shrug in the direction of the rest of the party.

"But I must see Miss . . ." Felicia protested, unable to recall if she knew the seamstress's name.

"Miss Carnworth. Later, if you please. She is enjoying her tea just now."

Felicia blushed in embarrassment. "Of course. I beg your pardon."

Stronbert waved aside her apology and shooed the young people out of the room, saying to Felicia as she left, "Have Williams show you to me in the library when you return and I will take you to Miss Carnworth."

"Yes, my lord," Felicia agreed with a shy curtsy.

Dorothy linked her arm with Felicia's and said, "He's a pet, really. Even when he scolds you he is never really cross, just . . . firm, I guess it is."

"He is very kind," Felicia replied. "Where do you come from, Miss Clinton?"

"You must call me Dorothy. I do not know your name."

"Felicia. I hope you will use it."

"What a pretty name. Well, Felicia, we are from near Bath. My mama is Lord Stronbert's sister. Mama has been sick with a nasty crack of influenza, but she is getting stronger all the time now. We had a very cheery letter from her just yesterday. And she has never had a weak constitution like Uncle Nigel's wife did, so I try not to worry over her so much. But Uncle Nigel thought we might enjoy staying at the court while she recuperates."

"My mama and I used to live near Scarborough, but we have just come to Tetterton. Mama has bought Mr. Dean's shop in the High Street." Felicia watched anxiously to see how her new acquaintance would accept this statement.

"Yes, Helen told me so. Shall you help her there?" Dorothy asked. She gave no sign of discomfort and Felicia relaxed somewhat.

"Not in the shop, but I plan to decorate some of the bonnets. Mr. Dean's taste in hats is not altogether pleasing," she giggled.

"Well, I shall come and buy one of your bonnets," Dorothy declared.

"I hope you will find one to like."

Rowland, who had been talking with his cousins, joined the two young women and asked Felicia if she would like to see the stables. Dorothy demurred, saying, "That is all Rowland is ever interested in, Felicia. Horses and carriages. You cannot want to soil your pretty dress in the stables."

"I should like to see what horses his lordship has, though," Felicia admitted.

"There, you see?" Rowland declared triumphantly. He was as blond as his sister but much taller than she. They were a handsome pair, resembling one another enough to be twins with their grave brown eyes and aristocratic noses. The firm chins were duplicates, too, but where Dorothy's mouth was small, his was wide.

"Do you really want to see them?" Dorothy asked, not nearly as loath to venture there as she had sounded.

"Yes, for I find it hard to believe that one estate could house so many fine animals as I have seen so far—the children's mounts, and Lord Stronbert's, to say nothing of the chestnuts which drew the phaeton."

Felicia was not disappointed in the stables. The hunters and carriage horses were as magnificent as the riding mounts. Helen and Matthew pointed out each of the horses, and knew their names and qualities. The tour went on for some time and Felicia thought she had never seen so many horses at one time, even in a coaching inn. The young people walked for a while past the kitchen garden, and a row of hothouses and along the home wood to the hill beyond, where a waterfall babbled over pebbles and down into a stream that ended at a lake near the deer park. Felicia was enchanted with the scene and longed to go farther but felt she should be returning to the court for her meeting with Miss Carnworth.

Williams showed her into the library where she found Stronbert seated at a rosewood cylinder desk. The leather-covered writing surface had been drawn forward from under the pigeon holes and his lordship was writing on cream-colored crested paper. He put down the quill immediately when Felicia was announced and rose to greet her. "I have spoken with Miss Carnworth and she will be expecting us. Are you sure you wish to do this, Miss Coombs? There really is no need; I could have the material sent to London. On the other hand, Miss Carnworth is the only one who knows my mother's size exactly and need not have her for a fitting to complete the outfit. You understand this is in the nature of a surprise."

Felicia grinned. "Yes, I understand that and I really am looking forward to designing a gown from such magnificent material. I was surprised that Mr. Dean stocked anything so fine."

"There is certainly little call for it in Tetterton, I should imagine." He walked with her now through the vast hall and into the west wing where she was soon confused by the turns they made. A gentle voice responded to his tap on the door and she was ushered into a cheerful suite where a middle-aged woman she had been introduced to in the gold parlor awaited them. The woman was dressed rather severely and spoke bluntly, "I understand that Lord Stronbert has at last decided to see that his mother has at least one decent gown. I could not count on both hands the gowns I have made up for her which I would gladly have consigned to the fire. I myself have no flair for design, but one could buy more attractive gowns ready made in a shop than the last one I worked on."

Felicia was rather alarmed by this outspokenness and darted a glance at Stronbert to see how he dealt with it. His eyes were laughing as he retorted, "Really, Miss Susan, I am surprised that you have not convinced my mother by now that her taste is execrable."

"Convince the dowager marchioness! You must be loose in the haft, young man. Come and sit at my work table, Miss Coombs, and show me what you have in mind. We will not need you further, Nigel," she dismissed him.

He accepted this brusque dismissal, but Felicia could not resist whispering to him as he turned to go, "I thought you told my mother she was biddable!" The sound of his warm laughter did not cease until he had left the west wing. Felicia obediently seated herself and accepted the quill and paper offered her. She talked as she drew and found Miss Carnworth easily understood her plans for the brocade. They both had a healthy respect for the quality of the material and the style Felicia suggested would both enhance it and its elderly wearer. Miss Carnworth nodded over the finished sketches and announced, "Now that is more in keeping. You are very clever, child. Did you make the dress you are wearing?"

Felicia flushed slightly. "Yes, Mama let me choose the material yesterday and I made it quickly so that I could wear it to tea."

"Are you in mourning? It is rather dark for one so young," Miss Carnworth remarked bluntly.

"Yes, ma'am. My father died some months ago. We are but just starting to wear colors."

Miss Carnworth examined the dress and commented approvingly, "You must be handy with a needle, Miss Coombs. I have always enjoyed making clothing myself, and I thought for a while that Lord Stronbert would object. But, there, he has been very accommodating. Not that they keep me busy at the court, you understand, but there is enough to indulge my fancy from time to time. Miss Helen is a pleasure to sew for. I understand you made her bonnet."

"No, no. I merely added the ribbon to enliven it."

"No matter. I can see from your sketches that you have the flair. Can you come back in a few days to see that I have everything as it should be?"

"I cannot say," Felicia hesitated. "I cannot very well run loose here."

"I shall send for you when I am ready," Miss Carnworth said firmly. "No one will object to your calling on me. Thank you, child. I look forward to this project with real pleasure."

Miss Carnworth herself escorted Felicia to the hall where Stronbert was lounging against the mantelpiece speaking with his niece and nephew. The latter darted off to get the phaeton. Stronbert sent an inquiring, quizzical glance at Miss Carnworth who said gruffly, "It will do very well," and retreated to her quarters.

"High praise indeed from Miss Susan," he complimented Felicia. "Rowland will drive you to the inn, but Dorothy wished to speak with you before you left."

"Could you ride with us tomorrow morning, Felicia? We often ride out about ten and we could come for you at the inn."

Felicia turned to Lord Stronbert for confirmation and he set his lips firmly. "You do not need my approval, Miss Coombs. If you think your mother would allow the expedition, I will have Rowland bring a mare for you."

"Oh, no. I can have a mare from Hodges," Felicia said stubbornly.

"Dorothy said you were especially taken with Dancer. We need the horses exercised, Miss Coombs." He eyed her intently.

Felicia hesitated; she knew her mother would prefer that she rode one of the inn hacks, but there was that in his lordship's eyes which brooked no opposition. "Very well, Lord Stronbert. I should love to ride Dancer."

Stronbert smiled approvingly and shook her hand as Rowland came to announce that the phaeton was ready. Dorothy walked out with them and watched her new friend climb up onto the high seat. Then she returned to the hall and gave her uncle an impulsive hug. "I am so glad you brought her, Uncle Nigel. I like her excessively."

"She is as stubborn as her mother," he muttered darkly, but his lips twitched. "Yes, I am glad she came and that you go on well, Dorothy."

Felicia chatted easily with Rowland as he tooled the phaeton along the carriage path. He was respectful of the horses and the new carriage, and his driving was adequate, if he had not the expertise of his uncle.

"You will ride with us tomorrow, won't you?" he asked.

"Oh, yes, and I am to have Dancer," she replied happily.

"Bit of a handful that one, but I dare say you can handle her if you were not afraid to take my uncle's chestnuts in hand."

"I *was* a little afraid, you know," she confessed. "But I should like to learn and Lord Stronbert was right there to help if I got in trouble."

"Uncle Nigel is a great gun. He has been teaching me how to fence. I thought at first that I should rather go to London than come to the court, but I'm glad I did."

"Have you been to London before?"

"Several times. There is always something to do there—the theater, and the parties, and the gaming houses, though I am not so lucky at cards. Have you never been?"

"No, but perhaps one day I will. Mama had expected to take me in a few years, but that will not be possible now. I do not mind so very much, really, for I love the country and I am not sure I would feel at ease in society." She flushed suddenly. "Of course, there is no question of that now."

"Why not?" he asked, puzzled.

"Because we are shopkeepers now," she retorted defiantly.

He gave a gust of laughter and touched her gloved hand with one of his, losing his concentration on the chestnuts. His intention was to reassure her, but the chestnuts took exception to the haphazard jerk on the ribbons and bolted to the right. Felicia clung to the seat as Rowland struggled to bring them under control. "Damn and blast, what a careless gudgeon I am," he swore. The carriage swayed as it touched the opposite bank and Felicia nearly lost her seat before Rowland finally brought the horses to a stand. He was red with exertion and embarrassment when he turned to assure himself of her well-being. Felicia smiled timidly at him and casually adjusted her bonnet.

"I *am* sorry," he muttered. "Are you all right?"

"Quite all right."

"And I thought I could be trusted with such a team." He was sunk in gloom and his despair communicated itself to his companion.

"I distracted you from your driving. Do not berate yourself," she said, her voice full of concern.

"I cannot think what Uncle Nigel will say," he moaned as he urged the horses to continue.

"Need you tell him? I shall not mention it to him."

"Well, of course I must tell him. He trusted me with his horses and I did something foolish. Besides," he said with a comic look of dismay, "I think I have scraped the off side of the carriage."

Felicia burst into whoops and was only just recovering when they drew up to the inn. Rowland handed her down and said ruefully, "I promise I will be more careful next time. Will you be afraid to drive with me again?"

"Pooh! Do not be absurd. Of course I shall drive

with you again . . . that is, if you ask me," she said in confusion.

"I shall ask you," he replied frankly.

"Thank you for bringing me back, Mr. Clinton."

"You called my sister Dorothy."

"Well, yes. Shall I call you Rowland?" she asked shyly.

"Certainly, for I intend to call you Felicia," he said boldly, but with an embarrassed flush.

Felicia saw her mother approaching and beckoned her over to the phaeton. "Mama, I should like you to meet Rowland Clinton, Lord Stronbert's nephew. This is my mother, Lady Coombs."

Alicia liked the young man's manner as they conversed for a few minutes. She agreed to the proposed riding expedition, though she raised a brow when Rowland enthusiastically described Dancer's merits. She did not say anything, however, until she and her daughter were once more in their room. "You are to ride one of Lord Stronbert's horses?"

"Yes, Mama, for I told him that I would have a hack from Hodges and he gave me one of those looks. I did not dare contradict him."

"I know just what you mean, my love," Alicia laughed.

CHAPTER EIGHT

Alicia officially became owner of the shop the next day. Mr. Dean spent part of his time working with her and the rest preparing to remove from the cottage. By now most of the residents of Tetterton and its surroundings were aware of the change of ownership. Alicia was faced with the curiosity that prompted an unusually large number of customers to visit the shop each day. Her demeanor assumed the respectful quality of most of the shop proprietors of the area and most of the gentry accepted her waiting on them as a matter of course. Lady Wickham from Tosley Hall, along with several of her cronies, did attempt to make matters hard for Alicia, demanding items which were not available, complaining of the price of stuffs, and generally relished making her uncomfortable with their comments. But Alicia bore this with a tolerable grace, only occasionally exploding with wrath when she returned to her room at the inn.

Felicia rode almost daily with Dorothy and Rowland Clinton, and frequently Matthew and Helen joined the party. The dowager marchioness's gown was completed and Felicia complimented Miss Carnworth on it. The gown was set aside for Lord Stronbert to decide when to present it to his mother. Lord Stronbert himself had left for Leeds where business would occupy him for some days.

The dowager marchioness occasionally visited the shop and even Mr. Allerton commented on her reasonable behavior. Once she was dissuaded by Alicia from choosing an inappropriate fabric for her age; on that occasion she refused to purchase the other materials presented to her, but she made no disagreeable comment, either.

Within the week Mr. Dean departed and Alicia, with the help of the innkeeper and his wife, found help to get their belongings into the cottage and have it thoroughly cleaned. Mrs. Harper suggested a former maid from Tosley Hall as their only helper. "For Lady Wickham has turned her off, my lady, and it will be hard for her to find another position. But it were no fault of the young woman's. 'Twere Lady Wickham's son kept pestering her until she lost her temper with him and tossed the handiest bowl at his head. Good aim she has, too, for it hit him and he complained to his mother and had Mavis turned off. But you need have no fear, for she is a hard worker and a pleasant person, daughter to one of Lord Stronbert's tenants over Beverley way."

"Would she cook for us? Neither my daughter nor I have the least experience in the kitchen. It would mean a great variety of work for her."

"'Twon't be the least problem for her, my lady. Shall I send for her to speak with you?"

Mavis was in her early twenties and expressed her gratitude when Alicia agreed to employ her. "Nonsense! Felicia and I are the ones to be grateful, Mavis, for we will depend on you to run the household completely. I will be at the shop all day and Felicia intends to do some work about the cottage, making covers for the chair seats and such, but she will also be decorating hats from the shop and goodness knows what else."

So the three women settled into a comfortable routine in the cottage, well satisfied with each other. On the day that Alicia received a letter from Lady Gorham, Felicia burst into the cottage at luncheon, her eyes burning with anger.

"Whatever is the matter, my dear?" Alicia asked anxiously.

"We met Lady Wickham's son while we were out riding this morning. He was so rude to me!" Felicia burst into tears.

"Then he is only taking a cue from his mother."

"He refused to acknowledge the introduction and rode off with Dorothy in such a way as to suggest that he would not be seen with me," Felicia sobbed.

Alicia gathered her daughter in her arms and murmured, "You must not let such an incident bother you unduly, love. You have been very fortunate to be so well received. It has made you forget that we expected this sort of snub. Having met Lady Wickham I am not at all surprised to learn that her son is odious." Alicia wiped away her daughter's tears and held her at arm's length. "Perhaps it was shaming you in front of Rowland and Dorothy which bothered you so much."

"Oh, Mama, I wanted to sink into the ground! Rowland was red with embarrassment for me and I would not have him discomfited for the world!"

"Rowland Clinton is a sensible young man and his sister has become your good friend, so I am sure they will understand."

"But, Mama, Mr. Wickham had the nerve to tell the others that there was to be a ball at Tosley Hall and they were to be invited. He sneered at me." Felicia furiously wiped away the new tear that formed.

"Well, we shall not have him to our housewarming then," Alicia declared grandly.

Felicia uttered a watery chuckle. "Do not be so absurd, Mama. I should not invite him to a rat chase!"

"Of course not, my dear. Beneath our observance, I assure you."

Felicia had recovered her spirits by now and agreed to sit down to her meal. Over the cold meats and fruit Alicia informed her that Lady Gorham was intent on visiting Tetterton. "And you will never guess with whom she has been invited to stay."

"The dowager marchioness."

"However did you know?"

"Dorothy said this morning that her grandmother is expecting a visitor with a daughter our age, and it turned out to be Lady Gorham. I can hardly wait to see Cassandra again."

"Is the dowager marchioness aware that Lady Gorham is acquainted with us?"

"No, and I told Dorothy not to tell her. I thought it would be a superb surprise for the dowager," Felicia admitted impishly.

"Not a particularly pleasant one, I fear," Alicia replied ruefully.

Less than a week later a traveling chaise rolled down the High Street piled with trunks and luggage. Lady Gorham and her daughter, accompanied by two maids, were seated within and the coachman was directed to halt the chaise in front of the shop which still bore Mr. Dean's fading sign. The footman leaped down to place the steps and Lady Gorham and Cassandra stepped out into the muddy street. Picking their way carefully they entered the shop with only slightly muddy slippers and surveyed the scene with curiosity.

Alicia, who did not immediately perceive them, was intent on explaining to a slightly deaf old man that the bicorne hat he was regarding with aversion had replaced the tricorne which they no longer carried. Mr. Allerton was attempting to placate a sharp-eyed elderly woman, the vicar's sister, who found it upsetting that she had found undergarments displayed in the rear room. Felicia had been importuned by Miss Helen into bringing her to the shop to look for a present for her father's birthday, and the two of them were discussing the merits of a gnarled walking stick versus a stick pin for his frilled shirts.

Lady Gorham cleared her throat magnificently and all three assistants turned their startled gazes to her. "Cassandra!" Felicia squealed and hastily excused herself to Miss Helen to throw her arms about her friend.

Alicia plunked several hats before the elderly man and murmured that she would be back in a moment, a statement which she was required to repeat at high volume.

She approached Lady Gorham with a sparkle in her eye. "You have caught us unawares, Lady Gorham. Welcome to Tetterton." Alicia caught a glimpse of the overladen chaise and exclaimed, "You have not been to the court yet? You are too kind."

"Much too kind," her older friend sniffed. "We have come at an inopportune time."

"No worse than any other," Alicia admitted as she led Lady Gorham to a comfortable chair provided for customers who had to wait. "Please do not leave. I can be with you in a moment."

Lady Gorham shrugged and said, "I have no intention of leaving, my dear, until I have had a word with you. But I do not need to seat myself; I shall be much happier having a bit of a look around."

Alicia smiled gratefully and returned to the old man who grudgingly agreed to purchase the bicorne hat and presently left the store. Felicia explained to Cassandra that Miss Helen was searching for a present for her father, and her friend accompanied her to where Miss Helen waited patiently.

"What does your father like to do?" Cassandra asked Miss Helen.

"Oh, he does everything," she confided shyly. "He reads books in the library, and does accounts with the steward, and visits tenants. He likes to ride and he drives a glorious new phaeton with the most beautiful chestnuts."

"And does he have some handsome driving gauntlets?" Cassandra asked.

"Just some plain ones that he has worn for years," Helen admitted. "Do you think he would like some?"

"I gave my brother a pair for *his* birthday and I vow he has used them every day since," Cassandra remarked.

Helen lifted shining eyes to Felicia and said, "Yes, I think that would be just the thing. Might I see some?"

While Felicia took out the driving gauntlets and Mr. Allerton discussed the weather with the vicar's sister as she studied the linens, Alicia joined her friend before the Irish poplins and colored paduasoys.

"You did not mention to the dowager marchioness that you knew us," Alicia said quizzingly.

"Well, you know, she is such a strange woman that I thought it better to simply mention that I had a friend in the area. You have quite a selection of materials for a country town mercer."

"Mr. Dean stocked even the most expensive fabrics. It seems the neighborhood people rarely bother to go to York or Leeds for their dressmaking."

"This is a very attractive French brocade," Lady Gorham commented.

"Hopefully you will see the dowager marchioness in it before very long," Alicia said with a grin.

"Truly? Her taste must have improved since I knew her," the older woman replied caustically.

"The marquis purchased it for her and had it made up without her knowledge. In fact, Felicia chose the style. It is all a secret, you understand."

"Not a word shall pass my lips. Tell me, Alicia, how are you managing?"

Alicia considered the question carefully. "Very well, actually. The shop is rather fun, the cottage is charming, and we have been accepted very well on the whole. Lord Stronbert allows Felicia to run tame at the court with his niece and nephew who are staying there. She has been upset a few times by snubs and rudeness, but for the most part leads a remarkably genteel life. I fear things will be harder when the niece and nephew return to their home, but now all is well."

"And you, my love? Have you made friends in the neighborhood?" Lady Gorham bent her penetrating gaze on the younger woman.

"You know, I have not even thought of it. I have

been so busy with the shop and the cottage that there has been no time for socializing. But I will make time while you are here, I promise. I am finally caught up on the books and have been working on the inventory. No matter. That would be of no interest to you." Alicia flushed and realized that she had become so involved in her work that she spoke of little else these days.

"I think it is more than time that you had a diversion," Lady Gorham commented pungently.

"I dare say you are right. Plan to come to tea tomorrow and I will broaden my horizons," Alicia teased.

"I shall accept, young lady, for Cassandra and myself."

"I would extend the invitation to all at the court, but Felicia said when she attended tea there that no fewer than a dozen people were assembled. And it was her impression that they were all resident. I should dearly love to meet Miss Carnworth, though," Alicia admitted.

"I shall induce her to come with me, whoever she is. And the dowager marchioness? She is my hostess, you know."

Alicia regarded her ruefully. "I doubt you could convince her to come, but you are willing to try. And do bring Dorothy and Rowland."

"I shall. Now I must be going, my dear. We are overdue at the court already, but I wished to see you straightaway."

"I am so glad you did." Alicia placed a salute on her wrinkled cheek. "I shall arrange to have time free to spend with you while you are here."

"See that you do," the older woman said gruffly, and bustled off to retrieve her daughter.

Felicia was delighted to hear that they were to entertain the next day. She was sent off to advise Mavis, who would need help from the inn. Mr. Allerton assured Alicia that he could manage in her absence but business had been so heavy recently that she hesitated. "Do you know of anyone who could come in for the afternoon? I think you should have some help."

"Young Jeremy Tomkins might be willing, ma'am."

"Yes, see if you can get him. I do not like to leave you shorthanded."

"I am used to being here alone. Mr. Dean was often too sick to spend much time in the shop," he explained.

"I know," she sighed, "but those such as Lady Wickham do not like to be kept waiting, even when they see that we are all busy."

Mr. Allerton allowed himself a grave grin. "As you say, ma'am."

Mavis, with Felicia's enthusiastic assistance, produced a vast array of cakes, biscuits, and tarts. The cottage gleamed with polish and several new seat covers adorned the chairs. There was a fire burning in the grate to offset the autumn chill, and its light glowed in the glass-fronted bookcase. Mr. Dean had even left a delicate little writing desk of mahogany inlaid with brass which had belonged to his wife. The handsome clock in its marquetry case chimed the hour and Alicia commented to her daughter, "You have wrought a miracle here these last weeks, my dear. I fear I have not thanked you as I should."

"I have enjoyed it. There are still several seat covers to be replaced, and you can be sure they will be noticed."

"But not commented on, thank heaven. Lady Gorham is well aware of our recent arrival. There is a carriage now. In fact, it sounds very like two carriages."

Felicia skipped eagerly to the window and twitched back the draperies, which would need to be replaced. "Three, Mama. Lady Gorham and Cassandra have Rowland and Dorothy with them. The dowager marchioness is riding in state, and Lord Stronbert has Miss Carnworth with him in the phaeton."

"Lord Stronbert! Perhaps he does not intend to come in but merely to leave Miss Carnworth," Alicia suggested hopefully.

"Oh, no, he is handing the reins to a groom. Do you not wish him to come, Mama? He is ever so nice."

"It is just that I did not expect him," Alicia admitted as she unconsciously patted her hair to make sure that it had not been tousled. "I did not invite him."

Lady Gorham was announced and whispered to her hostess, "I was sure you had forgotten to mention Lord Stronbert so I took the liberty of including him." She smiled mischievously. "It was the only way to get Evelyn here, and I felt she should be with me so early in my visit."

"Indeed," Alicia said with mock aloofness, then with more concern, "I doubt we have enough chairs."

A cool, lazy voice at her side said, "I shall not mind standing." But she had no time to respond as she greeted the rest of her guests. Finally she turned to Lord Stronbert and said, "How do you do, my lord? I am so pleased you could come."

"Are you? I thought you seemed rather horrified." He laughed down at her and resisted the impulse to raise her hand to his lips.

"I have just realized that we will need another chair. If you will excuse me, I will have the maid bring one."

"Do you have another?" he asked curiously.

"Frankly, I do not know," Alicia admitted helplessly. Chairs had already been brought from the dining room and she was not sure if the bedrooms had been canvassed as well.

"Go and entertain your guests. Let me see to the matter."

"I cannot do that," she protested.

"Your guests are awaiting you," he replied firmly.

"Yes, sir." Alicia retreated to the tea table and began to pour out as she spoke with Lady Gorham and Miss Carnworth. The dowager marchioness stayed a bit aloof, but not disapproving.

Lord Stronbert wandered into the dining parlor and found no chairs there. At the kitchen door he surveyed the activity within and drew back. He returned to the hall and hesitated before ascending the staircase. The first bedroom he entered was tidy if somewhat shabby. It contained no chairs. The second was strewn about with clothing, material, ribbons, and bonnets and contained a barely presentable chair. He surveyed it exasperatedly and bore it down to the drawing room with him. When Alicia saw him slip quietly into the room, she recognized the chair from her daughter's room and bit her lip with vexation. The man had had the nerve to invade her daughter's chamber, and probably hers as well! He gave an apologetic, helpless shrug and came forward to receive a cup of tea. "Thank you, Lord Stronbert. You might have sent a maid."

"They were busy," he responded calmly.

The young people had gravitated away from their elders and were making plans for an excursion the next day. Lord Stronbert drew a chair up to the older group and engaged Lady Gorham in conversation so that his mother was forced to make some effort with Lady Coombs and Miss Carnworth. Alicia was interested in what Tetterton had been like when the dowager marchioness had come to the court as a bride, and she found her guest surprisingly ready to satisfy her curiosity. It was not often people showed an interest in her forty-year-old reminiscences, and she felt strangely grateful to this young woman for hearing her out. She remembered two proprietors previous to Mr. Dean at the mercer's shop and told of the misadventures that had followed the greengrocer for years. Her mentions of her husband were softly spoken with a fondness which enchanted Alicia. Miss Carnworth sat through this monologue with patience but a noted lack of enthusiasm.

Abruptly Evelyn, Lady Stronbert said, "We are having a dinner to celebrate my son's birthday next week,

Lady Coombs. I hope you and your daughter will be able to attend."

Alicia was surprised and a little taken back by this gush of hospitality, and cast a nervous glance at Lord Stronbert. He was amused by her confusion but added his wishes that they would find themselves free to attend. "I am sure we would be delighted," Alicia finally managed to say. She was rewarded by an imperious nod from the dowager marchioness and an affable smile from the marquis.

Alicia took the opportunity to recover her scattered wits while she poured out more tea and the maids passed around refilled plates of pastries. The group had rearranged itself somewhat when she completed this task and she found an opportunity to speak with Miss Carnworth.

"Takes a fancy to someone now and then, does Cousin Evelyn," Miss Carnworth said bluntly. "Not that she shows it quite as someone else would, you understand. Not a bad soul, actually, though she puts people off with her odd starts. I've always thought it was a medical matter, but could you find a doctor to diagnose it? Never!"

Although Felicia had told her mother that Miss Carnworth showed not the least subservience to Lord Stronbert or his mother, Alicia listened to her wonderingly. Absently she offered the older woman a tart which was accepted as Miss Carnworth proceeded, "You will enjoy the food at the court, as I can see you are particular. Fancy chef we have there. Never less than two courses with four removes each, and dozens of side dishes. The number of pastries, jellies, creams, cakes, and suchlike is enough to bring on the palpitations. But there, Agatha and the general are extremely fond of them, as of course the children are."

"I can see I have a treat in store for me," Alicia remarked.

"One gets used to it," her companion muttered

darkly. "That is not to say that I do not appreciate it. And there are so many people to please, what with their different likes and dislikes. The general is uncommon fond of collared eels," she said, with a grimace of distaste.

"You could not possibly do the sewing for everyone there."

"Lord, no. I do some for the children and for Cousin Evelyn, but even they have most of their costumes made out. I would not have you think me a drudge. I love my sewing and wish there were more of it."

"Felicia has a passion for it, too. Years ago I admitted to myself that I did not really enjoy it and put my hand to other things."

"Felicia is a very clever child. Do you enjoy the shop?" Miss Carnworth asked with unwonted gentleness.

"You know, I do. It tires me sometimes, but I have taken a fancy to ordering the merchandise and to displaying it attractively," Alicia confessed.

"Surely there is a great deal more to it than that."

"Yes, and I cannot always like serving the customers. I have not the patience to wait for them to choose between the yellow silk and the purple satin. But I do not mind keeping the books; I was used to do so at the grange."

Miss Carnworth nodded her understanding and would have said more, but she received an unmistakable signal from Stronbert that he wished to speak with Lady Coombs, and she extracted herself by murmuring, "Must have a word with Lady Gorham, if you will excuse me," and a moment later Alicia found the marquis seated beside her.

"You were kind to indulge my mother in her tales of bygone days, Lady Coombs. The others at the court are not so patient with her, and she loves nothing better."

"I enjoyed hearing them, Lord Stronbert, especially

the tale of the butcher chasing your dog down the High Street," Alicia responded, her lips twitching suspiciously.

"When I dashed to Cuffy's defense and landed in the pond?" he asked ruefully. "Yes, I imagine that would amuse you. Those sausages cost me a month's allowance, I'll have you know, and the dog was not the least bit grateful. He very nearly bit me when I tried to take them away from him."

"Reprehensible," she murmured, "and your fawn corduroy coat and breeches ruined forever."

Stronbert regarded her with mock exasperation. "Mother remembers the most remarkable things. I was very proud of that outfit, though, for it was a duplicate of my father's, and it was never replaced. Some day I will show you the portrait that was painted of the two of us wearing them, while Cuffy chewed his way through my favorite boots as we posed."

"I would be honored to see it," she replied politely.

"Then you shall, at the birthday dinner, and I should warn you that I have requested that Mother wear her new gown. She has not seen it yet, of course, but she agreed to please me."

Alicia turned concerned eyes to his. "She will guess that Felicia designed it, will she not?"

"I imagine so."

"Then it might be wisest if we did not come, sir. I should not like to have such an occasion spoiled by our presence."

Laughing eyes met her gaze as he replied, "And miss all the fun? Never. It is most necessary that you and your daughter be there, I assure you."

"Felicia might be embarrassed by Lady Stronbert."

He considered her remark gravely and shook his head. "No, Mother would not upset your daughter, ma'am, you need have no fear. We are all grateful that Felicia has proved such a good friend to Dorothy, for my niece was rather lonely and worried over her mother's illness."

Alicia bowed her head and studied her hands as she said softly, "It is we who are grateful, Lord Stronbert, for the acceptance which has been accorded Felicia at the court. I . . . I have not always indicated my appreciation, I know, but," she swallowed nervously, conscious that his eyes were intent on her, "I pray you will understand how sincerely I feel your kindness." With difficulty she raised her head and met his gaze. In spite of the buzz of conversation around them, she felt very much alone with him, aware only of the warmth in his smile, the keenness of his eyes, the strength of his presence.

"If it were possible, I would welcome you at the court routinely, Lady Coombs. It is scarcely satisfactory for me to speak with you only in the shop." He ignored her distracted flush and continued, "You are busy, I realize, but you must arrange to visit the court while Lady Gorham is here. It is you she has come to see."

"I do intend to make time to see Lady Gorham," she murmured, unable to still the tumult his words had raised in her breast. It was nonsense of course to place too much significance on them. His observance was flattering, to be sure, but very confusing to her. Doubtless she was responding to his authority and capability having had to rely on her own wits for so long. And there was no denying that he was a handsome man with a thoughtfulness rare in her experience. He meant nothing more than to put her at ease because she was a shopkeeper, though gently born. With relief she noted that Lady Stronbert had risen and was moving toward her to make her farewells.

Miss Carnworth immediately rose also and soon the entire party was heading for the hall where the maids were waiting to dispense pelisses and bonnets. Lord Stronbert lingered to speak with his hostess. "We will look forward to having you to dinner next week, Lady Coombs. I trust you will forgive me for invading your bed chambers."

Alicia flushed slightly but said automatically, "Certainly, sir. I appreciated your finding the necessary chair."

When the two women were alone Felicia said sadly, "They have all been invited to the Wickham ball, Mama."

"I am sorry, my love. There will be other balls some day."

"Oh, I know. Cassandra said she would not go if I did not, but I told her not to be ridiculous."

Alicia hugged her daughter close and sighed. "You are brave, dear. We *are* invited to Lord Stronbert's birthday dinner next week. Shall you like that?"

Felicia brightened visibly. "Very much, Mama. Shall you?"

"Yes," Alicia admitted, rather alarmed at her own anticipation of seeing Stronbert again.

CHAPTER NINE

As arranged with the Clintons and Cassandra, Felicia, donning a blue riding habit, joined them the following day. Although there were sufficient horses housed at Stronbert Court to mount half the town, Alicia had suggested that during Cassandra's stay there, Felicia should hire Hodges's mare so that her friend might ride Dancer. The girl could see no logic to this exercise, since Cassandra could have her choice of half a dozen mares from the court stables, but she recognized that it somehow had to do with her mother's pride, and she gave in with a good grace. Rowland had protested, well aware of Felicia's partiality to Dancer, but she had remained firm.

The party met at the Feather and Flask stables and determined to ride north of town, since the weather was propitious and the way led by an inviting stream where they could all dismount and listen to the babble while seated on the pine-needled ground. Felicia suffered under the feeling that Cassandra and Dorothy would naturally be discussing the Wickham ball and the gowns they were to wear, if she were not with them. Several times the conversation did indeed drift in that direction, only to be brought up short as one or the other of the young ladies realized that it was not a discussion in which Felicia could take part.

Rowland grew impatient with his sister for her carelessness in making Felicia uncomfortable and suggested that they might like to visit the natural cave further up the stream.

"Never say you want us to troop up that muddy bank!" Dorothy protested. "My habit has never been the same since the day we went there."

"Oh, pooh," Felicia protested, her eyes sparkling with interest. "I have never been in a cave. Is it large?"

"The merest hole in the wall," Dorothy disparaged, "and muddy as can be."

"But it hasn't rained in days," Rowland pointed out. "I have no doubt it will be dry as a bone."

Cassandra took her cue from Dorothy, since she had no desire to despoil the brand new riding outfit she was wearing. "Another time, perhaps, Rowland. It is too pleasant just sitting here to even think of moving."

"And you, Felicia? Have you no spirit of adventure?" Rowland challenged.

Jumping to her feet immediately, Felicia retorted, "There is nowhere that you could go that I would not be able to follow. I climbed about the Scarborough cliffs as a child with our neighbors. Lead on, sir."

"You will ruin your pretty outfit," Dorothy cautioned with a grin.

"Oh, what can it matter compared with seeing a cave?" Felicia laughed.

Since there were no other takers, Rowland and Felicia followed the stream as it wound through the trees to the north. He took her hand to assist her over a fallen tree and did not release it as they continued, declaring stoutly, "The ground is rough hereabouts and I don't want you to fall."

Although Felicia would ordinarily have informed him that she was quite capable of looking to herself, she liked the warmth of his hold on her and made no protest. "Is it far?"

"Not very. Perhaps half a mile or so. Are you tired already?" He looked down at her with amused eyes.

"Of course not! I was merely interested. When did you find the cave?"

"Uncle Nigel took us there shortly after we came.

He often rides this way to visit the Tooker farm with Helen and Matthew. I'm glad you shall be at his birthday party, but you must not mind being left out of the Wickham ball, Felicia," he said seriously. "It will be dull indeed without you, but Lady Wickham is a stuffy old bag and her son is a nodcock. I daresay you won't miss a thing."

Felicia offered him a forced smile and a sigh. "Indeed. We are still in mourning in any case, and I suppose I could not dance, so it is better that I should not be there at all."

"Right you are." He pressed her hand encouragingly and they walked on in silence.

The murmur of the stream and the twitterings of the birds in the trees about them became more obvious now, and Felicia reveled in this chance to be entirely alone with Rowland. In spite of the fact that they rode almost daily, there were always others with them. Certainly Dorothy and Cassandra were her dearest friends (her only friends, she thought sadly), but Rowland was different. There were things she wished to share with him that she would never mention to the two young ladies. But now that she was alone with him she did not quite know how to begin; perhaps he would not wish to hear about her problems and her thoughts. She cast a sidelong glance at him and found him studying her. "Have I a . . . smudge on my face?" she asked anxiously.

"No, you look beautiful," he answered simply, then decided that perhaps he had been too abrupt and hedged, "Walking brings a healthy glow to the cheeks, don't you think?"

Felicia giggled. "I hope so. Is . . . is your mother better, Rowland?"

"I had a letter from my father yesterday, and he said she is recovering nicely now. I think you would like her, Felicia; she's a bit like Uncle Nigel—generous and kind, but she means what she says. Worries about us too much, of course, but I guess all mothers are like that. She laughs a lot and doesn't stand on ceremony."

Her eyes on the ground, Felicia said softly, "She sounds delightful, but I don't suppose I shall ever meet her."

Startled out of his own train of thought, Rowland regarded her earnestly. "Well, of course you shall. Comes to see Uncle Nigel once a year at least. Not this year, I suppose, because she's been sick, but certainly next year. Or you shall come to visit Dorothy."

"I could not leave Mama here alone even if Dorothy wished for me to visit," she protested, snapping a twig between her fingers. "Mama needs me to assist with the shop."

"Nonsense. You know perfectly well she does not even want you to go near it."

"Yes, but that won't serve, really. Everyone knows we keep the shop, so where is the good in pretending that I have no connection with it?"

"Felicia, your mother is trying to protect you."

"But she cannot, Rowland." Felicia turned troubled eyes to him; here was one of those things she wished to discuss. "Why should I not bear the burden of the shop with her, when it does no good to exclude me? You say I must not mind not being invited to the Wickham ball. Very well, I have to accept that, but the reason for it is that we keep a shop, and if I am to be cast in that light in any case, I might as well be of some use to Mama."

Rowland seized both of her hands and Felicia was struck by the seriousness of his countenance. "I am sure you are of the greatest assistance to your mother; it cannot be otherwise. But do not deny her the solace of knowing she is doing what she can to shield you from social distress. You owe her that much, Felicia, for it is difficult for her to see you unhappy, and it is the only thing she can do for you."

"Does it . . . bother you, Rowland? That is . . .

well, never mind." Felicia watched a tiny bird wing its way through the branches above, and did not allow her sad eyes to meet those of her companion.

"No, Felicia, it does not bother me, or Dorothy, or Cassandra, or Uncle Nigel, or Helen, or Matthew, or Miss Carnworth, or . . ."

A gurgle of mirth escaped her, and her eyes were shining when she returned them to his face. "No more, I beg you! You are all very kind to me."

"How could we be otherwise?"

The look in his eyes spoke more than his words and Felicia shyly tugged one hand from his grasp. "Is the cave close by now?"

"Only a step," he murmured as he led her forward.

During their inspection of the small cavern, the awkwardness of the moment before was forgotten. The dampness was not unpleasant, and the earth underfoot was no longer muddy, so Felicia inspected to her heart's content, bubbling over with questions on its formation and whether smugglers might ever have used it.

"*Now* you have a smudge on your face," Rowland laughed as they turned to leave. He gently rubbed away the dirt while their eyes held before he took her hand once more and they proceeded back along the twig-strewn path. Felicia chatted about Lady Gorham and Cassandra in an effort to keep their conversation on an impersonal basis, and withdrew her hand from his when they came in sight of her friends seated beside the stream.

"I see you have not muddied your clothes, Felicia," Dorothy called teasingly, "but was it worth the walk?"

"I found it fascinating. You should have come," Felicia retorted, though she was grateful that they had not.

On their arrival at the Feather and Flask stables they found Hodges speaking with a soberly dressed man of indeterminate years, but he promptly left the stranger and came forward to take the mare from Felicia. She waved a farewell to her friends after arranging to ride the following afternoon.

Even when Felicia saw the stranger again the next day, first at the stables and later riding in the same direction as their party, she thought nothing of the matter. After all, she and her mother had not been long in Tetterton, and he might well be known to others in the community. Only Dorothy and Rowland accompanied her, as Cassandra had chosen to go driving with her mother and the dowager. It was a golden autumn day, and they again chose to ride north, past the Tooker farm to the meadows beyond. The horses were tethered in the shade of a gnarled oak, and while Felicia and Rowland stood talking beneath the tree, Dorothy wandered off to gather cornflowers.

A gust of wind loosened several brightly colored leaves from the tree and they floated down, one settling gently on Felicia's head. "It is the same color as your hair," he commented with a laugh as he reached out to remove it. Instead, he stroked her hair, his eyes intent on her face.

He is going to kiss me, she thought breathlessly.

"Look at all the flowers I have gathered!" Dorothy exclaimed, arriving with her arms full of the beautiful blue plants. "We shall have enough to fill half a dozen vases."

Rowland and Felicia, startled from their enchantment, turned rather guiltily to her and Rowland said exasperatedly, "How are we to get them to the court? They are bound to wilt quickly in this heat."

"Not if we go directly there," Dorothy returned gaily. "I can have them in water in half an hour."

With a slight shrug of his shoulders and a crooked grin at Felicia, Rowland handed the two ladies onto their horses before he ungraciously wrapped the cornflowers in his handkerchief and swung himself onto his mount. "Hardly out long enough to exercise the horses," he grumbled.

Intent as they were on returning speedily to the court, the riders were not aware of the man they passed, hidden in the shrubbery alongside the road. This was not the first time he had followed them, but he was now satisfied with the information he had gathered and decided to return to his employer.

Francis Tackar was a very persistent and a very conceited man. He refused to believe that Alicia was not attracted to him, but he conceded that it might be difficult for her to assume the role he had outlined, when she had a young daughter whom she wished to see creditably established one day. It had become incumbent upon him to force the issue in his own way. Having no principles to obstruct him, he immediately began to devise a plan of action when he left Tetterton. He was not impatient and the length of time his machinations took to come to fruition merely added spice to his appetite.

His valet, Martin, arrived at Tackar's estate when his employer was seated after dinner thoughtfully sipping at his brandy. Since he considered his news to be of value, he slipped into the room and coughed discreetly. Tackar turned his cold eyes in the direction of the sound, and a gleam of interest appeared in them. "You have discovered something?"

"Indeed, sir. I thought you would wish to be apprised of certain findings I have made." The small man remained standing by the door, inconspicuous in the shadows away from the candlelight.

"Well, come over here, fool. I have no intention of breaking my neck to see you."

"Certainly, sir." Martin advanced to a respectful distance from the table. "As you know, Lady Coombs serves in the shop regularly, so I thought it wisest to concentrate on the young lady."

"I am not interested in what you thought. Tell me what you have found out," Tackar snapped.

"Miss Coombs rides regularly with the Clintons, a

niece and nephew of the Marquis of Stronbert, who are staying at the court. There appears to be an affection between the young man and Miss Coombs."

Tackar's brows lifted cynically. "You don't say. That could be useful."

"There is to be a ball at Tosley Hall, Sir John Wickham's place, on Monday. The Coombs ladies are not invited."

"She had no chance to retain her place in society when she took a shop. Better for her to have accepted my *carte blanche* in the first place, without all this shilly-shallying and coyness," Tackar mused, his irritation evident.

The valet coughed again, more discreetly than before.

"There is more?"

"Yes, sir. All of the others appear to be invited, and from the conversation I overheard between Miss Clinton and another young lady, it is likely that the day of the ball will be spent in preparations for it. Miss Coombs is unlikely to ride with them that day, as she normally would."

His employer nodded and sat staring vacantly at the epergne in the center of the table. Abruptly he asked, "Is it likely that Miss Coombs has ever seen Mr. Clinton's handwriting?"

"I should think it most improbable. They meet daily, and any necessity for correspondence would more properly be conducted through the sister."

"What of Lady Coombs's maid?"

"Her name is Mavis Carter and she lives with them, but her family is in Beverley." Martin allowed himself a wintry smile. "Unfortunately Miss Carter's mother is prone to attacks of asthma, and on such occasions Mavis is summoned to nurse her."

"Most unfortunate," Tackar agreed. "I think, Martin, that Lady Coombs is about to give up shopkeeping. I don't suppose you have found an appropriate spot."

"Now, there, sir, I was lucky. When I followed the young people today, it was necessary for me to leave the lane because Miss Coombs happened to catch sight of me riding behind them."

Tackar eyed him sharply. "She saw you? What did she do?"

"Nothing. I assure you she thought nothing of it, but I had no wish to be seen hanging about or observed when they returned toward town. They left the lane shortly after I did to wander about a meadow. Where I was hidden in the shrubbery I found an abandoned shed."

"Can it be secured?"

"With very little effort."

"I will come with you tomorrow to see it."

"Very good, sir."

"Where does the girl get a horse? From the Feather and Flask?"

"Yes, she hires one particular mare there."

"Excellent. You have done well, Martin." Tackar dismissed him with a wave of his hand and remained seated at the table, languidly caressing his brandy glass, a satisfied smile on his lips.

The afternoon of the ball found her mother in the shop and Felicia working needlepoint seat covers in the cottage. She was feeling blue-deviled, much as she was determined to keep herself busy and cheerful. Mavis answered a summons at the front door and came into the drawing room to hand Felicia a note. "There is a man waiting out front for your response, miss."

Felicia tore open the note and read: "Dear Felicia, I knew you would miss your ride today, so I have sent your favorite mare from the inn. If you will ride on the lane north of town you will find an old oak a half mile farther on from the Tooker farm. I have left you a surprise there which I hope will cheer you. Rowland."

Felicia grinned. How thoughtful of him! She was

too excited to pay any particular attention to the nicely dressed man standing out front with the mare but directed him to tie the horse to the fence as she would have to change into riding dress. Then she whisked upstairs and changed so quickly that it was but a matter of minutes before she was downstairs again to inform Mavis that she was going for a ride.

The day was cold but there was no rain in the air. A gallop brought color to Felicia's cheeks and she eventually let the mare slow to a trot as they passed the Tooker farm. After a while she began to scan the side of the lane for an oak, her excitement rising. Then she saw it, an old gnarled tree with a yellow ribbon tied about it. She smiled in anticipation and reined in the mare. Since she could see nothing from her perch, she jumped down and tied the reins to a nearby sapling.

As she approached the tree, a dark figure loomed out from behind it, and she thought for one astonished moment that Rowland had met her there. She was speedily disillusioned, though, for in the next instant she recognized Tackar's features and her reflex was to run. He grasped her wrist before she could turn, and she struck him with her other hand. An uttered oath succeeded her strike and she opened her mouth to scream, but his hand was immediately across it. When she bit him he smashed her to the ground and sat on her back with one hand pushing her face into the fallen leaves until she thought she would not be able to breathe.

With his other hand he drew a rag from his pocket and slid it down under her face; then he used both hands to pull it into her mouth along with some leaves. She lay there choking until he rolled her over and turned the cloth so that the leaves fell out. But the grit which remained in her mouth was painful to swallow and her fear was overwhelming. He had her hands pinned down at her sides, and her struggles were to no avail. Taking both her hands in one of his, he drew a rope from his pocket and wound it around her wrists, at length using both hands to tie it securely. Then he stood over her menacingly and growled, "I want no more nonsense from you, girl."

Tackar lifted her to her feet and shoved her in front of him. "Just walk past those bushes." Felicia made one last attempt to run, darting around him in the faint hope of reaching her mare. She felt a searing sting across her back and turned in astonishment to see that he had picked up her riding crop and lashed her with it. Even while she stood frozen he grasped her bound wrists and dragged her after him, half walking, half crawling to the shed behind the bushes. He shoved her in so that she sprawled on the floor, her skirts in disarray about her thighs.

The late afternoon light streamed through the door and he stood panting, his eyes fastened on the firm white thighs. He reached in his pocket yet again and drew out another length of rope and grasped her ankles. After he had bound them, he ran his hands up her legs while her eyes dilated with terror and her cries were muffled by the cloth in her mouth. His eyes were attracted by her heaving breasts and he grasped them so tightly that she winced. He seemed to come to his senses then and laughed. "Later. Now I have plans for your mother. Strange I did not think of the benefits of this particular plan before." Felicia closed her eyes to block out the evil light in his, as he stuffed her bonnet into his pocket.

"I shall return," he promised her smugly, "and then you will learn something new." He reached down and felt between her legs. He nodded, satisfied. "Yes, something new." Before Felicia could control the shuddering aversion of her body, he was out the door and she heard him slam the bar to. She huddled up into a ball and wept. How could she ever have thought it might be pleasant, when she was married, to have a man touch her! And her mother! He was going now to force himself on her mother. The bitter tears would not cease.

Tackar strode confidently to where he had left his horse and swung into the saddle. He then ripped the yellow ribbon from the oak and grasped the reins of Felicia's mare as he passed it and led it behind him. As he passed the Tooker farm he noted that someone was coming out onto the lane and he turned his head aside and urged his mount into a canter, the little mare following suit. The other rider paused at the entrance to the lane and did not issue forth, but Tackar kept up a steady pace for some time before cutting across the fields so that he would not have to ride through town to reach Alicia's house.

It was more than an hour after Felicia left for her ride that Mavis answered another summons to the door. It was a different man, but he was leading the mare Felicia had left on. Mavis exclaimed in her alarm, "Do not say anything has happened to Miss Coombs!"

"No, no," Tackar soothed her. "Miss Coombs was passing the inn when a message came for you. You are Mavis Carter, are you not?"

"Yes," Mavis answered suspiciously.

"From over Beverley way?"

"Yes," more curiously now.

"Miss Coombs was informed by the messenger that you were needed at home. Your mother is ill. Miss Coombs had met some friends with a mount for her, so she asked that I bring you this horse for your journey."

"My mother," Mavis said, alarmed. "And Miss Coombs wished me to go to her?"

"She was most emphatic about it," Tackar assured her smoothly. "She would have come herself, but I told her I should not mind bringing the mare, and her friends were eager to be on their way."

"Why, I do thank you, sir. I'll just run over to the

shop to tell Lady Coombs that I must be off, and get the key to lock up."

"I think you should start immediately if you want to reach your home before night falls," he urged her. "I am acquainted with Lady Coombs and will inform her when you are on your way. Just run along and get your wrap while I hold the horse." He managed to inflect a slight note of superior impatience into his voice, and Mavis's years of training in genteel households prompted her to obey him. When she had passed out of sight down the lane, he beckoned to his valet who was seated uncomfortably behind a hedgerow down the lane awaiting this signal.

"Follow her. Do not let her stop anywhere. I cannot think she is suspicious, but one can never be sure. Use force if need be," Tackar instructed coldly.

"Yes, sir," the valet murmured respectfully. He had spent years with Tackar and was paid well for obedience and punished severely for any insubordination. When he too had disappeared from sight, Tackar casually entered the house to await Alicia.

CHAPTER TEN

It appealed to Tackar's sense of humor to check in the kitchen for what the maid had been preparing for dinner. The soup had been left simmering and the partridge appeared nearly finished on the spit. There was an apple pie sitting near the window ledge. Adequate, he thought.

Tackar then made a tour of the house. He knew that it would be an hour yet before Alicia returned. The neater of the two bedrooms he determined to be hers. He rested a proprietorial hand on the bed. She would do better to accept his offer, he thought scornfully as he surveyed the shabby furniture. Then he went through the house to make sure that all the draperies were closed and finally settled comfortably in a chair in the drawing room to wait. His glance at the clock told him that he still had some time to wait, but there was a noise at the door and he sprang to his feet, alert.

"Felicia? Mavis?" he heard Alicia call.

Tackar stepped into the hall and faced her. "There is no one here but me."

"What are you doing in my house? Get out!" Alicia cried.

"I cannot think that would be wise, Alicia," he said insinuatingly. "If I were to leave, how would you learn where to find Felicia?"

Alicia's face drained of blood. "What have you done with her? Where is she?"

"She is safe. I will tell you where she is when we

have spent the evening together." He reached out a hand to grasp her wrist but she leaped away from him. "Alicia," he said softly, "if you do not cooperate, your daughter will not be returned to you a maiden."

Alicia cast a pleading look at him. "You would not, could not do that. Please. She is but a child."

"And you are not. Cooperate, Alicia, and you shall have her back intact."

Alicia shuddered and shrugged helplessly. "As you wish. The bedroom is upstairs." She moved reluctantly toward the stairs.

"There is no hurry," Tackar purred. "Mavis has left supper in the kitchen and I am feeling a trifle sharp set from my afternoon's activities."

"Where is Mavis?" Alicia asked bluntly.

"She seems to have taken the notion in her head that her mother is ill and has gone home to nurse her."

Alicia felt completely demoralized by this knowledge. Not that Mavis's presence would have helped her, but that Tackar had planned the whole so carefully.

"Please, it cannot matter to you. Let us get it over with now."

"It does matter to me," he assured her, his eyes wandering slowly over her body. "I will come with you to the kitchen and you will serve our meal in the dining parlor. Then you will understand how it could be with us, my dear."

Alicia shivered but went directly to the kitchen and began to serve the food into the waiting dishes. Tackar lounged against the door, occasionally putting an arm around her and rubbing her breasts through her dress. Alicia stiffened at his touch but continued with her task without a murmur. When they were seated at the table opposite one another he said softly, "Take off your bodice."

Alicia gazed at him in horror and sat rigid. "I said, take your bodice off," he reiterated slowly. When she continued to sit unmoving he rose and walked to the hall. He returned to toss Felicia's bonnet in the center of the table. Alicia slowly and awkwardly removed her bodice. "To the skin," he instructed. She undid the drawstring of the chemise and lifted it off over her head. Her eyes were fixed on her plate.

"Excellent. You have further improved my appetite," he remarked smoothly. His eyes caressed her breasts as he lifted each bite of food to his mouth and dabbed at his lips with a napkin. "You are not eating."

"I am not hungry."

"Nonetheless, I should like to see you eat." He touched the bonnet with a languid finger.

Alicia picked up a fork and awkwardly lifted a bit of partridge to her mouth. She was horridly aware of her naked body. The bonnet in the center of the table hypnotized her. Chew as she might, she could not swallow the bite. Eventually she put her napkin to her mouth and inconspicuously removed the food. Tackar seemed satisfied with her one attempt. He continued to work his way through his meal, his eyes seldom straying from her breasts. Eventually he put his fork down and rose from his seat; Alicia did likewise. "No, sit there," he ordered and came round the table to stand behind her. He reached a hand around her and gripped a breast firmly, flicking the nipple. Slowly he did the same with the other. "Now," he said, "we will proceed to your bedroom."

Alicia stooped to gather up her clothes and press them against her naked chest. He wrested them from her. "Don't be absurd, Alicia," he laughed.

Alicia's limbs felt as though they would not support her, but she knew he would carry her if she did not ascend by herself, so she made a supreme effort. It was growing dark now and Tackar lit a branch of candles to carry with him. Alicia put a trembling hand on the doorknob and opened the door carefully. She then walked into the room and stood by the bed, her mind frozen, her body shivering.

"Are you cold?" he asked with mock solicitude. "I shall light the fire Mavis has conscientiously laid. But first I want the rest of your clothes off. Do I need to fetch the bonnet?"

Alicia removed the remainder of her clothing with shaking hands. She did not know where to look when she stood there naked. Tackar walked around her, touching her nipples, her waist, her thighs. "Beautiful. Better than I had imagined even."

He left her standing there and went leisurely to light the fire and the candles in the room. When the fire was going well, which seemed to Alicia to take an inordinate amount of time under his unskilled hands, he turned to her and said, "Get on the bed." His eyes followed her eagerly as she obeyed his instruction, and he rose to join her.

A voice from the doorway said with cold fury, "Stay away from her, Tackar." Alicia knew the mortification of being fully exposed to Lord Stronbert's view when Tackar sprang away with an oath. But the marquis kept his eyes on the man opposite him. "I have your daughter safe, Lady Coombs. Get under the covers. I will send her to you."

Alicia crawled under the covers and hid her head in a pillow before giving way to the shuddering sobs which wracked her. Even then she was aware of Stronbert's voice. "You will meet me in the morning, Tackar. Seven o'clock at your oak. If you do not arrive, then you had best spend the rest of your miserable life outside of England, for I will find you. Now get out."

Tackar could not understand how his plans had gone awry, but he did not stay to find out. There was murder in the marquis's eyes, and Tackar had a healthy respect for his own skin if for no one else's. He sneered with bravado at his opponent, who stepped aside to let him pass and followed him down the stairs. Alicia heard the door slam but it was some time before she heard steps on the stairs again. She was unable to lift her head until she heard her daughter's voice whisper softly, "It is all right now, Mama. Here, I have brought you a glass of brandy. Lord Stronbert will see that Mr. Tackar goes away, and then he is sending for Lady Gorham to come to us."

Alicia turned then and surveyed her daughter's tear-stained, exhausted face. "Oh, my love, he did not harm you, did he?"

Silent tears streamed down Felicia's face, but she shook her head mutely. The two women sat on the bed for a long while holding each other and murmuring comforting sounds, while their tears exhausted themselves. Eventually Alicia spoke. "Can you tell me what happened?"

Haltingly Felicia told of the letter and of her meeting with Tackar. She did not hold back anything and her mother ached for her and comforted her. "He meant to have you too, after all. How did Lord Stronbert find you?"

"He was coming from the Tooker farm when he caught a glimpse of Tackar. It made him suspicious that Tackar turned his head away and that he was leading the mare I hire from the inn sometimes. There was still daylight then and he began to ride along the lane calling for me. When I heard my name I tried to answer, but with the rag in my mouth it was useless. I felt so helpless." Her tears began to flow again. When she could finally speak, she whispered, "He had dismounted where he saw the sapling torn from the ground and I could tell that he was close from his voice. I beat against the shed with my feet, over and over, and then he was there.

"Oh, Mama, I had been so afraid. I was afraid for you but mostly I was afraid for me. I could not stand his hands on me. I wanted to die. When Lord Stronbert released me, I could not talk. When I tried, there were only sounds, and he held me and he kept running his hands over my hair as you do when I am upset and saying, 'Go ahead and cry, Felicia. It will help you.' And I was not afraid of him, for he held me like you do and then I cried. It was more like screaming, really. Or an animal caught in a trap. And

I was ashamed for him to hear me like that but he kept saying, 'Good girl.' "

She drew a shuddering breath. "When I could talk again I told him we must come to you. I am so sorry I could not talk before, Mama. We could have been here much sooner. But Lord Stronbert said we were in time." Her eyes anxiously questioned her mother.

"Yes, love, you were in time."

"Lord Stronbert made me wait in the drawing room in the dark. But I did not mind so much, except that I wanted to be with you. When the door slammed he came in to me and lit the candles and told me you were all right. But he sounded so strange that I was afraid for you. He told me to be brave and take some brandy up to you and that he would send Lady Gorham if his messenger could get there before they left for the ball. When he is sure Mr. Tackar is gone, he will wait in the drawing room."

Alicia sipped at the brandy her daughter offered her again and motioned for Felicia to have some too. "It's like drinking fire!" the girl exclaimed.

"Yes," Alicia smiled faintly. "But it helps put some starch in you when you feel like a limp rag. Have a little more."

Felicia did as she was bid and the color returned to her cheeks. "Shall I get you your dressing gown, Mama?"

"No, my clothing." When Felicia made to bring her the outfit which had been discarded on the floor, she shuddered and said, "Those are to be burned. All of them." At Felicia's anxious look she said softly, "I could not wear them again. They would remind me." *Of my humiliation and my terror,* she thought. *Of the degradation and helplessness. I will kill another man before I let him touch me,* she vowed. Aloud she said calmly, "Choose something from the wardrobe, love."

Felicia busied herself at the wash basin while her mother began to dress. When she was called, she helped to complete her mother's toilette. "Would you like to go to bed now?" Alicia asked softly. "You have had a very difficult time."

"No, Mama. I do not want to be alone yet," Felicia admitted. Her mother took her in her arms and held her until the sounds of a carriage stopping outside were succeeded by the murmur of voices in the drawing room.

"I must go down now," Alicia said gently. "Come with me a moment and then you and Lady Gorham can come up while I speak with Lord Stronbert."

The two women descended the stairs slowly and were met at the parlor door by a shaken Lady Gorham. She silently gathered Alicia into her arms and murmured, "My poor dear."

Alicia noted the ball gown she wore and said, "You are very kind to come, Charlotte. Would you take Felicia upstairs while I have a word with Lord Stronbert?"

"Of course, love." Lady Gorham, pleased that Alicia had finally used her name, then hugged Felicia to her and after a moment led the girl back up the stairs, murmuring gently.

Alicia walked into the well-lit room to find the marquis gazing out into the night through the pulled-back draperies. He turned slowly at the sound of her entry, but did not move toward her. "You should not be up," he said kindly.

"It was necessary that I speak with you," she replied. Her attempt to meet his eyes was not entirely successful.

"Let us be seated, then," he suggested. He drew the two winged chairs in front of the fire he had lit in the grate. When Alicia had seated herself, he did so and kept his gaze on the leaping flames.

"I want you to know," Alicia began hesitantly, "that I can never thank you enough for what you did for my daughter and myself today. Not just rescuing her, but . . . helping her to cry out her fear and shame and distress. I think she will be able to handle it better because of that."

"Would that I could do the same for you."

"I am older and I have been married," she replied stiffly. "It is not the same for me."

"When you first came to Tetterton I saw Tackar accost you in the High Street."

"And you thought that what Mr. Parker said was true?" she gasped.

"No, Lady Coombs, quite the opposite. That is why when I saw him leading the mare I was worried. He is an unprincipled villain."

"Yes, that is the other thing I have to speak with you about. I realize that in your anger you have challenged him. I cannot allow you to take such a risk because of his behavior toward my daughter and myself. He is beneath your dignity and you have a family to think of."

"I will meet him, Lady Coombs." His tone reminded her of those words spoken in the bedroom.

"He killed my husband in a duel. I will not have him kill you, too. It is none of your affair."

"I have challenged him, and I will meet him."

Alicia turned from the fire to face him. "I cannot be responsible for another death." Silently tears rolled down her ashen cheeks to be brushed furiously away by an impatient hand. Stronbert handed her a handkerchief, careful not to touch her as he did so. She wiped away the tears and blew her nose.

"You will not be responsible for my death, or for his. You were not responsible for your husband's."

"You do not know!"

"Then tell me," he urged gently.

"I cannot!"

"You think Tackar dueled your husband because of you?" When Alicia did not answer he said, "Perhaps you think you unwittingly encouraged him."

"Never! I have always held the man in contempt!"

"Then there is no reason to think that you had anything to do with their meeting," he said reasonably.

Alicia set her chin firmly. "You are right, of course, Lord Stronbert."

"I have no wish to force your confidence, Lady Coombs. I could hope that it would be given freely, for nothing you tell me will go any further."

"It would do no good to tell you, my lord."

"You should tell someone. It was but a moment ago that you told me what good it did Felicia to let loose her emotions. Can you not see that the same applies to you? I would be honored to stand your friend."

"You are a man!" she cried accusingly.

A slow grin curved his lips. "Too true. But do not take that too much to heart. I am also a son, a father, a brother."

"I told my brother," she whispered.

"About Tackar?"

"Yes, and he wanted to kill him, too. I would not let him. I cannot let you."

"And what protection did you think your brother could offer you? He does not live nearby, I expect."

"No, he lives in Oxford. It was for Felicia's sake that I told him—in case she should have to go to him." Her voice was so faint that he had to concentrate to hear her. Suddenly she said more clearly, "I do not want anyone else to know what happened today."

"Are you upset that I had Lady Gorham come?"

"Oh, no. She is my dear friend and I could have asked for no one better. But I should be mortified if all those people at the court were to know about it. You will not tell them," she begged.

"I shall not spread the story about, but it might be wise if I spoke a little with Rowland. Felicia is like to be skittish with him and he could inadvertently cause her distress."

Alicia considered this carefully. "You may be right. I shall leave it to your judgment," she said seriously.

He would have liked to tease her about this, but knew the moment was not right. He replied with due gravity, "I promise to broach the matter delicately. Now you really ought to get some rest, Lady Coombs. I shall spend the night here but I will be gone early. You can provide a bed for Lady Gorham?"

"Yes, I will share with Felicia. There is no need for you to stay," she said uncertainly.

"There is every need for me to stay," he replied with finality. "Go upstairs now and try to relax."

"How can I relax when you are intent on fighting that creature?" she blurted.

"Your concern for my well-being is flattering, Lady Coombs." He dropped his jesting tone when she flushed. "I am not unfamiliar with pistols, ma'am. You will allow me to handle this matter in my own fashion, if you please."

Alicia was not proof against that steely tone. She bowed her head in acquiescence. "I will bid you good night, my lord. And godspeed." Her sad eyes rested on him for a moment, and then she was gone.

CHAPTER ELEVEN

Lord Stronbert did not pass a particularly restful night. The sofa was far too short for his lanky form, and he found the floor confoundedly hard. It was not these matters that disturbed him most, however. Several times during the night he had heard stifled, heart-rending sobs from the floor above him and he longed to have the right to share in the comforting of the girl. For he was sure it was Felicia and not her mother who was sobbing, though he knew Lady Coombs was suffering silently. He had never known before the rage which had swept over him when he found Tackar with her, that defenseless naked body being attacked. The deep-seated fear of men that he had already sensed in Lady Coombs had been strongly, violently reinforced for her and might never be overcome.

There was a light tap on the drawing room window at six. The footman from Lady Gorham's carriage had been sent home with a message to Stronbert's valet to present himself with his dueling pistol case at that hour. Stronbert silently rose to let in the valet, who had a change of clothing for him in addition to the pistol case. The valet eyed Stronbert warily. "And who might you be meeting at this hour?" he asked with acerbity.

"My dear fellow, it is none of your business. And no one else's. You are to be there only to prevent any dishonorable attack. Help me into this coat, will you?"

Alicia had spent a disturbed night and heard the movement downstairs when the valet arrived. She quickly donned her clothing and crept to the window in time to see Stronbert leave. There was nothing in his bearing to suggest that he was out for more than an early morning ride; he sat his horse with his usual casual elegance. But there was that ominous case which the valet carried to remind her of his destination. A sound between a sob and a sigh escaped her, and she returned to the bed to see that Felicia was sleeping before going downstairs. She had the remains of that grotesque meal to remove before the others awoke.

Stronbert turned to the valet and asked, "Did you hear if the group that went to Tosley Hall enjoyed themselves?"

"Your lady mother's dresser said milady was proper annoyed with you that you didn't attend, and that you drew Lady Gorham off as well. But the young folks seemed pleased. Sounds as though half the county was there. Though I did hear some comments on Lady Wickham's nip-cheese ways from Mr. Clinton. Not enough to drink, I gather."

"And was there speculation at the court as to why Lady Gorham and I were absent?"

"Not as much as you'd expect. Lady Gorham said very little, I gather. Just that she must needs go to Lady Coombs. Some thought a death in the widow's family, others thought an accident to Miss Coombs." The valet pressed his lips together disapprovingly.

"Hmm. I shall suggest the latter to Lady Coombs, and you will support me if necessary, will you not?"

"As you wish, sir."

They continued their ride in silence. Stronbert had chosen to arrive well before seven, as he had no intention of being taken at a disadvantage by the unprincipled Mr. Tackar. The sun was bright but the air was freezing, and the frost on the ground promised slippery footing. Stronbert scouted for a likely spot, deciding on a reasonably flat stretch of ground not far from the shed. When he returned to the oak he could see Tackar and his man driving toward him in a phaeton as garishly colorful as any he had seen.

Tackar's ordinary air of self-confidence was slightly shattered, but the vindictiveness he felt gave him dutch courage. He had soundly whipped his valet, though the miscarriage of the plan had been through no fault of his. Mavis had indeed arrived at her parents' home without stopping and had not been allowed to ride back in the dark owing to the concern of her family.

Stronbert watched Tackar's approach grimly. The man's insolent air made Stronbert want to strangle the suave popinjay with his own hands. Stronbert's valet, James, had taken the pistols from the case for the purpose of loading them. He blew gently through the muzzle to carry away any loose dust collected in the barrel and ascertained that the touchhole in each was clear. One at a time he put the hammer at half cock and stopped it; then poured in from a measure the quantity of powder required. The ball he rammed gently in place with a piece of the finest kid glove leather, and he kept his thumb on the touchhole so that no powder might escape. James knew this art to a nicety and informed Lord Stronbert when the pistols were ready.

"You may practice with each of them, Tackar, and choose your weapon," he said coldly.

Tackar took sight on a fence post some fifteen yards distant and his shot was successful. He smirked as he raised the other pistol and fired again, another hit.

"Are you satisfied?"

"Yes. They are nicely balanced weapons. I shall use this one," Tackar replied, retaining the one with which he had just shot.

When James had reloaded the pistols, Tackar watching him closely, the adversaries stationed themselves fifteen yards apart and positioned themselves right sides forward. Tackar had fought three previous duels: once, in Sir Frederick's case, having killed his opponent, and in both other cases having wounded his adversaries. Stronbert had never been called upon to settle a matter of honor before, but he stood steadily, easily facing Tackar. James had thoughtfully provided him with a black coat, had even changed the buttons to black during the night. Tackar was darkly dressed as well, as he had been the previous day, but his buttons glittered in the morning sunlight.

James, sick at heart, stood ready to drop a handkerchief. The two men raised their pistols and aimed. As the flutter of white descended, the marquis pulled the trigger, moving only his knuckle joint so that the motion should not disturb the muscles of his hand and arm and shake the pistol. The two shots roared almost simultaneously. Stronbert felt Tackar's ball graze along his shoulders and pass on. Tackar fell.

James automatically hastened to his employer, but Stronbert waved him to where Tackar had fallen and followed more slowly himself. Tackar had received the ball under his right arm and it had lodged in him. He was alive but very pale.

"We shall have to get him to Dr. Carmichael. Put him in his carriage." Tackar's man and James lifted the insensate man carefully and carried him to the waiting phaeton. Stronbert turned to James to inform him, "I will drive his carriage. Bring the pistols and the horses." To Tackar's man, "Hold him as steady as you can, else the ball could do more damage."

The slow procession wound its way to a house east of Tetterton where Dr. Carmichael resided. He was breakfasting when Lord Stronbert was announced. "This is a surprise," he commented as his friend entered the room.

"I have a severely wounded man for you to attend to, Hamilton."

Dr. Carmichael pushed back his chair and rose to accompany Stronbert to the carriage. "Take him to the surgery. I shall be with him immediately." He threw Stronbert a querying glance.

"There is a ball lodged in him," Stronbert said.

Dr. Carmichael raised his eyebrows slightly and hastened after the patient, saying calmly over his shoulder, "Help yourself to breakfast, Nigel. I shall be with you when I can."

Stronbert had completed a hearty repast when Dr. Carmichael returned. "I have removed the ball. He will live, though he would probably rather not for some time for the pain. Was this necessary?"

"Yes," Stronbert replied, "quite necessary."

"I should not have liked it to have been you lying there on the table. He missed you?"

"No."

"Then let me have a look at you."

"It is nothing," Stronbert said with finality. "A mere graze."

Dr. Carmichael had attended Stronbert from his youth and recognized the tone in which these words were spoken, but ignored it. His keen eyes even across the room had noted the slight wince when Stronbert had shrugged. He came to stand behind the younger man and ordered, "Take your coat off."

Stronbert exasperatedly flung up a hand. "I tell you it is nothing, Hamilton."

"I shall decide that," the doctor rasped, glaring at his friend.

"Very well," Stronbert grinned. "If you must." He removed the coat and was instructed to remove the shirt as well, which he did.

Dr. Carmichael surveyed the graze with annoyance. "You are right. There is little damage done, but I shall bathe it. Stay here." He left to return a few minutes later. "Sit down and hold still."

Stronbert complied and winced as the astringent was applied. "I might have known you could not let me go without torturing me," he grumbled goodnaturedly. "Are you finished?"

"Yes."

"Then I must go." Stronbert replaced his shirt and shrugged into his coat. "I hope you will not find it necessary to mention this incident."

Dr. Carmichael bent bushy-browed eyes on the younger man and replied with asperity, "I shall not feel the least necessity. And I hope it will not happen again."

"Yes," Stronbert agreed thoughtfully, "I found no pleasure in it. I have never shot at a man before, and I found it disconcerting, no matter what the cause. If Tackar does not pay the reckoning, send it to me." He shook hands with his friend and strode out of the room and the house to find James awaiting him. "He will live," was all he said to the valet before he swung himself onto his horse and headed silently for Lady Coombs's cottage. James merely grunted.

The three women were seated in the dining parlor partaking of the breakfast which Mavis, having left her home at first light, had prepared for them. The maid announced him and was directed to have him brought to them. Alicia felt her heart lurch at sight of him and her relief was only slightly marred when she noticed the tear across the shoulders of his coat. He was alive, he was walking, he was talking, he was not pale or in any obvious pain. She heard him ask Lady Gorham if he should send James for the carriage for her, and nodded when the older woman regarded her inquiringly. No one else knew that Stronbert had dueled Tackar that morning; she had no intention of telling anyone.

"Lady Coombs, might I request a word with you?" he asked blandly.

"Certainly, my lord." She led him to the drawing room, but first he went to speak with his valet before joining her there.

"Mr. Tackar has been wounded but will survive," he informed her bluntly.

"I thank you for sparing him."

"I had no intention of sparing him," he said with annoyance. He took a turn about the room and stopped before her with a comically raised eyebrow. "But I am glad he is alive. I should not like to have to leave the country. I have little fear that word of the duel will spread. It might be wise if we were to explain Lady Gorham's presence here as having been on account of an indisposition or accident of Felicia's. Have you any objection to that?"

Alicia did not answer him directly. "And your presence here?"

He shrugged. "It need not be known. If it is, there is the chaperonage of Lady Gorham. I would not think on it. No one is likely to ask me where I spent the night," he said with a grin.

Alicia smiled, if faintly, for the first time since the harrowing experience had begun. "I suppose not. How simple it is for men!" Her face clouded and she said sadly, "Perhaps Felicia had a riding accident which stunned her. I think there is no need for details. She is better now."

"Precisely." He watched her twist her hands in her lap. How could he comfort this frightened woman, who refused to allow him to share her burdens? He could not take her in his arms and hold her, for his very touch would undo her. She would resent any familiarity or help he offered; part of her anxiety now was that she had been in need of his assistance the previous day. He knew that she was upset that he had found her in such a distressing position as she had been when he opened the bedroom door on her and Tackar. For all her gratitude it would be difficult for her to forgive him that—the sight of her naked and being attacked without being able to raise a hand to defend herself. Time. She would need a lot of time.

Alicia raised her eyes to him inquiringly. He had been regarding her, unspeaking, for some minutes. "Is there something further, Lord Stronbert?" she asked hesitantly.

"No. I hope you and your daughter will still be able to come to dine tomorrow. We have quite a celebration. It is the custom at the court to feast the servants and tenants on the current lord's birthday. Felicia would enjoy the fireworks there are in the evening," he said gently.

"I should not like her to miss such a treat, but she will have to decide. I thank you again, sir, for everything you have done for us."

"Let us not speak of it henceforth, Lady Coombs. It was my pleasure to be of service where I could." He bowed formally and took his leave. Alicia rejoined her companions in the dining parlor.

Lady Gorham eyed her speculatively but said nothing. Felicia smiled at her mother and said, "Lord Stronbert is kind to come and see how we go on. You will not go to the shop today, will you, Mama?"

"Not if you need me here, love," Alicia responded.

"Oh, pooh," Felicia said defiantly. "If you wish to go to the shop, I shall go with you . . . if I may."

"Lord Stronbert will give out that Lady Gorham came to us last night because you had a riding accident and were stunned, but that you are all right now. You shall not mind?"

"Only to have my riding so maligned," Felicia retorted with a slight smile. "Yes, that will be fine. I cannot like to think that people will know what really happened."

Lady Gorham eyed the two of them exasperatedly. "So you shall go on as though nothing had happened? I would have spent the day in bed with my vinaigrette and cold compresses for my brow!"

"You know you would not, my dear," Alicia laughed. "You would be about your business as usual. Your carriage will be here shortly. I am sorry you missed the Tosley Hall ball, but I cannot thank you enough for coming."

"Nonsense," Lady Gorham replied gruffly. "Where else should I be at such a time? I cannot own to have missed seeing Lady Wickham or her disagreeable son, or even her mild-mannered husband. My hostess is like to be annoyed with me, though," she said gravely, her eyes twinkling.

"No doubt. I have the strongest desire to see her in the gown Felicia designed for her." Alicia stopped abruptly and continued more slowly. "We shall see how we go on before deciding whether we will dine at the court tomorrow."

Felicia sat up straight in her chair and glowered at her mother, saying stubbornly, "I am sure *I* shall be right as a trivet. Of course, if you are not up to going I shall stay at home with you."

Lady Gorham grumbled, "You might have known, Alicia. I hear the carriage. If you need me, do not hesitate to send for me." Then with a last aggrieved shrug she commented, "I shall see you both at the court tomorrow evening, no doubt."

Alicia accompanied her to the door. Before Lady Gorham descended the stairs she turned and asked slyly, "Did Stronbert kill Tackar?"

Astonished, Alicia mumbled, "How could you possibly know they would duel?"

"How could they not?"

"Well, they did, but Tackar will live."

"More's the pity," Lady Gorham murmured angrily.

"How can you take it so lightly? Can you not see that Lord Stronbert might have been killed himself?"

The anguish in Alicia's voice drew Lady Gorham's sharp attention. "You are fond of Lord Stronbert?"

A blush stained Alicia's cheeks. "Well, yes, of course I am. He has been very kind to Felicia and me," she hurried on to say. "What position we have in Tetterton is due solely to him, you see."

"Yes," Lady Gorham replied as she allowed the footman to assist her into the waiting carriage, "I believe I do see."

CHAPTER TWELVE

Stronbert rode back to the court preoccupied. As he had said, there was no one to ask him where he had spent the night, though he would not put it past his mother to do so. The prospect did not daunt him. however, for as much as he loved her he had no intention of allowing her to meddle in his life at his age. Nevertheless he entered the court through a back door in an attempt to avoid the rest of the household. Before he could ascend to his room he was accosted by Miss Carnworth.

"Lady Gorham has not returned as yet," she informed him.

"She will be here presently."

"They are all right, are they? Lady Coombs and her daughter?" she asked anxiously.

"Quite all right," he informed her lazily, then, noting her very real concern, he added, "I have no doubt you shall see them tomorrow at dinner."

"I am so glad," she responded, her face strangely puckered. "Thank you for helping them."

Stronbert eyed her closely, wondering if she had any idea what had really happened. Then he said gently, "I shall always do what I can for them, Miss Susan. I think you know that."

"Yes, yes. But they will not always accept your help. If that should ever be the case and you are at a stand, I hope you will allow me . . . that you will tell me so that I can do my possible," she said firmly.

Stronbert pressed her hand comfortingly. "You are

very wise, Miss Susan. Be sure that I shall call on you when . . . and if . . . the time comes."

Miss Carnworth nodded unsmiling and disappeared into the west wing. Stronbert realized that she felt a kinship with the two women in Tetterton, and was especially attached to Felicia. He continued to his room and found James there ready to assist him out of his depressingly dark outfit. After he had washed he sent James away so that he might lie down for a while and sleep.

There was a light tap on the door which awoke him, but he did not respond. Then he heard his nephew's voice through the heavy panels, "Uncle Nigel? Are you there?"

"Yes, come in."

Rowland entered hesitantly, surprised to find his uncle stretched full-length on the bed in his drawers. "Would you rather I came another time?"

"No, sit down. I want to talk to you a moment."

"Is Felicia all right? I heard she had a riding accident," Rowland asked gravely, not taking his uncle's advice to seat himself.

"She is fine now. But she did not have a riding accident."

Rowland looked at him inquiringly. His uncle had donned a dressing gown and seated himself on the edge of the bed. He obeyed this time when his uncle waved him to a chair. "What happened to her?"

Stronbert considered how he might best put the matter and found no easy solution. "What I tell you now is for your ears alone. Not for your sister or anyone else. Do you understand that?"

"Yes, sir."

"I tell you only because I think you need to know so that you will not distress the girl in all ignorance. I do not want her to know that I have told you. If you feel you cannot manage that, I shall not tell you."

"I can manage," Rowland responded hotly.

Stronbert said only, "I hope you can. I shall depend

on you to do so. Felicia was abducted yesterday."

Rowland's face paled and his annoyance of a moment before dissipated. "By whom? What happened?"

"I shall not tell you by whom. I do not think you need to know. Suffice it that I have handled the matter."

"Is he dead?"

"No, he will live. Now listen carefully, Rowland. Felicia was not harmed. That is to say, she remains a virgin. However, she was handled grossly and knew the fear of being raped. It is no small fear with a woman. I do not think a man can ever have such a similar fear. It is more than being insulted, more than being assaulted, though it is both of them. There is a shame and a helplessness involved which may not perhaps be duplicated in any other action between human beings. You have, no doubt, a concept of how you would feel if something of the nature happened to Dorothy. But you can never know just how shattering such an experience is, nor can I." He frowned sadly as he remembered the anguished cries Felicia had uttered when he had held her.

"But she was not raped?" Rowland asked timidly.

"No, I found her before anything happened. But the fear will be there for a long time. It will not be easy to overcome. She will not feel the same toward men for some time. Even the most casual touch might upset her—being lifted onto her horse, dancing, placing her hand on your arm." He was not altogether thinking of Felicia, of course, but the same could apply to either of the women. "I do not say that these things are necessarily true. She is a young woman and may be flexible enough to shrug the whole incident away. I doubt it, though."

"What do you suggest I do?" Rowland asked, his voice shaking.

"Be gentle with her. Do not let her know that you are aware of the incident, for she would then be embarrassed with you. *Ask* her each time if you can help her onto her horse or if she would like to take your arm. Do not take some of those things for granted any longer. And give her time, as much time as she needs."

Rowland sat very still for a long while. "I am extremely fond of her."

"Yes, I thought so. But she is only sixteen and has seen nothing of the world."

"You mean nothing of other men," Rowland surmised sadly.

"In part. Where the proper degree of attachment exists it will last," Stronbert said gently. "I am your uncle, Rowland, and not your father, so I may be out of line in what I am about to say, but I feel the circumstance warrants it." He observed his nephew give an encouraging sign. "Some men treat a woman's body as their right when they marry—and even when they do not. There is never any excuse for such an attitude. Our society is premised on a family, land handed down from father to son. Sometimes men, out of passion or out of an excess of determination to beget heirs, treat their wives as objects for this purpose alone. And they treat them roughly. A woman's body is to be respected, no less sacred to you than your own body. It is a fragile thing, more so than your own, and yet it can bear children which yours never can. Because of the constant chaperonage and the lack of discussion, women often come to marriage with little concept of the way their bodies will be used." Stronbert stopped as his nephew flushed. "Would you rather I did not discuss this?" he asked calmly.

"No, sir. That is, I pray you will continue."

"Many women are sold into marriage to all intents and purposes and their husbands treat them as any other item they might buy. They use them to their own pleasure with the end sometimes, sometimes not, of begetting heirs. It would be cheaper and more humane to go to a prostitute who understands what is expected of her, and who is often well paid for the service she provides. On the other hand, even men who are sincerely attached to their wives often treat them roughly,

simply out of lack of knowledge. If one day you should
marry Felicia you would no doubt find her timid of
your advances because of the experience she has gone
through. She will require patience and love and gentleness even more than another woman might. But every
woman does, Rowland, and it is your responsibility
as a man to learn to give those things, or you should
not marry. You should learn how to treat a woman's
body so that you give and not only take pleasure. Many
women do not even know that their bodies can experience pleasure," he said somewhat sadly, "and they
are ashamed of themselves for feeling it if they do.
Poppycock! A woman *can* receive pleasure and should
not deny it to herself. But you will have to teach her
that because she is not like to learn it elsewhere. That's
all I have to say. Do you have any questions?"

Rowland contemplated his uncle wonderingly. "Yes,"
he said. "Just how am I to learn all that?"

Stronbert let out a roar of laughter. "A good question, Rowland. There is no simple way of gaining the
experience, for you cannot come by some woman who
will allow you to practice on her. Forgive me, I should
not laugh about it. Have you never had a woman? No,
I have no right to ask you such a question. Ignore it."

But Rowland had no intention of ignoring the question. "I have, you know, in London. Twice. Jimmy
Drew introduced me to them."

Stronbert admirably controlled the smile he felt sur-
facing and said, "And did they teach you anything?"

"*Teach* me?" Rowland asked incredulously.

"I can see that they did not. You had best choose
more carefully in future."

"Well," Rowland protested, "they were not expensive and they were willing."

"That is not enough. With an inexperienced man
a woman of experience has a lot to offer. She can
teach you how to be gentle and how to give her pleasure. And when you give her pleasure," he said, with
a smile which mocked himself, "you will be repaid in

kind, I assure you. I could have Colette recommend someone for you. It would not be inexpensive, but if your allowance did not run to it, I would see you had sufficient funds."

"I am sure I can manage," Rowland said stiffly.

Stronbert stood abruptly and put his hand on the young man's shoulder. "It is not only you I am thinking of, Rowland. It could be important for your Felicia. I did not mean to insult you. Perhaps you would rather we dropped the whole idea."

"No," Rowland said slowly, imitating his uncle's usual method of speech, "the idea intrigues me."

Stronbert laughed. "Run along, rascal. I shall see what I can arrange."

The celebration for Lord Stronbert's servants and tenants began early in the afternoon with bowling on the green, quoits, and a cricket match in which Stronbert participated. The general organized the various activities; he had assumed this task when he arrived at the court seven years previously and guarded his domain with jealous vigor. Agatha Trimble in turn had assumed the responsibility for the feast when she arrived two years after the general, and the two activities were kept entirely separate. A meal was served at four o'clock which consisted of thirty-one pigeon pies, twenty-four sirloins of beef, six collars of beef sliced, ten cold hams sliced, two hundred forty-four chickens, six dozen tongues sliced, ten buttocks of beef, eleven edgebones of the same, thirteen quarters of veal, forty-four house lambs, fifty-six pounds of cheese, eight pounds of chocolate, five pounds of coffee, twenty dozen bottles of strong beer, ten hogsheads of the same, three hogsheads of wine, and two of punch. In addition there were three dozen each of mince pies, apple pies, tarts, jellies, boiled puddings, cheesecakes, and custards. No one was able to keep count of the bread and fruit consumed. For some reason Agatha Trimble had found over the years that the vegetables were largely ignored and she now only had set out a dozen large salads, which were not always finished.

Alicia and her daughter arrived at six as requested, both in gowns made especially for the occasion which they had been working on for a week. Felicia had convinced her mother that a burgundy velvet fabric in the shop would be most becoming; Felicia had chosen a navy blue satin and at the last moment had made it more demure than she had originally intended. Her mother sympathized with the change and made no mention of it.

The Coombs were shown into the lavender parlor where the rest of the party, consisting entirely of the residents of the court, were assembled, with the lone exception of the dowager marchioness. Lord Stronbert greeted them himself and introduced Alicia to his various relations. Miss Carnworth whispered, quite loud enough for the marquis to hear, that Cousin Evelyn had been a bit recalcitrant but was expected to appear momentarily. Stronbert's eyes danced as he heard this, but he gave no other indication of his amusement.

Felicia was welcomed by the young people, and since none of them seemed to know of her terrifying adventure but inquired instead as to her recovery from the riding accident, she soon relaxed. They explained that Lord Stronbert had suggested that they not call for a few days to give her a chance to recover completely, but they were hoping that she would feel up to riding with them the next day. Felicia gladly accepted, but her eyes on Rowland were wary enough that he readily accepted his uncle's advice about treating her carefully. It was difficult for him not to blurt out his outrage and his concern for her, but the effort was worthwhile, for later Felicia timidly placed her hand on his arm for him to take her into the dining parlor.

The dowager marchioness made a grand entrance. Since only Miss Carnworth and the marquis himself knew of the gown, the others were astonished to see Lady Stronbert arrive in an extremely attractive, fashionable French brocade. The general was heard to exclaim, "Egad! Who would have known she was such a handsome woman?" The others settled for complimenting her, while Felicia's eyes shone with pride and she shared a speaking look with her mother across the room.

Stronbert crossed to her and murmured, "Thank you, Mother. I have never seen you looking better."

The dowager marchioness eyed him sternly and tapped his sleeve with an ivory fan. "I know Cousin Susan sewed it, but you will never convince me that she designed it. Was it the girl—Miss Coombs?"

"Now, Mother, surely you could not ask me to divulge the secret?"

"I shall ask *her*," she retorted stubbornly.

"As you please, ma'am," he drawled, and dinner was announced before she could make a move in Felicia's direction. He offered his arm and led her, proud as could be (even if the chit *had* designed the gown) into the dining parlor.

Dinner was magnificent, as Miss Carnworth had prophesied, and Alicia watched to see that Felicia was enjoying herself. The girl was seated between the general and Rowland, both of whom seemed intent on entertaining her with stories of the day's activities—the cricket match especially. Alicia was seated to the marquis's right, with Mr. Jacobs, an elderly gentleman of the cloth whose health had forced him to retire, on her other side. While Stronbert conversed with Lady Gorham, Alicia was treated by Mr. Jacobs to many of the same cricket-match anecdotes as her daughter. When his flattering references to Stronbert's performance drew the marquis's attention, Stronbert entered their discussion.

"You must not allow Mr. Jacobs to cozen you into believing that I am above average as a cricketer, Lady Coombs. There is a great deal of revelry in our games which is what makes them amusing, not the sterling performances."

Mr. Jacobs had turned away to respond to a remark made by Miss Carnworth, and Alicia replied quizzingly, "I trust you would not cozen me yourself, Lord Stronbert."

He studied her seriously, a faint smile curving his lips. "Never, ma'am. There is that about you which inspires the utmost trustworthiness in me." At her helpless gesture of denial, he turned the conversation. "You will see there above the mantel the portrait I mentioned. Although Cuffy is portrayed as a most fierce hunting dog, he was in fact very amiable. My father gave him to me as a puppy to train and I fear I did not succeed to admiration. I think it was rather a joke of Father's to have him shown as he is, for as I told you he spent the time we were posing destroying my boots."

Alicia could not repress the gurgle of laughter she felt when she compared his story with the scene in the portrait. The previous Lord Stronbert was a distinguished-looking gentleman, not unlike the present marquis in his facial features, and his hand rested on his son's shoulder, the dog beside eagerly poised to run. The younger Stronbert's eyes were excited and mischievous and Alicia could visualize him tumbling into a muddy pond in his effort to rescue his dog from the butcher. Embarrassed by the emotion the portrait and story evoked in her, she remarked formally, "You resemble your father considerably; more so, perhaps, than Matthew does you."

"Yes, Matthew has more of his mother's family about him, I would say," he conceded easily. "Felicia, on the other hand, is the image of you."

"Certainly we share some likenesses," Alicia admitted, "but Felicia is undoubtedly possessed of a most unique combination. You remarked yourself that she is . . . attractive," she finished proudly.

"Beautiful, I believe I said, Lady Coombs, but without her mother's maturity of countenance."

With an attempt at lightness she rejoined shakily,

"That is merely another way of saying old, Lord Stronbert."

"Not at all," he retorted. "Innocence is beguiling, amusing, but experience is compelling. You give Felicia an example in courage and resourcefulness which will stand well with her for the future."

"I give Felicia very little," she sighed, as her eyes wandered to her daughter. "She deserves a great deal more than I am able to provide."

"There is little of use to her that she does not receive from you. I admire what you have done."

"You are kind to say so, Lord Stronbert, but she should be looking forward to a season in London, to a place in county society. Instead she decorates bonnets and knows the rejection of not being invited to balls."

"It is hard for her, I know, but no less difficult for you."

"Nonsense! I am beyond the need for the diversions of the young."

"Surely not past the need for friendship?" he asked seriously.

"No," she faltered, "I could not bear to be without a friend such as Lady Gorham . . . or . . . you, my lord. I do not mean to be presumptuous," she flushed, "but you have indeed stood our friend on numerous occasions."

A slow smile spread over his face. "I am honored that you should consider me your friend, for I mean to be." And more, he thought wryly, as he sipped a silent toast to her, which she shyly acknowledged.

"I would never trade on your friendship," she assured him earnestly. "That is, I would not speak of it with anyone else, for it could only lower you in another's eyes to be known to have befriended a shopkeeper and her daughter. But I . . . feel reassured by your concern."

"I doubt my consequence will suffer from my concern for a 'shopkeeper,' " he remarked exasperatedly, "and you have my permission to use my name in vain on any occasion where it will assist you."

He regarded her so fixedly that she dropped her eyes before his gaze. "You are gammoning me, my lord," she replied stiffly.

"No, Lady Coombs, I am not. I am granting you and Felicia the same privilege that each member of my household has, and as with them, I trust you not to abuse it."

"Well, of course we would not abuse it," she protested, "but we are not members of your household and do not deserve such notice."

"As your friend, I could do no less. You would do the same for me, would you not?" he asked searchingly.

"Why . . . yes, of course I would," she asserted breathlessly, conscious of the people all about them. With an effort at self-composure she laughed uncertainly. "I cannot imagine your ever needing my assistance."

"It is enough to know that you would offer it if I did," he replied gently. His brown eyes, warm with affection, held hers for a moment that was exhilarating yet frightening. She suspected that her own betrayed more than the friendship she professed, for he gave a satisfied nod and allowed Mr. Jacobs to claim her attention.

When the ladies withdrew, Lady Stronbert immediately approached Felicia and drew her aside. "Miss Coombs, I can get no straight answer from my son, to say nothing of Cousin Susan. I wish you will tell me if you designed the gown I am wearing."

"Why, yes, ma'am, I did," Felicia admitted nervously.

"Then I should like to tell you, young woman," the dowager said sternly, "that I have never owned such a fashionable costume."

"And you are not happy to do so?" Felicia asked, puzzled.

"Of course I am happy. Can you not tell?" the old woman asked with a most unflattering leer. Then she chuckled and said, "Everyone thinks I am going to clapperclaw about it. I just wanted to thank you and to ask . . . if you would consider designing some day dresses for me."

Felicia uttered a little laugh of relief. "I should be happy to do so, ma'am. I enjoy nothing more."

"Good. You are a clever little puss and if I am jealous you must put it down to my advanced age. We shall discuss it further another day. This is not the time." The dowager kissed her cheek a trifle awkwardly and walked away.

When the gentlemen joined them there was music, each of the young ladies performing in turn on the harpsichord. The men joined in the singing of glees, catches, and madrigals until Rowland suggested that they all join the dancing which was underfoot in the barn. Stronbert always attended the dancing for some period during the evening, and a number of the household decided to accompany him. Those who remained settled down at the card tables.

Alicia found Stronbert at her side, presenting his arm. "If you will allow me?" he asked politely.

"I . . . yes, very well," she mumbled and placed her fingertips gingerly on the bottle-green sleeve of his handsome coat. Alicia was silent for a while as they traversed the lawns to the strains of music issuing forth from the barn. Stronbert kept up a gentle flow of small talk the while. When they arrived there was a general cheer for the marquis and he was urged to take part in the Slingby's Reel just forming. He turned questioning eyes on Alicia but she shook her head mutely. He led Dorothy into the set. Alicia saw her daughter refuse Rowland and stepped up to her to promote her participation. "It is not a formal dance, love, and I am sure no one would take exception to your participating."

Felicia turned alarmed eyes to her mother, but Alicia

smiled encouragingly. Rowland waited patiently for her decision. They both watched her swallow nervously and turn to the young man, her lip trembling so slightly as to be hardly noticeable. "If you please, then, I should like to dance," she whispered, though it was obviously not completely true.

Rowland led her to the set in which Dorothy and his uncle, as well as Cassandra and Mr. Cooper, were positioned. The fiddler struck up his tune and Felicia soon found herself caught up in the swirling movement, her hands lightly touching those of the men about her as she went through the dance. Her cheeks were flushed and her eyes sparkling when the tune ended. Stronbert solicited her for the Tristram Shandy and Mr. Cooper for the Macaroni. Breathless then, she returned to her mother's side to confess that she had not enjoyed herself so well for months. Alicia blinked back the stupid tears which threatened and pressed her daughter's hand. "Yes, my love, there is nothing like music and dancing to pick up one's spirits."

"Then may I hope that you will honor me for this next?" Stronbert queried at her side as the Spaw Stag Chase was announced.

"Oh, do, Mama. You will enjoy it excessively," Felicia urged, her eyes pleading with her mother.

Stronbert kept his eyes on Alicia's and nodded. Although he did not say a word, it was one of his commands and she silently obeyed. Felicia giggled and said mischievously, "You see, he can do it even without speaking."

"It is lamentable," her mother agreed as she walked off with his lordship.

But she, too, felt relief in the rhythm and swing of the dance and forgot for a while the cares that pressed on her. Rowland and Felicia had joined the set as well, for it was to be the last of the evening. Stronbert shared a hopeful glance with his nephew when the dance ended. Then the party returned to the terrace of the court to watch a display of Roman candles, gillockes, and girandoles light the night sky. Felicia was struck dumb in her awe, and her mother, who had never seen fireworks before either, was amazed at the sight.

Alicia spent a moment speaking with Lady Gorham and Cassandra before she announced that they must be leaving. Lady Gorham walked aside with her a bit to ask, "May we come to see you tomorrow, my dear? We must leave the next day."

"So soon? I shall be sorry to see you go. Yes, do come to us for tea tomorrow, just you and Cassandra and the Clintons."

"Felicia seems easier. I cannot tell about you," the older woman complained, her sharp eyes scanning Alicia's face.

"I try not to think on it. Do not be concerned for me," Alicia replied with a faint smile.

"You would not, I suppose, consider giving up your shop and coming to live with me permanently?" Lady Gorham asked diffidently.

"No, my dear, I could not do that," the younger woman said gently.

"I thought not. Well, we shall see you tomorrow."

Stronbert came then to tell Alicia that the carriage was ready. She and Felicia expressed their thanks to the dowager marchioness and to him for the lovely evening and were escorted by Stronbert to the front steps. "I shall be away for a few days," he remarked lazily. "I hope, Felicia, that you will feel free to ride Dancer whenever you choose. The gown was a great success and I thank you. I do not believe, Lady Coombs, that I have received a reckoning for the service." He made a languid gesture while his eyes laughingly mocked her.

"I must have overlooked it, sir. Have no fear that it shall be sent."

"Oh, Mama, I do not wish to be paid for such a thing," Felicia cried, her face flushed.

"It is a matter of principle," Stronbert said gravely.

"Indeed," Alicia agreed, but her lips twitched slightly. "Come, my love, we must not keep the horses standing."

Stronbert returned to the house amused and exasperated. He had counseled his nephew in patience, but he wondered if patience would be enough with Lady Coombs.

CHAPTER THIRTEEN

Jane Newton was in the morning parlor when she was brought a letter from her sister-in-law. Alicia had written that the shop was prospering and that she and Felicia were comfortable in their cottage. Felicia, she wrote, had made friends with some young people at Stronbert Court and rode with them almost daily. They were both invited to dinner there the next day, when the gown Felicia had designed for the dowager marchioness was to be displayed. Alicia wrote in a humorous vein about her more obstreperous customers and neighbors. There was one special note to her brother which his wife did not understand. It read: There has been a little trouble with Mr. T, but that is now taken care of. Jane was sure that the name of the man from whom Alicia had purchased the shop was Dean, so she could not mean him. She puzzled over the note for a while, and as she was finally setting it aside the maid came to announce a visitor.

"The Marquis of Stronbert," the girl repeated nervously.

Jane knew a moment's fear but managed to say in a level voice, "Send him in, Janet. And try to find Mr. Newton. He will wish to see our visitor." Stronbert, that was the name of the court Alicia had mentioned. She rose as the door opened again and curtsied as the handsome, lanky man entered. Somehow she had expected him to be older; he could not be forty. She moistened her lips to utter some polite inanity, but what came out was far otherwise. "Lady

Coombs and her daughter? There is nothing wrong, is there?"

"No, no. Do not be alarmed. When last I saw them they were leaving the court in good spirits." His gaze wandered curiously about the small, cheerful room, its furnishings old but well polished.

Jane, relieved, remembered her duty as hostess and asked the marquis to seat himself. "I have sent for my husband."

"Thank you. I should like to have a word with him," Stronbert commented easily. He proceeded to ask Jane about her family and to tell her about Alicia's shop in Tetterton, about which she was fascinated. His casual air put her at ease almost immediately, though she had been intimidated by his title when he was announced. She rang for tea and was pouring when her husband arrived. After she had introduced them she exclaimed, "Is it not a coincidence, Stephen? I have just had a letter from Alicia this morning."

Stephen did not particularly like the coincidence, but he sat with them over tea for some moments before signaling to his wife that he would like to be alone with Stronbert. She immediately excused herself and softly closed the door behind her.

Stephen spoke abruptly. "You have come about Alicia?"

"Yes. I should like to discuss with you an incident that occurred the other day. It might be wise for you to read her letter. I cannot know if she would write you of it," Stronbert said thoughtfully.

Stephen lifted the letter from a side table and perused it carefully. His lips compressed over the note directed to him. "She says only that there has been a little trouble with Mr. T but that it is now taken care of. I presume that is what you refer to?"

Stronbert cast his eyes heavenward in a gesture of despair. "She told me she had confided in you about Tackar. If this is in the nature of a confidence you must be severely lacking in information."

"She would hardly write more when my wife was to read the letter," Stephen replied stiffly. "Alicia discussed his proposition with me when I last came to see her."

Stronbert's eyes narrowed. "It was not a matter of a proposition this time, Mr. Newton; it was an attempted rape. And not only of Lady Coombs, but of her daughter as well."

Stephen paled visibly and his voice shook as he asked, "But they were not harmed?"

Stronbert shrugged an angry shoulder and said, "They were not raped, no, but they were both handled—ungently. It was only by good fortune that I was able to intervene."

"I should have killed him," Stephen groaned. "She made me promise that I would not."

"I tried to, but he will recover. I thought it necessary to speak with you about the situation, Mr. Newton, because I was involved in it, and I did not think your sister would enlighten you. And I see she has not." Stronbert studied the man opposite him who bore a faint resemblance to his sister. "I imagine Lady Coombs would not approve of my coming to you, but then I did not ask her. She had mentioned that you lived in Oxford and it was no difficult matter to find you. However, I will proceed only with your permission."

"You have it," Stephen said shortly.

"Less than a week ago Tackar sent a note to Felicia, purportedly from my nephew, which led her to ride out to an old oak north of town. It was not to be an assignation but in the nature of a surprise awaiting her there, since she had been left out of a ball given in the neighborhood. Tackar captured, bound, and mishandled her, leaving her in a boarded shed with the threat that he would return to rape her. I was visiting a farm in the area and saw Tackar ride by leading a horse Felicia frequently hired from the inn. Since I had previously had reason to believe that he was annoying your sister, I found the circumstances suspicious and began a search for Felicia. When I found her and loosed her she was hysterical for some time. After a while she urged me to save her mother and we arrived at their house to find that we were in time. In time to save her from actually being raped, you understand, but not from the ignominies preceding it."

Stephen felt sick, and he looked pale. Stronbert asked if there was any brandy available and Stephen numbly walked over to a cabinet and withdrew a bottle and two glasses. He poured these out and offered one to the marquis, who accepted it and set it down. Stephen reseated himself and sipped at the fiery beverage gingerly. He had not spoken a word.

Stronbert continued gently, "I told Tackar to meet me in the morning. It was a most irregular duel, with no seconds and no surgeon, just our valets. Lady Coombs refused to allow it, saying that she would not have another death on her head. I want to know what she meant."

Stephen considered the amber fluid for a moment. "Why did you not ask her?"

"I did ask her and she refused to tell me. She said she had told you. Come, Mr. Newton, this is not a game we are playing."

"My sister is a very private, very stubborn woman."

"I know that. Can you not see that she needs protection? You can be of no assistance to her in Oxford. I wish to have that right, but I know she will not grant it to me now."

"You wish to protect her? You wish to marry her?" Stephen asked faintly.

"Yes, but I have not asked her because I know she will not accept me now . . . perhaps never. I am asking you for the right to protect her and her daughter, Mr. Newton, because she needs protection and because she has no one else to do so."

"How would you protect her?"

"By doing whatever I could whenever necessary. I

do not wish to incur her displeasure, nor do I wish to abandon her to the unscrupulousness of a man such as Tackar. I wounded him severely, but he will live. To wreak vengeance another time perhaps."

Stephen drew a weary hand across his brow. "I asked her to come to us instead of buying the shop, but she is well aware of our limited space and resources and would not do so. Why would she not have you?"

"For many reasons. She is trying to accept a reduction in her station because she keeps a shop. Therefore she thinks me above her. She might think that I wish to marry her to save her from such a life, or to save Felicia. In other words that I would do so out of pity."

"Would you?" Stephen asked curiously.

"I might," Stronbert drawled.

Stephen wished to pursue this matter, but the glint in Stronbert's eyes stopped him. "Are there any other reasons?"

"I cannot be sure that she likes me," Stronbert admitted ruefully. "But the largest obstacle is the fear she now has of men. I had noticed it even before this occurrence, but it is of course much worse now. Felicia, too, is suffering the effects of the attempted rape and both of them will take much time and patience to bring to a more natural view of males. Will you tell me what Lady Coombs said to you about Tackar?"

Stephen hesitated no longer. "When the grange had to be sold . . . Well, perhaps you do not know that Sir Frederick made a will leaving half of his property to his mistress, who had a son, and half to my sister. Alicia had to sell the grange in order for this disposition to be made, for Sir Frederick had spent lavishly. Alicia managed his estate for some sixteen years," he said angrily. "Sir Frederick seldom came there; in fact, she had not seen him for two years before his death. She is convinced that it was Tackar who killed him in the duel," Stephen said skeptically.

"It was."

"How could you know?"

"A friend of his told me so. I doubt he lied."

Stephen sighed and set down his brandy glass. "That, too, then. Tackar bought the grange, though Alicia did not wish to sell it to him and had gotten a better bid than his original one. He overbid the other party and purchased it for more than its worth. He then came to Alicia and proposed that she stay there and receive him when he chose to come to her, is how she put it." Stephen watched the pulse in Stronbert's neck throb as the man pressed his lips firmly together. Stephen continued, "That is all she said, except that she would never speak to me again if I killed him. She meant it."

"She would," Stronbert managed to say, but the bile in his throat almost gagged him. He should have blown Tackar's head off. "You understand the situation now, Mr. Newton. No one can really give me the right to protect Lady Coombs but herself, of course. Since she is not like to do so I would like your assurance that you are agreeable to my intentions. Are you?"

"How could I be otherwise?" Stephen asked dismally. "I can do nothing for her myself but have her here, and she will not come. I can only be thankful that you are concerned."

"I want you to understand that my protection will be as unobtrusive as possible and that it will continue as long as I feel there is any danger to either of them. I am very fond of Felicia, as are my niece and nephew. My nephew . . . well, we shall see. Felicia is but sixteen and cannot know her mind yet, especially after this incident. I am a widower myself, with two children—a son of twelve and a daughter of ten. Perhaps Lady Coombs mentioned in her letter that my niece and nephew are staying for several months. At the court a few more or less make little difference. My mother is there as well as a vast array of relations. It would not perhaps be the sort of home that Lady Coombs would choose for herself, but it would undoubtedly be more comfortable than their cottage. Felicia is a favorite of everyone. I tell you these things in the event one day that I am able to convince your sister to wed me." Stronbert gazed out the window for a moment and then said more slowly, "Since the succession is assured it would be possible for me to wed your sister without making any demands on her, but I had rather not have things come to that pass."

Stephen felt his eyes widen in astonishment at this statement. If he were not the age he was he would have thought to redden at such plain speaking. Stronbert noted his discomfiture and said softly, "Forgive my bluntness. I wish only to arrive at the source of Lady Coombs's distress about men. Perhaps it is only Tackar, but I feel that is not all. As her brother I had hoped you might be able to enlighten me, but I know it is a distressing subject and I shall not press you." He made a gesture of dismissal and lifted his brandy glass to take a sip.

Stephen was sure he had not suffered such embarrassment since he was a youth. And yet he could not feel the impertinence that should have been in the question, for it was a question. He was being asked to discuss his sister's physical relations with men. Another sip of brandy fortified him somewhat. "I realize," he said faintly, "that you feel justified in asking such a question, but it is hardly a matter in which my sister would have confided overmuch in me."

"I should welcome your impressions. Mr. Newton, it cannot be for the best to allow your sister to go through life afraid to give her hand to a man if it can be prevented. She is as skittish as a filly about even the most formal of social touches from men, except the very young and old." Stronbert sighed. "No matter, I will be patient." He made a move to rise, but Stephen waved him back into his chair.

Through dry lips he spoke haltingly. "My parents sold Alicia to Sir Frederick. That is what it amounted to. She was just turned seventeen and did not care for him at all, but he took a fancy to her when he met her here in Oxford. My parents used the money they received to set out for America. We have never heard from them since and do not know if they are alive or not. Sir Frederick was nearing forty then and Alicia's youth appealed to him. She was shy in those days and I protested my parents' decision. They brooked no argument from me or from Alicia, who was locked in her room for two weeks before she agreed to accept him." Stephen bit his lip and sighed. "And so they were wed. I visited her some six or seven months later and found her distraught. Sir Frederick was due back that day from a trip to London and I could see that she was anxious. When he arrived, although we were sitting at tea, he took her by the arm and drew her out of the room. I have seldom seen such terror in a girl's eyes."

Stephen took another sip of the brandy and continued, "She was already with child, and I was distressed enough to follow them. He took her to his room and even from down the hall I could hear her pleading with him." Stephen shut his eyes in an agony of remembrance. After a moment he moistened his lips but did not open his eyes. His voice was a faint thread of sound. "I heard him tell her, roar at her, to get on her hands and knees and uncover herself. And I heard her screams. I felt helpless to interfere. She did not speak of it, of course, when she returned to me some time later. I wanted to take her off with me, but she said he would only come to get her. I stayed longer than I had intended to, but my presence was no deterrent to her husband. When he wanted her he came and took her away to his room, whether I had been sitting with her or not. I lingered until he became totally intolerant of my stay, and then I feared that I did her more harm than good. I had a wife and young child at the time, with another on the way. I did not visit Alicia again until after her child was born.

"At that time she seemed stronger and more resilient than I had expected. She told me that on the day Felicia was born Sir Frederick came to her room and slapped her repeatedly all the while shouting that she should have had a son. He had wagered five thousand pounds that he would have a son. She told him never to touch her again, and, perhaps because he found a mistress in London soon after, I think he never did. Of course, she had threatened to kill him if he did, which may have influenced him," Stephen remarked with grim humor.

Stronbert had sat through this discourse with his head bowed. He did not wish to have his gaze interrupt the long-suppressed flow of Stephen's agony for his sister. Now he spoke, his steady, steellike voice bringing reality back to the scene. "I appreciate what it has cost you to tell me this, Mr. Newton. I promise you will never regret your confidence and that I will do what I can to see your sister safe and happy. I will write you, if I may." Stephen nodded his acquiescence. Stronbert continued, "I would prefer that your sister not know as yet that I have visited you."

"Certainly. I will explain to my wife." Stephen rose to take the other man's offered hand. "I wish you well, and can only thank you for your concern for my sister and my niece."

Stronbert left Oxford with a heavy heart. Matters were worse than he had presumed. Perhaps it would be best, after all, to offer Lady Coombs marriage without its obligations. She had suffered far too much in her physical relations with men already. And he might be able to convince her of the advantages for Felicia of such a match. He had schooled himself over the years in patience and gentleness with his own wife, and he had been rewarded with success in some measure. But she had not been well for some years before her death and afterward he had taken a mistress occasionally in London. The thought of an unfulfilled marriage with Lady Coombs was bitter indeed, and he was not sure that he had the strength for it.

He could not believe that his own personal charms were great enough to overcome the hatred she must feel of a man's touch on her body. A lopsided grin replaced his frown when he contemplated Lady Coombs's reaction to his suggesting that she marry him in name only and allow him his pleasure with Colette. Somehow he could not think she would take to it kindly. But it was a possible solution and he decided to consider it. Not that he cared a fig for Colette, who was a very high-priced courtesan, but he knew his own needs and the proximity of Lady Coombs was not like to damp them.

London was relatively quiet at this season of the year and Stronbert approached his town house as the lamps were being lit along King Street. The house, at the corner of Park Street, was of a dark red brick with stone quoins outlining the three portions brought forward. Stronbert recalled the first time his daughter had seen the building, with its classical portal supported by two elongated caryatids. After staring in amazement for some time, Helen had cried, "Oh, Papa, the poor ladies must be frightfully tired." Matthew, with the superiority of his advanced years, had proceeded to inform her that she need not waste her pity on statues, so Helen had counted the thirty-three identical windows on the facade instead, but had given each of the "ladies" a reassuring pat on her way into the house.

As he himself was let in, Stronbert wondered momentarily what Lady Coombs would think of the house, with its black-and-white marble entrance hall and its dozens of elegant rooms. He relinquished his hat, gloves, and driving cape to the footman as he instructed, "A light supper in the library, Thomas. Is all well here?"

"Yes, milord. Shall I put the knocker up?"

"No, I shall only be here for a day or two and have no intention of receiving."

"Very good, sir." Thomas strode ahead of the marquis to open the library door and put a taper to the fire laid there, then he quietly withdrew.

When a tray was brought in quarter of an hour later, Stronbert was seated in a comfortable leather chair staring at the fire, his booted feet thrust out before him. He thanked the footman, but made no move toward the meal for some time. With half a dozen commissions to execute in town for his mother, including the purchase of a pair of long white kid gloves, he could not well leave for the court the next day in any case. So he walked to the desk and sat down to pen a note in his typical bold hand. If Colette were free the next afternoon, he would take the opportunity to visit her.

Colette was indeed free to receive him, and Stronbert regarded the vivacious little brunette with amusement as she struck a pose for him. "You see," she cried, "Emma Hamilton is not the only one who can be a poseur! Do you not think me the image of Venus?"

"A pocket Venus, perhaps," he retorted with a smile, regarding her diminutive form.

"Ah, well, maybe one must be taller to be a poseur," she pouted, aware that this made her dimples prominent. "I overheard a very fine lady once say that she found it difficult to take short people seriously. Do you take me seriously, Stronbert?"

"No, my dear, how could I?"

"Wicked man! Is it because I am short?" she asked curiously.

"No, I shouldn't think so. I have no difficulty taking short people seriously."

"Really? But then, it makes no difference, mon cher." Colette provocatively twitched the gauze drapery she had flung about her. "Perhaps you could take me more seriously were I . . . less hampered with these robes."

"It is possible."

She wagged her head with mock despair, and allowed him an alluring view of her bosom by rearranging the draperies. "I know what it is! You find it difficult to take anything seriously all trussed up in that skin-tight coat and breeches. Nothing is so conducive to serious thinking as being unrestricted, I promise you." Dextrously she relieved him of these offending items, in addition to his remaining apparel. "There, I told you so. You are thinking better already," she announced proudly, with a swish of her draperies, as she vaulted onto the bed. "You must not try that," she cautioned. "When Sir Geoffrey did so the whole bed went whoosh-bang! This is a stronger bed, of course, but he had to pay for it, and I should not like the inconvenience of having to have yet another bed made, though I know you could afford it."

Colette made room for him to slide into bed beside her. The problem with Colette, he thought ruefully, was that she never stopped talking. Her enthusiasm could not be faulted, nor her skill, but her talent for mimicry seemed to burst into flower under the influence of sexual excitement, and he was treated to Sir Geoffrey's more inane maxims and Lord Clafford's most daunting observations on Greek culture, all delivered in perfect tone of voice.

"Ah, yes, I like that," Colette murmured before quoting Lady Bufton's comments upon spying Colette in Bond Street with her Scotch terrier. "And do you know, she has not the least right to complain of my Muffit, for I have seen her myself driving in the park with the silliest little chihuahua perched on her lap. And such a lap! Ralph Drew said . . . Oh, Lord . . ." Momentarily speechless, Colette regarded him with enormous eyes.

"As you say, my dear." When he could tell that she was recovered enough and about to launch forth once more, he stayed her by placing a finger on her lips. "If I don't ask you now, I fear I won't have another chance. My nephew is coming to London and I think he would benefit from acquaintance with an experienced woman . . . and one who would not bend his ear, Colette," he said mournfully.

"Bah, everyone says I talk too much. It is not that I talk too much, Stronbert, but that sometimes I forget who I am talking to. Once I mimicked Sir Geoffrey to Sir Geoffrey! You would think that would cause a catástrophe, no? Well, it did not! He did not even recognize his own words, paperskull that he is. Now when I did the same with James Akers, he leaped from the bed, red in the face and still . . ."

"Colette. Do you mimic me?"

She cocked her head to one side and regarded him pertly. "You? You never say enough for me to catch the right inflection." Folding her hands demurely, she leaned back on the pillows and commanded, "Speak to me and I will memorize your every word for my next performance."

Stronbert cast his eyes heavenward. "Give me strength. Do you have anyone in mind for my nephew?"

"But certainly. Mrs. Frazier is just the one. So charming, so attractive, and she used to be a governess," Colette declared virtuously.

"Perfect," Stronbert replied dryly, but his eyes acknowledged her mischief. "I must leave if I am to finish my errands in town and be off tomorrow."

"I shan't see you again?"

"Not this trip."

"And do you not take me more seriously now?" she asked with a grin.

"Only so long as I am unrestricted by my clothing."

CHAPTER FOURTEEN

After Lady Gorham and Cassandra left Tetterton for Peshre Abbey, Alicia renewed her determination to finish putting the store in order. She suggested some rearrangements of merchandise to Mr. Allerton for his opinions. This led to a general reorganization that absorbed her days completely.

Felicia continued to work in the cottage decorating various bonnets and other items—slippers, parasols, fans. In addition she made the rest of the seat covers for the chairs and relegated to the tiny attic those pieces of furniture which were unsightly. Her rides with the Clintons continued daily, and she was a frequent visitor at the court, where the dowager marchioness occasionally asked her to design a gown or day dress from some disagreeable material she had accumulated over the years. Felicia patiently rejected the materials offered and brought swatches from the shop which she thought more appropriate. The dowager usually gave in reluctantly, and Felicia would then discuss with Miss Carnworth what she had in mind and leave sketches.

When Stronbert returned to the court, he found Rowland anxious to speak with him. The young man ran a distracted hand through his blond hair and said, "Felicia does not seem much easier with me, Uncle Nigel. She talks to me and rides with me, but she seems almost afraid to smile at me or to let me lift her down from a horse."

"It has only been a few weeks, Rowland. She is

probably afraid of encouraging you. She is too young to understand that you would not take advantage of her." Stronbert sighed. "I have spoken with Colette and will give you the name of a woman to contact in London if you wish to. That is your own decision."

Rowland did not meet his uncle's eyes but murmured, "Thank you. I thought to visit London after returning home."

"How is your mother? Is Dorothy anxious to return to her?"

"Mother is well and seems to miss Dorothy. I think we won't stay above a week longer now," he said sadly.

"You are welcome here at any time, Rowland. Go to London and Bath. Your parents will be desirous of seeing you and I have no doubt you have friends in the neighborhood. When you tire of that, come back here. It will probably be easier for Felicia to mend with you away. She is going to be lonely when you and Dorothy leave, though." He sat thoughtfully silent for a while. "Perhaps we should have a party with dancing for the young people before you leave."

"So that Felicia will meet all the young men in the neighborhood?" Rowland asked bitterly.

"And their sisters, nephew. Would you rather she had no entertainment when you left?" Stronbert eyed his relative gravely.

Rowland shamefacedly muttered, "No, sir, of course not. I want her to be happy."

"Good. I will speak with Dorothy and my mother about whom to invite." Stronbert placed a firm hand on his nephew's shoulder and said encouragingly, "As I said before, where the proper degree of attachment exists, it will last."

"You do not think I should speak with her about . . . how I feel?"

"It would be very unwise. I would simply tell her that I intended to return." Stronbert shrugged elaborately. "God, Rowland, you must act as you see fit. No one can make these decisions for you."

"I know," the young man said with a grin. "But you always seem to know what is best."

"Far from it," Stronbert replied soberly. His gaze wandered to the window for a moment before he recalled himself and said indolently, "But when I was your age I thought I did."

Rowland laughed. "I used to think I did, too, before I met Felicia."

"Fine. There is hope for you." Stronbert watched his nephew stroll from the library as he tried to imagine what he could possibly need from Lady Coombs's shop that day.

Alicia experienced a moment of profound relief when she looked up from the thread drawer to see Lord Stronbert entering the shop with Miss Carnworth. It was ridiculous to endow him with magical powers, she scolded herself, but he had been gone and somehow she felt safer when he was around. Stronbert did not miss the brief expression. He identified it for what it was and ruefully decided that it was better than nothing. His smile was relaxed, unconcerned as he greeted her. "We have determined to have a party for the young people in a few days. My niece and nephew must return to their home. I hope you and Felicia will honor us with your presence."

"How kind of you. I am sure we have no other engagements to stand in our way," she replied, her eyes mocking.

"And I hope that you will feel it proper for Felicia to join the dancing. Dorothy would be disappointed could her friend not take part."

"Why, yes, I could not deny Felicia such a treat. She deserves a chance to enjoy herself with people of her own age."

Stronbert nodded his agreement. "I have asked Miss Carnworth to make Dorothy a new gown for the occasion. Perhaps you would help her select a fabric."

"And perhaps Felicia would assist with the design," Miss Carnworth contributed bluntly.

"Have a look around and I will fetch her," Alicia suggested, as she gently closed the thread drawer. "I will be but a moment." She ignored Stronbert's look of protest and left through the rear of the shop.

When she returned with Felicia, the girl beamed on Stronbert and exclaimed, "Mama has told me of the party! I shall look forward to it." Her face clouded then and she said, "But I shall miss Dorothy and Rowland. They have been so good to me."

"And they will miss you, my child. I think Dorothy would like to pack you away in a trunk and take you with her," Stronbert said.

Felicia laughed, and Alicia wondered that her daughter could be so at ease with this man when she was still so timid with Rowland. Perhaps it was that he had comforted her when she was so upset, or again that she thought of Lord Stronbert more as a father. The thought made Alicia flush and she turned to Miss Carnworth to assist in the selection of a fabric. A sapphire-blue velvet was chosen and Felicia mused, "I have just seen the most delightful creation in one of the magazines, Miss Carnworth. It would have to be modified slightly for Dorothy because of her height, but I believe it would be just the thing. Would you mind coming to the cottage with me for a moment?"

"Of course not," the good lady replied stoutly. She turned to Stronbert and said, "Perhaps you have other errands to run, Nigel. I should not be above half an hour."

"There is no hurry," he replied easily.

When Stronbert made no attempt to leave and the women had disappeared, Alicia turned to him somewhat nervously. "Can I show you something else, sir?"

"No. I will wait here for Miss Susan, if you have no objection, that is."

"Of course not." She searched for some topic of

conversation and settled at last on, "I presume Mrs. Clinton is well, since Dorothy and Rowland are going home."

"Yes, she has completely recovered."

There was a pause and Alicia asked hesitantly, "Did you have a good trip?"

He studied her thoughtfully and replied, "I am not sure, frankly. The results remain to be seen."

"A matter of business then."

"Not precisely."

"Oh." His gaze on her was disconcerting and she turned aside to replace a bolt of cloth they had been considering. "I heard from Lady Gorham yesterday. She had a great deal to say about the roads, but I gather they had a relatively uneventful journey home. I miss her."

"We shall have to convince her to come again soon then."

"There is little likelihood of that. She has family still at home and the holidays are not so far away now. She has invited us to go to her then, but I do not see how we can."

"Why not?"

"I cannot simply abandon the shop, Lord Stronbert," Alicia said a little sharply.

"I daresay Mr. Allerton could manage," he drawled.

"Not for so long," she retorted.

"Could he manage for a few hours tomorrow?"

"Why?"

"So that you might go riding with me."

"Whatever for?"

"Because you have been working so hard that you are beginning to snap," he said firmly. "You need some fresh air and exercise."

"I am flattered that you should concern yourself, but I assure you that I am perfectly healthy." Alicia grew uncomfortable under his uncompromising gaze and said faintly, "Perhaps you are right. I do need to get away from the shop for a while, but there is no need for you to trouble yourself. I can ride with Felicia."

"I will bring a mare for you tomorrow at twelve, at your cottage." His tone was insistent but his eyes were gentle. "The weather is like to hold fine. I will bring a picnic hamper."

She nodded slowly. "As you wish. Thank you."

Stronbert then assumed the direction of their conversation, talking of the members of his household and their backgrounds. He had counseled patience for Rowland, and he had thought to pursue the same course. It was not impetuosity that led him to this move, however, but the sudden realization that Lady Coombs would become more resolved in her fear the longer she was allowed to live with it in isolation. Her daughter was young and without previous male contact. Lady Coombs had suffered altogether too much of the wrong sort of male contact. He was determined on a course of re-educating her. When Miss Carnworth returned, he bid Lady Coombs farewell and they took their leave.

Alicia and her daughter each chose a fabric to make new gowns, although Alicia laughed that they would never show any profit at this rate. When Felicia put back the fabric she had been examining and said, "I do not really need a new gown, Mama; I have the blue satin," Alicia hugged her.

"Do not be a goose. I was merely jesting, my love. The reason we have the shop is that there will be some income for our out-go. Otherwise our funds would have lasted but a few years. With the shop we may live reasonably and for as long as we work." And so Felicia took the two pieces of fabric to the cottage and sat down to consider some really special design for her mother.

When Alicia arrived, her daughter had sketched a gown with low neck, high waistline and a skirt tighter and shorter in front than in back. There was to be ruching at the wrists and a diadem of fall flowers.

Felicia was so enthusiastic about it that Alicia's feeble, "Do you not think perhaps it is a little revealing?" was brushed aside.

"Heavens, no, Mama. Come and see these pictures in the magazine. Why, this is all modesty by comparison."

Alicia did not protest further, but thanked her daughter for the design. "Oh, I intend to make it for you as well, Mama, as you will be busy. You can help me in the evenings sometimes. Though really," she said thoughtfully, "you should more beneficially take a walk in the evening. You are cooped up too much in the shop."

"So Lord Stronbert informs me," Alicia said dryly. "He is to take me riding tomorrow."

"Good for him. Is he not the kindest man?"

"Yes, my dear." Alicia bent over the sketches determined to think no more of his lordship.

She did, however, don an attractive riding dress the next day at her daughter's insistence. Felicia would not countenance the drab beige outfit her mother had taken to wearing. She had been almost impatient with her mother, and had gone herself to retrieve from the wardrobe the riding dress Alicia had had made shortly before her husband's death. The royal blue jacket was molded to her form, with a velvet collar and a waistline in its proper place, flaring out below. The high-crowned hat had a buckle and the dress was not so full as her previous riding outfits.

"Much better," Felicia pronounced. "There is Lord Stronbert now. You are just in time."

Alicia felt unaccountably nervous in the becoming outfit. And the admiration in Stronbert's eyes made her more so. He did not attempt to hide it; it was part of his training program. "We have a lovely day for our ride, Lady Coombs, and you grace it perfectly," he said lazily as he assisted her onto the horse he had brought for her. "The mare's name is Muse, and she is rather spirited. I thought you would prefer that."

Alicia assented and ran a hand over the black mare's neck. "You have no hamper," she said accusingly, not because she feared that she would not eat but because she had hoped that a groom would be riding with them to bear it.

"I have had it left at our picnic spot," he informed her as he mounted.

"And where is that?"

"On the estate. I think you will like it."

Once they reached the lodge gates and entered, Stronbert led the way to the west away from the carriage path. Without consulting her, he set his horse to the gallop and she gladly did likewise. It had been a very long time since she had ridden a horse like Muse, highly bred and mannered, with easy paces and controlled power. Stronbert drew in as they entered the home wood and smiled at her. "She's an excellent little goer, is she not?"

"I have not ridden better," Alicia admitted, returning his smile.

They rode around a hill and came upon the waterfall, with the stream rushing off below. There was a hamper set out on a cloth, a bottle of wine in the stream. Alicia exclaimed involuntarily, "What an enchanting spot!"

"I thought you would like it." He dismounted and stood by her. "May I help you down?"

Alicia agreed and felt his firm hands about her waist. They dropped from her the moment her feet touched ground and he said, "Would you rather walk about for a while or have luncheon now?"

"The ride has given me an appetite," she confessed, "and I do not know that I shall have time for a walk."

"I feel sure you will," he responded gently. "Will you set the food out?"

Alicia opened the hamper and grinned at the assortment of treats within. "Did you tell them that there were only two people to eat all of this?"

"I have a remarkably large appetite," he retorted laconically. "These are my favorites," he commented as he lifted a stuffed mushroom. "Will you try one?"

Alicia silently extended her hand for the mushroom he held out to her. Their fingers brushed as she accepted it and her eyes met his as she lifted it to her mouth.

"You are not cold, are you?" he asked, obviously concerned at her shiver.

"No, no." She continued to chew the bite in her mouth while he retrieved the wine from the stream and produced two glasses. "I am not sure that I should have any wine," she protested.

"I think you should. Just a little."

"Lord Stronbert . . ."

"I think it is time you called me Nigel."

Alicia was honestly shocked at the idea. "I could not."

"As you wish, of course," he drawled.

Alicia busied herself with arranging the items on the cloth. She spread them out so that they formed a barrier between her and the marquis. He reached across it to set her wine glass beside her, somehow making the barrier very ineffective indeed. "We have all manner of fruit and vegetables from the hothouses most of the year," he said conversationally. "Would you pass me a chicken wing?"

When she lifted the container closest to her he said, "Oh, just hand me one." She set the container down and lifted a chicken wing from it which she extended across her barrier. Again their fingers brushed; she did not shiver. "Excellent," he said approvingly. "I do think that one should be informal at a picnic."

Stronbert spoke of the hothouses and the stables and the deer park and the lake. He requested items of food from her and offered her others. "Do have a sip of your wine. It is extraordinary." Alicia lifted the glass to her lips; it was indeed the most mellow she had ever tasted—fruity but not sweet. "I like it."

"My father had it laid down years ago."

"You should have saved it for a special occasion," she said guiltily.

"I did."

Alicia did not know how to respond to this, did not want to think about its significance. Through the whole of the meal she had the strangest feeling that something was expected of her, and she could not understand what. Stronbert did not say anything, but there was a patient, waiting look about his eyes when they rested on her. In her confusion she lifted a tart and took a bite of it. The flaky crust and the raspberry filling were delicious. She reached down and handed one across the barrier to Stronbert saying, "Here, you must have one of these."

The smile with which he rewarded her made her feel pleasantly fluttery inside. She had pleased him somehow and the brush of his fingers as he accepted the tart was not frightening but reassuring. "Ah, here are the children," he said a moment later. "I promised them they might join us if they did not come before we finished eating."

Matthew and Helen rode toward them gaily waving and burst into speech before they stopped, "We have not come too soon, have we? We thought for sure you would be finished by now."

"Well," Alicia laughed, "I for one could not touch another bite."

The children looked inquiringly at their father, smiling impishly, and he beckoned them to join him. "No doubt you have already eaten, but Lady Coombs has discovered that the raspberry tarts are very special and you may each have one if you wish."

The children seated themselves at the ends of the barrier and Alicia handed each of them a tart.

"May I have a sip of your wine, Papa?" Matthew asked.

"You give them an inch . . ." he murmured helplessly. "One sip, young man."

In an effort to make this the largest sip possible the boy choked on the wine and had to be pounded on the back for a moment by his father. Matthew raised an embarrassed face to Alicia and said quietly, "Forgive me, ma'am."

"I think it is only to be expected at one of your father's picnics," she said judiciously. "We are very informal, you know."

The children giggled and began to chatter about previous picnics they had made. Alicia listened to them as she packed the remaining food into the hamper. Then she sipped at her wine, feeling Stronbert's eyes on her. When she had finished, she put her glass in the hamper, asked him if he was finished, and leaned over to take his glass from him. The barrier was no longer there, of course. Stronbert rose and held out his hand to her. She took it and was lifted easily to her feet. He gave her hand a firm squeeze before letting it go.

"Have you time to walk to the deer park, Lady Coombs?" he asked gently.

"Y-yes, I should like that."

She placed her hand on his offered arm and was very aware of his strength. For a moment she hesitated, but he appeared to take no note of it and in a while she was more relaxed. After all, the children were there. She had nothing to fear.

Later, when they returned to the horses, the children rode off and Stronberg assisted Alicia to mount. They rode back to town companionably discussing the coming party and which neighbors had been invited. Stronbert seemed to know some anecdote about each of them, and Alicia knew them all from the shop. As they approached her cottage, Stronbert said seriously, "I should like to make a special effort to introduce Felicia to some of the young people. She is like to be lonely when Dorothy and Rowland leave."

"Yes," Alicia replied, a note of sadness creeping into her voice. "But you know, Lord Stronbert, that you are an exception in accepting her. Lady Wickham and her son have been otherwise."

"It can do no harm for her to be seen at the court."

"No, I am sure it can only be beneficial."

Stronbert jumped down and came around to her. He did not ask this time, but she allowed him to lift her down, and his hands fell away as quickly as they had before. "Thank you," she said shyly. "I enjoyed the ride and the picnic tremendously."

"I'm glad. I have business tomorrow, but I hope you will ride with me the following day. No picnic. We cannot expect such fine weather to last at this time of year. Shall I come by at one?"

"Yes, please." She was offering him her hand before she was aware of doing so and gazed wonderingly at it. He shook it gravely, only his eyes acknowledging her bemused expression.

CHAPTER FIFTEEN

Lord Stronbert's business the next day was arranging for Lady Coombs's protection. He was pleased with the small progress he had made with her, but reminded himself that leading her to accept normal social contact was far different than accustoming her to the idea of marriage with its more intimate demands. There was a long way to go, and he had no intention of neglecting her protection while he trod the careful path. Stronbert sent for several of his most trusted employees, separately, and set them about the tasks he had determined on.

Felicia spent as much time as possible during the next few days with Dorothy and Rowland. It made her sadly dashed down to think that they would be leaving soon. She cherished their friendship. But her feelings about Rowland especially were confused. Before Tackar had abducted her she had shared a special sort of companionship with him. She had not allowed herself to think ahead to the future precisely. But she often thought of their talks while she was sewing and going about her tasks. She had especially dwelt on the afternoon when Dorothy had wandered off to pick the blue cornflowers in the meadow where they had paused. Again and again her mind dwelt on the scene of Rowland standing with her under the gnarled elm and telling her that her hair was the color of the falling leaves. She could almost feel his hand as he stroked her hair. He had been about to kiss her, and she had wanted him to. And now?

After the experience with Tackar she shied from even the most casual touch from Rowland. Somehow the memory of his touching her hair now embarrassed and frightened her. At first she had feared Rowland because he was a man, and only a man could be capable of what Tackar had intended. As her sight began to clear a bit, she acknowledged that Rowland was not the kind of man Tackar was. She became ashamed of herself for her lack of faith in him. But she still dreaded the thought of her body being touched so intimately and being defenseless. She would always be defenseless. There was no help for that. So her confusion continued, and although Alicia spoke gently with her sometimes to try to ease her worry, she was not able to speak of her fears. It was useless to cherish her nebulous dreams of Rowland, for she would never be able to be a—never a wife to him. When she had put it into words she scolded herself for being so foolish. It was a childish dream. Rowland was four years older than she, a man grown, and no doubt had plenty of pretty, well-to-do young women to choose from, should he decide to marry. He would never wish to marry the daughter of a shopkeeper, surely, no matter how gently born. *And even if he did,* she thought, sobbing quietly in her bed one night, *I could not marry him or anyone. Could not again be put in a man's power, no matter how kind he might appear.*

Alicia heard the muffled sobs and went to her daughter. "My love, what has distressed you so?" she asked as she pushed the tear-dampened hair from the pretty young face. Her daughter had, for a time after her abduction, wakened from horrifying nightmares, but these had seemed to cease.

"I cannot bear it that Dorothy and Rowland are to leave," Felicia whispered as she allowed her mother to cradle her.

"Yes, that is hard. But they must return to their home, you know. I cannot doubt they will come to visit the court again sometime."

The girl's lips quivered uncontrollably. "I almost feel angry with them for leaving me here alone," she confessed softly.

Alicia smiled in the dark. "I can understand that, love, But I hope you will not let them leave knowing you are upset or angry. You must make new friends at the party and show your old ones a smiling face when they leave. Can you do that?"

"I hope so, Mama."

"It grieves me to keep asking so much of you, Felicia. I would that I could make your path smooth. But I cannot."

Felicia was silent for a moment and then she asked hesitantly, "Will the others at the party accept me? We were not invited to Tosley Hall."

"I am sure most will see the wisdom of accepting you, if you are invited to the court. Doubtless Lady Wickham will snub you, but then why should you care? She is a disagreeable woman and you could have no wish to enjoy her friendship, or her son's."

"I have met a few of the others while riding with Dorothy and Rowland. Most have been civil, but they have never invited me to their homes."

"But then you have spent all your time with the Clintons. When they are gone, well, perhaps others, knowing you are free, will invite you. I cannot warrant it will be so," Alicia said sadly.

"I know, Mama. Do not fret for me."

Alicia could not prevent herself from suffering along with her daughter. Felicia had been mercifully granted a respite from facing the ordeal of lowering her station, but she would have to face it now, when it was harder. Alicia did not sleep well that night and she looked drawn when Stronbert called to take her riding.

"Is something the matter, Lady Coombs?"

"It is only a headache, Lord Stronbert," she replied with an attempt to smile.

"It may come on to rain, too. Would you prefer to put off our ride to another day?"

Alicia's eyes rested on the frisking mare for a moment. Muse had pricked her ears forward at the sound of Alicia's voice and was attempting to nuzzle her. "No, let us ride, even if for a short while."

The late November afternoon was cold with an icy breeze through the almost-bare trees. Their ride took them past the fields, forests, and farms to the west of Tetterton. They talked easily as they rode, and Stronbert pointed out the local landmarks of interest. When the rain started they were several miles from town and Stronbert suggested that they shelter under some trees a way off the road. He saw the doubt in her eyes and said, "Come, Lady Coombs, you do not wish to spoil your riding habit, do you?"

But the skies opened up just then and by the time they reached the trees they were both soaked. "I *am* sorry," Stronbert apologized. "I did not think we would have such a heavy rain. Nor did I think," he added exasperatedly, "that it would turn to hail."

Alicia gave a doleful chuckle as she felt the icy balls beat against her. Stronbert dismounted and imperiously held his hands up to her. She allowed them to grasp her waist and lift her down. Even the cover of the trees was little protection; her riding habit proved more stylish than warm or proof against the icy slush driven against her face and body. Stronbert held her eyes for a moment and said gently, "I am going to hold you. Please do not be afraid of me." Alicia opened her mouth to protest, but the imperative look in his eyes froze her words. She felt his arms encircle her, his hand turn her face to his shoulder before he leaned with his back against the tree that the wind lashed around. He made no move to caress her. With one arm about her shoulders he folded her small cold hands in his other large warm one against his chest. She could feel the warmth of his body against her shivering form. He spoke to her in a calm, dispassionate voice, of the Yorkshire storms he remembered. She did not hear him at first, for her fear enveloped and panicked her. He could feel the tautness of her form gradually relax as his voice went on and on. The worst of the storm passed after fifteen or twenty minutes and he matter-of-factly set her aside from him to comment diffidently, "I must get you home before you catch your death."

Alicia kept her head bowed until he was ready to hand her onto her horse. She met his eyes then and her lips quivered slightly as she said, "Thank you, Lord Stronbert."

He only smiled his acknowledgment and swung himself onto his horse. They maintained a swift pace back to Alicia's cottage. "Will you not come in and warm yourself at the fire?" she asked.

"I should like to, but I had best see that the horses are rubbed down as soon as possible."

She nodded, thanked him again, and scurried into the house. Mavis clucked over the soggy riding outfit, and over her mistress, whom she bustled up the stairs and helped out of her clothes. "I've a good fire going in the drawing room, ma'am, but I can have one for you here in a jiffy."

"No, I will come down to the drawing room. Can you do anything with my habit?"

Mavis regarded it skeptically but assured her she would do her best. Alicia went to sit in front of the fire in her dressing gown, slowly drying her thick auburn hair before its heat. Her thoughts however strayed to the scene beneath the trees when Stronbert had held her. How frightened she had been at first. Which was foolish, really, since she knew that he was not a man who would take advantage of her. He had a way of inducing her to do things she did not really mean to do, though. When he looked at you in that certain way, it was as though he knew he was right and any opinion you might have on the subject was frivolous. She shook back her steaming hair and decided that she must go to the shop.

* * *

The dowager was seated with Miss Carnworth in the winter parlor, a merry blaze on the hearth to warm the room. "I think perhaps my new gown should have a flounce," she announced abruptly.

"Evelyn, when will you learn to accept someone else's judgment? Felicia has designed you the most charming and appropriate gown imaginable and you must needs try to destroy it. A flounce! Do you wish to challenge the young people at the party with your youthful flounces and spangles? Nigel has told me that he finds your gown admirable."

"Has he now?" The dowager raised her head from the fringe she was knotting and stared inquiringly at her companion. "When did he see it?"

"Only yesterday. Felicia and Dorothy brought him to my room for that precise purpose."

A cross expression flitted over the dowager's features. "He has more faith in that child's taste than in my own. Surely he owes more respect to his mother than that."

Miss Carnworth's lips pressed into a thin line. "Don't be absurd, Evelyn. His respect for you has nothing to do with your taste—or lack of it," she murmured dryly.

"These last weeks he has neglected me," the dowager complained.

"You astonish me! Did he not execute your every commission in London?"

"Why should he have gone away at all?" the old woman asked petulantly.

"Why should he not? This is his home, and we are all here by his generosity alone. Never did he suggest that you retire to the dower house when he was married. Quite the contrary. He has taken in every needy relation who has applied to him, and some who have not. I cannot blame him if he wishes to shake the dust of the place from his heels now and again, Evelyn. A young man, a widower, must regard this as something of an old people's home, and wish for a little amusement."

The dowager's face set stubbornly. "He is thirty-eight recently and should settle down to his home and his children."

Miss Carnworth threw her hands up in despair. "Good Lord, I cannot believe you could say such a thing! One would think he went roaring off to town every other week to hear you talk. He cannot have made more than half a dozen trips from home in the last two years. And his attentions to you and his children are quite remarkable."

"He has divided his attentions widely of late," the dowager complained, pulling overfiercely at the knot to set it in place. "Here are his niece and nephew claiming his time, to say nothing of Felicia. And I believe he has been riding with Lady Coombs recently." The old woman cast a suspicious glance from under her lowered eyelids to see how this comment would affect Miss Carnworth.

"About time someone did," she retorted with asperity. "Lady Coombs has been working altogether too hard in the shop. It is not a life she is accustomed to, Evelyn."

"I know, I know, but it need not be Nigel who undertakes her amusement. Surely the young people could invite her to join them."

"I doubt she would interfere with their youthful exploits. She would fear to dampen their spirits with her presence."

"She is little more than a child herself," the dowager protested.

"Only in comparison with us, Evelyn. She must be close to Nigel's age."

With a dark look the dowager transferred her gaze to the window. "The rain has stopped. I have no doubt Nigel will be soaked to the bone when he returns. He will need a fire in his room."

"He is perfectly capable of sustaining a wetting,

Evelyn. Shall I instruct that a fire be started for him?"
she asked as she rose.

"Now where are you going? I can very well give
orders to the servants, Susan. Everyone treats me as
though I were too old to be of use," Lady Stronbert
said fretfully.

Miss Carnworth offered an incredulous snort. "I
think the weather is addling your brains, Evelyn. Dorothy's gown is in need of another hour's work and I
should like to see it finished. On my way through the
hall I shall order a fire in Nigel's room."

"See that he is told I wish to speak with him when
he comes in."

"Yes, after he has changed to dry clothing, cousin,"
Miss Carnworth agreed repressively.

When Stronbert received word of his mother's wish
to see him, he was shaking himself out of a dripping
greatcoat. "Tell her I have returned and will be with
her shortly, if you will, Williams." Taking the stairs
two at a time, his topboots squishing at each footfall,
he was unaware of any discomfort from his condition.
Gladly would he have suffered a soaking daily if it
provided him an opportunity to hold Lady Coombs in
his arms and encourage her confidence in him. He had
not purposely put them in such a situation, but he
could only view the experience with satisfaction. With
the party but a few days away, he was unlikely to
have a chance to ride with her again soon and he hoped
their afternoon's adventure would work to his advantage.

His valet promptly divested him of his wet clothing,
and would not accept thanks for the warmth of the
blaze. "Your lady mother instructed that it be started,
milord."

Stronbert shook his head exasperatedly. "Then she
probably wants to see me to assure herself that I have
not sustained damage from my soaking. Had you best
rub my face with rouge, James?" he asked quizzically.

"Give over, sir. You be in the pink of health and

well you know it. Her ladyship do treat you like a boy at times," he said disgustedly, as he gave a final tug to the set of Stronbert's coat. "Fair lucky she never heard word of the duel."

"Yes, and I appreciate your discretion in that matter, James." With a nod of thanks he left to present himself to his mother in the winter parlor.

"Ah, there you are, Nigel. It would have been wise not to ride out on such a threatening day," she admonished him.

"No, do you think so? I quite enjoyed myself, though I was grateful for the fire you ordered in my room." He stooped to kiss her cheek before seating himself on a green-velvet-covered spoonback chair near her. "Did you wish to see me in order to scold me?"

Her piercing gaze took in his unperturbed countenance and relaxed attitude. "It would not do the least good, I dare say. Nonetheless, I did have in mind to mention that I think you have been neglecting your family."

Stronbert raised a brow. "Do you? In what way, Mother?"

"You have not spent enough time with your children."

"I have ridden with them every day since my return, to say nothing of participating in numerous games of barley break; prisoner's bar; My Daughter, Jane; and whoop and hide." He considered her thoughtfully. "Do you feel that I have neglected you, Mother?"

"I was not speaking of myself, Nigel."

"Perhaps it is merely that everyone has been busy preparing for the party," he suggested.

"I could see no need for your trip."

"But then, I wished to make it," he said gently, "and it provided an opportunity to bring you some items you desired from London."

"I could have done without them," she mumbled. "Things are not the same here. I can feel it."

"You need never fear that we do not all hold you

in affection, Mother, and we shall always continue to do so, no matter what changes occur. If you feel the demands placed on you by the party are too great, you need only say so, and I will arrange for more help for you."

This remark, calculated to provoke her, succeeded very well. "More help? Do you think I am incapable of managing a country entertainment? I am plagued with offers of assistance from morning to night, Nigel, and I assure you I am adequate to any demands such a function will make on me."

Stronbert rose and rested a hand on her shoulder. "I know you are, my dear. Everyone wants to have a hand in it, and you are a past master at organizing our resources." Moving toward the door, he remarked casually, "Felicia and Dorothy showed me your gown. I congratulate you; it is exquisite."

The dowager, momentarily diverted from her complaints, smiled proudly as he bowed and excused himself. It was only after he left that she realized she had obtained no information on the subject in which she was most interested. Certainly he had assured her of his unchanging affection, but he had not mentioned Lady Coombs. Even the dowager, with her habit of outspokenness, was not prepared to ask him straight out if he had intentions in that direction. She had no wish to receive a set-down from him, and she greatly feared that if she so trespassed on his private life, he would not hesitate to give her one. With a sigh she returned to the knotting of her fringe.

CHAPTER SIXTEEN

Francis Tackar gazed out over the lawns of his estate as he addressed the minion awaiting his pleasure. "Take this tray away and send Martin to me." As the man disappeared out the door, Tackar absently rubbed his hand over the newly healed wound. For the first week after it had been inflicted he had suffered agonies which he did not long to dwell on, but he prided himself on his quick recovery. Few men of his acquaintance would so soon be riding again. Even fewer would have been contemplating the revenge he now planned.

Martin knocked discreetly on the door and was bade to enter. As usual, his face was devoid of any expression.

"Where the devil is that brother of yours?" Tackar demanded coldly.

"I expect him within the hour, sir."

"Have him shown to me immediately he arrives."

"Very good, sir."

Sending Martin's brother had been a necessary precaution; the valet himself was too likely to be recognized in Tetterton. Tackar had no desire to arouse suspicion in the community, though he thought it likely that his attempt on Lady Coombs's virtue, as well as the duel, were not common knowledge. When he bent to retrieve the book he had set down earlier, he relished the twinge of pain he experienced. Lady Coombs would suffer for that.

Although Tackar proceeded to open the book and stare at its pages, his mind was not on reading. His physical desire for Alicia had been extinguished by the pain that had wracked his body, but his desire to wreak vengeance on her had been kindled. No matter that it was Lord Stronbert who had foiled his well-organized plot and fired the ball which very nearly killed him. It would be foolhardy to take on such an opponent; moreover, it was merely a matter of coincidence that the marquis had become involved at all. Tackar realized belatedly that it had been Stronbert who had seen him as he rode away with Felicia's horse. No, he could not fault the marquis for his subsequent actions. It was Alicia whom he would ruin—not physically this time, but financially.

The matter was very simple. She had obviously invested the majority of her money in that ridiculous shop in Tetterton. Without it she would have to beg for charity. Not that she could come crawling to him. Tackar had an enjoyable vision of such a scene, where he would laugh in her face. The proud Alicia, who had scorned his generous offer to provide for her as his mistress, would suffer greatly from the indignity of poverty.

When Martin's brother was ushered into his presence, he regarded the sloppily dressed fellow with disgust. "Well, what have you found?"

The man shuffled his feet awkwardly before the exquisitely dressed Tackar. "Nights there's hardly no one about on the High Street. Few locals in and out of the Feather and Flask. Shop closes at dark usually, though sometimes the lady stays on a bit in the back office."

"I know all that," Tackar rasped impatiently. "Did you find nothing of interest?"

"Goin' to be a party at the court on Tuesday. Seems the whole neighborhood is invited or working there for the night."

"And Lady Coombs? Is she invited?"

"Sure to be. Thick as thieves with the folks at the court."

Tackar's exasperation was growing. "Did you make no effort to find out positively?"

"Heard the young lady talking about the ball gown she was making," the fellow offered.

Tackar sighed. "Very well. Is that all?"

"Dull place. Nothing much happening there."

"Oh, for God's sake! Get out!"

In spite of his annoyance, Tackar was convinced that the information was sufficient for his purposes. A party at the court would leave Tetterton as nearly deserted as made no matter. Undoubtedly the Coombs ladies were to attend, if the girl was making a gown. There could be no better occasion to carry out his plan, and this time he would do it without assistance. He was intrigued with the slight element of risk involved; it lent spice to the venture.

Tuesday afternoon, the afternoon of the party, Tackar established himself in a village not far from Tetterton. When dusk fell and he could be reasonably sure of being unrecognizable, he rode into Tetterton and stationed himself at the far end of the green from the shop. His horse was left in a copse of trees, but he emerged to study the scene in the High Street. There was very little movement there after dark. He saw a carriage from the court come through town and stop down the lane where Lady Coombs lived. Shortly afterward the carriage bowled off again to return to the court, presumably. Tackar was well satisfied.

Still, he waited another hour for all activity to cease in the street. Even the Feather and Flask seemed light of company. He retrieved his horse and rode along the green and down the lane alongside the shop. The horse was tethered to a tree before he silently retraced his steps to the corner. No one was in the street now and he covered his hand with a gunnysack to smash a pane of glass beside the door. The noise sounded loud in his ears and he glanced around for any sign of its having attracted attention. When he could perceive no movement, he slid his hand through the empty space and reached around to unfasten the door. This presented no difficulty and he slipped quietly inside the shop.

Tackar surveyed the bolts of flimsy, flammable fabric with smug satisfaction. He set to work at once pulling lengths from a dozen of them toward the middle of the shop. When he was satisfied that there were enough to keep the blaze going, he spilled a small quantity of gunpowder on top and lit it with a flint. As the fire took hold, he dragged more lengths of fabric toward it and sprinkled gunpowder sparingly about. The sight of small poufs of flame breaking out about the shop thrilled him and he had to take hold of himself to admit that he had accomplished what he came for and prepare to leave. He glanced into the street before he stepped out the door, but he still could see no one. The green across from the shop was deserted; there was not a soul to see the fire until it had consumed the building entirely, he thought.

Jeff Thomas was not entirely happy with his assignment to protect Lady Coombs. He thought Lord Stronbert exaggerated any danger to her, and he certainly felt it unnecessary to take up his post on a night when Lady Coombs was not even at home. He liked the marquis, and he liked the additional pay which came with this assignment, but it was getting cold at night and he thought he might just slip over to the Feather and Flask for a little something to warm him. Jeff had not been dismayed when he saw a man ride up and tether his horse in the lane. Folks did that sometimes to save the small expense of leaving it at the inn for a short while. Even the sound of breaking glass was not particularly sinister, although it was not the sort of thing he was expecting.

But the longer he sat there in the cold garden across from Lady Coombs's cottage, the more his legs ached from their cramped position, the more he considered the possibility that he should perhaps walk about a little to warm himself. And it could do no harm to investigate that tinkling noise, even if it had nothing to do with Lady Coombs. Once he was in the High Street perhaps there would be no harm in slipping into the Feather and Flask for a quick one.

Even as he rounded the corner of the lane into the High Street he sensed the smell of smoke, and the sight of an eerie light coming from the shop alerted his cold-numbed senses. The movement at the shop door made him draw back momentarily. The marquis had cautioned him that Tackar was not one to be treated lightly and an element of surprise could not come amiss. Jeff flattened himself against the laneside wall of the shop and listened to the hurried footsteps approaching him. When the man was rounding the corner into the lane, he struck a blow at the head, and his opponent reeled with the shock. But Tackar did not go down. Instead he turned savagely on his attacker and reached for the pistol stuck into his waist. Jeff aimed a kick at his hand and waist which knocked Tackar to the ground, and Jeff fell upon him, wresting the pistol away. He aimed the weapon at the gasping Tackar and roared, "Get up!" Before Tackar could comply the young giant hauled him to his feet and shoved him before him into the High Street.

A sense of urgency had stolen over Jeff as the acrid smell of smoke filled his nostrils. He grasped Tackar's hands behind him and used the gunnysack to tie them before roughly marching him toward the inn. "Harper!" Jeff cried as they arrived at the inn. "Hurry!" The landlord appeared immediately at the door and stared at the sight confronting him.

"This fellow has set fire to Lady Coombs's shop. See he is guarded until I can take him to a magistrate. And send me men to fight the fire!"

The landlord did not hesitate. He knew Jeff and accepted his word without comment, in spite of the indignant protests squealed by Tackar. Harper accepted the pistol from Jeff and led Tackar away, rousing the household all the while to fight the fire. Soon men and women were forming a line of buckets to the pump. Jeff returned to the shop where the fire was blazing mainly in the center of the building. Smoke drifted out the hole left by the broken windowpane. Jeff opened the door and entered the smoke- and heat-filled room. He ripped his cravat from about his neck and tied it over his face. First he ran to close off the second room by the doors which were always left open. Then he began to make his way along the sides of the room, tearing down the bolts of fabric that had caught fire.

The door burst open again as the first of the men with buckets of water entered. "In the center. Put it out there first," he called as his gloves began to smolder against a burning bolt of fabric. More men were streaming in now and several of them, after emptying their buckets, followed his lead in wresting the burning fabrics from their shelves. Jeff raced outside to draw in great mouthfuls of air before returning to the shop to continue his efforts. The blaze was dying now and most of the smoldering bolts lay in the center of the shop being carefully doused with buckets of water. "Shall we have them all down just in case?" a man asked him.

"No," Jeff replied roughly. In the dim light it was difficult to tell if there was further danger. "Have some men stand guard with filled buckets, though. I will see they are paid well. Let's not ruin any more of the stock than is absolutely necessary," he said, his voice discouraged. "I will ride to the court to inform Lady Coombs."

The dancing was well under way when Jeff arrived at the court. Stronbert had led his niece out in the first set, and then Felicia. He had taken care to introduce Felicia personally to several of the young people there. Alicia had watched anxiously as her daughter spoke shyly with her neighbors. She relaxed somewhat when she realized that Felicia was not going to lack for partners. Alicia herself was determined not to dance; it was a party for the young people and she aligned herself with the matrons. Lady Wickham continued to ignore her, but the attention paid her by the dowager marchioness and the other members of the household at the court induced many others to speak with her. She was especially pleased with a young woman about her own age who had come with her two daughters. Mrs. Maple was a regular visitor to the shop and had always been pleasant to Alicia, but they had never before had the opportunity to converse at any length. While they spoke, the marquis was called from the room.

He was gone for some time and when he returned he approached Alicia, who was laughing over something Mrs. Maple had said.

"Lady Coombs."

Alicia glanced up at his grave face and her eyes flew immediately to Felicia, who was dancing quite unconcernedly further down the room. "Yes, Lord Stronbert?"

"I must have a word with you in private if Mrs. Maple will excuse us."

Mrs. Maple, puzzled, nodded her head as she noted his grave demeanor. She impulsively squeezed her new friend's hand as Alicia rose to allow herself to be led from the room. Stronbert did not speak until he had seated Alicia in his library.

"What is the matter?" she asked faintly.

"It is your shop. There was a fire set there and a great deal of damage has been done."

Alicia's face paled. "Tackar?" she asked numbly.

"From the description, yes. He has been apprehended and will be turned over to a magistrate. The fire has not burned the building much, but I fear most of the stock is burned or spoiled by the smoke," he said gently.

Alicia wanted very much to be brave about this and gazed for a moment at the ceiling so that the tears would not overflow her eyes. But this meant ruin for her and Felicia and her spirit rebelled at the unjustness of it. After all her effort, after all the pain of stepping down to such a position, that she should be broken by the maliciousness of someone she had never done the slightest harm to. There were not sufficient funds left to replace the inventory, let alone whatever damage the fire might have done to the building. She put her head down on her arms and wept.

Stronbert extracted a handkerchief from his pocket and moved to stand by her. His hand rested reassuringly on her shoulder and he said gravely, "Perhaps the damage is not as great as Jeff fears. He closed the doors to the second room before the smoke could invade it entirely, and the flames did not reach there at all."

"Wonderful!" she sobbed bitterly. "The most expensive fabric is always kept in the front, so as to be seen."

"I realize that," he replied sadly. He regarded her bent head despairingly. He could not offer her the financial assistance she would need. She would not accept it from him. He could not ask her to marry him. She would reject him, seeing the offer as pity for her. Her sobs were abating now and he placed the handkerchief firmly in her hand. She rubbed furiously at her eyes and her cheeks, annoyed with herself for her weakness.

"What time is it?" she asked abruptly.

Surprised, Stronbert consulted his watch. "Eleven thirty."

"We can safely leave at midnight. I will not tell Felicia until then. Let her have another half hour to enjoy herself."

"As you wish. I will drive back with you to assess the damage."

"That is hardly necessary, though I appreciate your offer. You have guests to see to," she said calmly. "I cannot very well go back to the ballroom in this state.

Ask Mrs. Maple, please, if she will just keep an eye on Felicia and bring her here to me at midnight."

"Certainly. I will have the carriage ready for you."

"Thank you, Lord Stronbert. You are very kind."

Stronbert muttered an unintelligible oath and departed. Alicia sat alone in the library attempting to accept this new calamity. Her tears were past now, but her mind refused to offer any solution. She could make no decisions now, tonight. But soon she would have to, and there were few choices left.

Alicia heard a clock chime somewhere and she sighed as the tap came on the door. Stronbert held the door for Felicia and announced at the same time, "The carriage is ready, Lady Coombs."

Felicia curiously surveyed her mother's face. Something was wrong. She turned instinctively to Stronbert. "Why has Mama been crying?"

"She has had some bad news. She will tell you about it in the carriage." He waited while they received their cloaks and walked with them to the door. "I will come round in the morning."

It was a statement and Alicia accepted it with a nod. She politely thanked him for the evening and climbed into the carriage. Stronbert pressed Felicia's hand and said, "Help her," as she climbed after her mother into the vehicle.

Felicia took her mother's hand and held it while she waited for Alicia to speak. The carriage jolted as it started and then swung into a rhythm over the graveled drive. "There has been a fire at the shop, my love. I fear most of the merchandise is ruined. We have not the resources to meet such an emergency," Alicia said softly. "I am not sure what we are to do. In the morning we will survey the damage and make some decision."

"A fire! How could such a thing happen?" the girl asked indignantly.

"It did not happen; Mr. Tackar started it. Lord

Stronbert said he has been apprehended and will be brought before a magistrate."

"Good! The hateful creature. Why must he persecute us like this?" Felicia wailed.

"I daresay he did not like being thwarted in his designs," Alicia grimaced.

Felicia sighed. "I daresay. Well, perhaps this will be the last of him."

"I certainly hope so. It will be too dark to see much tonight, but let us have a look at the shop." She gave the order to the coachman and within a few minutes they drew up before the building. There were two men standing in the doorway talking, and they came forward to greet her.

"We're so sorry, Lady Coombs, about the fire. Jeff asked that we stay to make sure it did not break out again," one explained. "Everything seems fine now."

"Thank you. And I must thank all of you for getting the fire under control so quickly. I am indeed lucky there is so much left." She considered the blackened paint inside the store and the mass of fabric drowned in the center. The counters were charred; she could tell from running a finger along them. The shelves were mostly empty. "If you think it is safe to leave now . . ."

"I think so, ma'am," the second man said gruffly.

"In that case, please come by in the morning and I will see you are paid."

"Oh, no, ma'am. Jeff said as how he'd take care of it," the first man said stubbornly.

"Who is Jeff?"

"Jeff Thomas, ma'am. He be the one who caught the fellow. Well, good night then, ma'am." The two men bowed politely and sympathetically to her and shuffled off in the direction of the Feather and Flask.

Felicia had wandered about the shop while her mother talked to the men, but she returned now to say, "How ugly it is! It will take weeks just to clean it up. The back room is not as bad. Many of the fabrics there could be salvaged, though I fear they will smell of the smoke."

"Let us go home. In the daylight we will be able to assess the damage better. I feel extraordinarily tired."

It was some time before the rest of the guests had left the court. When the last carriage had pulled away and the residents were sighing with the relief of being alone, Stronbert asked that his mother, Miss Susan, Dorothy, and Rowland join him in the library. Everyone else thankfully trudged off to bed.

"I thought it best that the four of you know what has happened this evening. Lady Coombs's shop was set fire and a great deal of damage done. The culprit has been caught and is being brought before a magistrate." He paused while they each expressed their horror and indignation, ranging from the dowager's fiercely raised eyebrows to Rowland's fist pounded against the chair arm. "I fear that Lady Coombs has not the resources to withstand this financial burden. I would, of course, be willing to assist her, but I cannot believe she would accept my help. Therefore, Mother, I have a favor to ask of you—a very tiring one."

"Well, what is it?" she asked when he paused.

"I should like you to go to Lady Gorham first thing in the morning. I will send a letter explaining the situation, and asking that she suggest to Lady Coombs a silent partnership with her for providing the necessary funds to restore the shop. The details can be worked out by a solicitor. Would you be willing to undertake such a journey?"

"I suppose so," the old woman grumbled.

"I could take your letter, Uncle Nigel," Rowland suggested eagerly.

"You and Dorothy are to leave in the morning, Rowland."

"I should not mind delaying our departure," Dorothy protested.

"No, but your mother is expecting you. I would rather Mother went, but Miss Susan might go in her stead if she were willing."

"I said I would go," the dowager proclaimed with a majestic wave of her hand, "and I shall."

"In that case, Cousin Evelyn, perhaps I might accompany you," Miss Carnworth suggested.

"As you wish, my dear. I am sure the company would not come amiss," the dowager admitted.

"Excellent," Stronbert approved. "I would have suggested an early start, but after such a late night it might be wise to start later and plan to spend the night at Peshre Abbey and return the following day."

"Nonsense," his mother said scornfully. "I am not so old that I cannot be up and about early." The dowager marchioness typically rose at ten and was not seen outside her chamber before noon. Stronbert regarded her skeptically, and she responded smartly, "We can leave at nine, can we not, Cousin Susan?"

"I shall certainly be ready by then," her relation said flatly.

"I thank you both. I shall have the letter ready for you in the morning."

When the others had left, Rowland stayed behind to ask, "Is there nothing I can do? Who set the fire? Why?"

"It was the same man, attempting to cause further trouble. I do not see any way in which you can help, Rowland, though I imagine you and Dorothy will wish to stop by to see Felicia before you leave. Rest assured I will do what I can for them," Stronbert said wearily. He toyed with a quill for a moment before replacing it on the desk.

"I know you will, sir. Thank you."

Stronbert rose to shake his nephew's outstretched hand. "Take care of yourself, Rowland. I shall expect to see you here again in the not too distant future."

When his nephew had left him he sat down again

at the ordered desk to compose his letter to Lady Gorham. It was not a simple letter to write. After considering for some time he dipped the quill in the standish and began:

Dear Lady Gorham,

I regret to inform you that still another calamity has befallen Lady Coombs. Mr. Tackar set fire to various goods in the shop tonight which caused a great deal of damage. I do not believe that Lady Coombs's resources can handle the necessary repairs and replacement of stock. I feel in part responsible, as I had undertaken her protection, a matter I had discussed with her brother in Oxford. Mr. Tackar has been apprehended and I shall do what I can at the next assizes to make him responsible for the damage, but the immediate necessity for funds is great. I do not believe that Lady Coombs would accept any assistance from me and I do not wish to ask her to do so. On the other hand, I cannot imagine that you would have the ready amount to assist her, even if you desired to do so. Therefore, I would suggest that we draw a private understanding between us in which I will advance the funds and you will permit that they appear to come from you, as a silent partner in the business, to be paid off when possible over a lengthy period of time. If you are agreeable, you need only send a letter with my mother and I will see that all is arranged. My intent is not to deceive Lady Coombs but to spare her feelings. I have every intention of marrying her if she will have me, but the time is not ripe to put my suit to the touch. I would prefer that no one else know of our arrangement, should you agree to it, and I sincerely hope that you will.

Your most obedient servant,
Stronbert

He could not feel entirely satisfied with the letter but decided it would have to suffice. He would send a letter to Stephen Newton when he knew the situation better, but that would be more difficult to write and he did not mind that it would have to wait.

CHAPTER SEVENTEEN

Mr. Allerton, who lived in a village a mile northeast of town, arrived at the shop unaware of the previous evening's activity. Alicia entered to find him standing horror-stricken by the sight, which even at her second viewing made her cringe. She carefully explained what had occurred, stressing that she did not as yet know how she would handle the matter. "But I shall have to start clearing the mess and do what I can until I make a decision. I do not know if I can continue to offer you a job, Mr. Allerton," she said helplessly. "And I am embarrassed to ask you to help with this," a hopeless gesture of her hand to the pile of soaking fabric, "for it is not what you are employed to do."

"If you are thinking that it would be beneath my dignity," he said with a rueful smile, "you are very much mistaken. I shall find a smock from the second room, where things appear a bit less damaged, and start to work."

Alicia smiled warmly at him and said simply, "Thank you."

Felicia arrived with Mavis, who was determined to help wherever she could, and the three women donned aprons. "For the time being we shall carry everything damaged to the backyard. Then we will inspect for items which may be salvaged," Alicia remarked, sadly surveying a charred paduasoy which ran twenty guineas the yard.

She had made two trips, the water soaking through her apron to the old gown she had worn, her face streaked with soot, when she glanced up to see Stronbert enter the shop. With a blackened hand she pushed the straggling auburn tresses back from her face and attempted to greet him with a cordial smile. "Ah, our first customer for the fire-damage sale."

It was necessary for Stronbert to keep a tight rein on his emotions. He wanted to shake her and hold her and tell her to get the hell home and leave this work for others to do. He did none of those things. "I have come to offer my services," he said, as his eyes met hers following a brief scan of the damage.

Alicia took in his immaculate buckskins, ruffled shirt, and riding jacket with amusement. "I think you are not dressed for the role."

"Well, to be perfectly honest with you, I had not actually intended to lug sodden bolts of fabric about, as I wish you would not either." He did not miss the lift of her chin and continued calmly, "I had hoped you might sit with me a moment and allow me to arrange for some carpenters and painters."

Alicia sighed as she glanced at the damaged counters, the burnt hole in the floor, and the singed paint all about the shop. "Yes, that will have to be done, even if only to find a purchaser for the shop. Come with me to the office and we shall make a list of what is necessary. I would not know where to begin contacting people for such repairs."

"I am hoping that my knowledge of the area will be useful."

"I am sure it will. Which reminds me, do you know this Jeff Thomas who apprehended Mr. Tackar?" Alicia asked him curiously.

Stronbert nodded carelessly. "Yes, a good man."

The very casualness of the gesture made Alicia suspicious. "Just how well do you know him? Why did he come to you?"

"Because he is an employee of mine." Stronbert was forced to stop as the woman leading him toward the rear of the shop swung about.

"How providential that he should have been here at just the right time," she said sharply.

"Yes, I thought so."

"The men who stayed behind after the fire said Jeff had instructed them to do so. He also said they would be paid for their time. That was my responsibility," she said angrily.

"I am sure he will allow you to reimburse him," Stronbert replied placatingly.

"You shall send him to me so that I may." There were bright spots of color on her cheeks.

"As you wish, Lady Coombs."

"Lord Stronbert, did you have this man . . ." but Alicia found it impossible to ask the question. Her companion regarded her inquiringly, at ease. She lowered her eyes and turned toward the office again. "Never mind. Let us make the list of necessary repairs."

Stronbert was relieved that she had not brought the matter to a head. He would not have hesitated to tell her the truth, but he definitely preferred not to. She would resent his interference and he could not blame her. It was becoming a very tricky situation.

Alicia mentally chastised herself for allowing her imagination to run rampant. It was ludicrous to think that Stronbert would have set a man to watch her property or herself, especially on a night when she was not even to be at home. She sat down at her desk and calmly discussed with him the necessary repairs. He undertook to put them in hand immediately. As they walked back to the front of the shop he waved her thanks aside.

"I think you will find that there are many in Tetterton who will come to your assistance in this emergency, Lady Coombs. I hope you will not be too proud to accept their help." His eyes were serious and troubled as they rested on hers.

Alicia flushed. "I do not like to be beholden to people," she replied stiffly.

"You must learn to be. They will come in all sincerity to offer what they can, and I would be ashamed for you to spurn their kindheartedness out of stiff-necked pride."

He had never spoken so roughly to her, and she could feel the stinging behind her eyes that promised tears. His voice softened as he continued, "It is a tradition here to give support when a neighbor undergoes a setback. I am sure you would do the same yourself."

"Yes," she whispered, unable to meet his eyes. "I will not reject anyone's help."

"Good girl. Here is Jeff now. I should like to introduce you to him."

Subdued, Alicia advanced to meet the young giant approaching them. To her surprise he was apologetic. "Oh, ma'am, I should never have let the fire get started at all," he groaned. "I heard the breaking glass, but I did not for a while realize what it meant."

"I am sincerely grateful to you, Mr. Thomas. It is owing to you alone that there is a shop standing here this morning at all."

Jeff made to protest, but the warning in Stronbert's eyes was heeded. "Well," he murmured, shuffling his feet nervously, "I am glad it was no worse."

Alicia noticed his bandaged hands and her face lifted to Stronbert inquiringly. "Jeff suffered some burns in attempting to quell the blaze," he told her calmly, while the young man flushed crimson. "They are not severe."

"No, ma'am. They'll be right as anything in a day or so," he proclaimed stoutly, almost beseechingly.

Alicia did not wish to embarrass Jeff further. She thought of speaking with him about the payment for the two men, but could not bring herself to do so in the face of his discomfort. So she offered him her hand and took his carefully with another word of thanks, and he gratefully escaped to await Lord Stronbert outside the shop.

Stronbert rewarded her with that smile which made

her feel fluttery inside. There were others coming in now to console her on her troubles and offer to set the shop to rights, and she barely had time to say good-bye to him before it was necessary to organize the work. The morning passed in a flurry of activity, and before it was over, a carpenter and a painter had appeared to survey what was needed.

Dorothy and Rowland had their traveling carriage stop in the street outside. Rowland's lips became a tight line as he surveyed the damage, and his sister looked as though she wished to cry. She ran to Felicia and caught her in her arms, wet and sooty as the girl was. "I wish I could take you home with me, away from all this!" she exclaimed.

Felicia's eyes twinkled. "Actually," she confessed, "I am quite enjoying the bustle. Ever so many people have come by and they are all so kind."

Dorothy regarded her with mock exasperation. "I might have known that you would find something good about it, my dear. We would stay to help but Uncle Nigel said he will do what he can, and Mama is expecting me. You do not think us poor spirited to desert you at such a time, do you?"

Felicia's eyes softened and she said fervently, "You are the best friends I have ever had and I cannot thank you enough for all the kindnesses you have shown me. I shall miss you excessively." Her glance included Rowland shyly.

"And we you," Dorothy cried, her eyes sparkling with tears. "I must say good-bye to Lady Coombs," and she scurried off.

Felicia stood sadly before Rowland, her heart aching. "Felicia," he said softly so that she would raise her eyes. "I shall be back in a month or two. I hope you will not forget me."

"Never," she breathed, as she extended her hand shyly to him.

Rowland took the offered hand gently and raised it

to his lips, never taking his eyes from hers. "We must leave now, but it will not be so very long before I return. Take care of yourself."

"And you," she replied softly, her face showing a tendency to crumple.

Rowland abruptly released her hand and turned to make his farewells to her mother. Felicia could not see them leave very well because of the tears in her eyes. Alicia joined her and put her arm about the girl's shoulders comfortingly. "Go home with Mavis for a while, love, and see to some luncheon for us." Felicia nodded mutely and left the shop. Her mother sighed, but was recalled to the pressing demands of those about her and soon involved herself in directing the removal of the damaged counters.

When Mr. Allerton had had a chance to eat his meal, Alicia slipped away to the cottage for a few moments of peace and something to sustain her. It was there that Mrs. Maple and her two daughters found her. Fortunately Alicia had caught sight of herself in a glass and had hastened to scrub her face and tidy her hair before the visitors arrived.

"We have just heard of the fire, Lady Coombs, and hoped that we might be able to help you in some way," Mrs. Maple suggested. "Samantha and Tabitha thought perhaps your daughter could drive with us a while if she is not too busy."

Felicia entered the drawing room at that moment and smiled shyly at the two girls. "That was very kind of you," she said softly, "but I plan to return to the shop now."

"No," her mother said firmly. "You have done your share and a drive is just what you need."

"But, Mama, there is so much to do!"

"It will be there tomorrow," Alicia retorted.

"Do come with us," Samantha begged. "We have the loveliest fur rug in the carriage so we need not even feel the chill."

Felicia wanted to go with them but she did not wish to leave her mother to cope alone with the shop. Alicia, as though reading the girl's thoughts, said, "You forget that Mr. Allerton is more than capable of supervising everything without either you or me."

Felicia agreed then to go with the Maples. She changed into a becoming blue dress and bundled herself in a warm mantle and matching scarf. Alicia watched them leave with relief; Felicia would have some friends after all. But would she even be in Tetterton to enjoy them? Alicia could see no way to retain the shop, when doing so would mean the necessity of replenishing the expensive stock. She could not allow herself to become discouraged, though, with so many kind people coming to their assistance. So she returned to the shop with a determined smile on her lips to continue the clean-up.

When Stronbert joined Jeff Thomas outside the shop, he paused to send a messenger to the court before they mounted their horses to ride to Tosley Hall where Sir John Wickham was a local justice of the peace, and the magistrate before whom Tackar was to be brought. Sir John was a weak and ineffectual man, if not unkindly. He was dominated by his wife and taunted by his son, and had allowed a vagueness of manner to isolate him from these annoyances. Stronbert was shown into his library and received a jovial welcome, which was somewhat marred by the nervous twitch Sir John's eye suffered when under stress.

"My lord, what has brought you today? Not that I am not honored by your visit, you understand. Flattering, most flattering. Good of you to call," Sir John mumbled enthusiastically.

"I came in regard to the fire in Lady Coombs's shop last night. I understand the culprit is to be brought before you this morning."

"Yes, yes, indeed, he has been." Sir John would

not meet the marquis's eyes, but regarded his shelves of books as though they might enlighten him on how to handle the matter.

"Already? But I have just ridden here with Jeff Thomas, who apprehended him," Stronbert remarked calmly. "I should have thought you would wish to hear him speak before you made a disposition."

"No need, I assure you. Had his statement from last night." Sir John's eye began to twitch in earnest.

"I see. And is Mr. Tackar to be turned over to the next Assizes?" Stronbert asked softly.

"No, no. Case of mistaken identity. Wasn't the right man at all. This man Tackar was merely walking along the street when Thomas attacked him. 'Twas another set the fire."

"Was it, indeed?" Stronbert's voice was ruthlessly scornful. "Whatever induced you to believe such a thing?"

"Thomas's statement said he did not see the man in the shop, just at the door. Could have been anyone set the fire."

"You cannot possibly believe that."

Sir John's eye was almost continually closed now, giving the impression of a preposterous wink. "Certainly I can," he retorted with weak spirit. "Man is wealthy, well known. Why would he set fire to a poor widow's shop? Hardly the thing, you know."

"Mr. Tackar is not likely to consider such niceties. Had you made the effort to have Mr. Thomas present he might have explained to you that he was currently assigned to prevent Mr. Tackar from doing just such a thing as he did."

Sir John regarded him with unfeigned astonishment. "You had set a watch for him? Why would you do such a thing?"

"Tell me, Sir John, did Mr. Tackar admit to knowing Lady Coombs?"

"I did not ask him." Sir John's face had begun to twitch, too. "He protested any knowledge of the whole affair; said he was only going for his horse in the lane."

"And his reason for being in Tetterton?"

"He gave none. Can't very well ask an Englishman why he's in an English town."

"When he is charged with arson, a very serious crime, I do believe it would be possible, even necessary. What have you done with him?" Stronbert asked, his tone dangerous now.

"Let him go, of course. Can't very well hold a man for a crime he didn't commit," Sir John said stubbornly as he pulled out his handkerchief to wipe his brow.

"Did your wife have any opinion on the matter?"

"She could tell right off he was quality," Sir John pronounced proudly. "And Lawrence knew him by repute from London—quite the dashing fellow, I hear."

"I will have you unseated for this," Stronbert said coldly, rising to take his leave. "And if any further harm comes to Lady Coombs from that man you will answer to me for it."

"Here now! You cannot threaten me!" Sir John blustered, his face white.

"You are supposed to represent the law in Tetterton. You have deliberately ignored a crime to which an honest, straightforward witness has sworn. Instead of locking the fellow up to await his just punishment, you have licked his boots. I shall take the matter to a higher authority—the matter of Tackar and the matter of you." Stronbert strode angrily to the door, pulled it open, and left. Sir John slumped in his chair and cursed himself for the fool he was.

Jeff had never seen Lord Stronbert as he appeared at the door of the hall. His eyes were blazing, his mouth grimly pressed, and the grip on his gloves was furious. Jeff himself had always been treated obligingly by his employer, and any rebukes had been justly deserved and never given in anger. He watched with amazement while the marquis brought his temper under control, strode over to the horses, and motioned for Jeff to follow him. "Am I not to speak before Sir John, then?" he asked anxiously.

"There is no need. Sir John has set Tackar free." The voice was level.

"Free? He can't do that. Is setting a fire no crime?"

"Sir John does not believe Tackar set the fire. You were mistaken in attacking him. I wonder that Tackar did not think to set the law on you." Stronbert's hard-won control deserted him for a moment in the sarcasm of this speech.

The enormous young man turned uneasily in his saddle to face Stronbert. "You do not believe that, do you, sir? I am sorry I was so slow to act, but I made no mistake in the man."

Stronbert sighed and grimaced. "Forgive me. I did not mean to upset you, Jeff. You must know that I believe you and that I am well pleased with all you did. Neither of us expected an attack on the shop. I might have thought of it, but I did not. It is such a cowardly act, and Tackar faced me bravely in . . . No matter. I did not expect him to stoop so low. It was my fault and none of yours."

The young man breathed a sigh of relief. "I could see no need to be there last night," he admitted, "what with her ladyship at the court. I had even thought to have a quick one at the Feather and Flask." His face flushed with shame at the memory.

Stronbert shrugged. "No matter. We all misjudge situations from time to time. It was the women them-selves I concentrated on. I even had the coachman carry a weapon last night."

"Well, you were not wrong that he meant trouble. Will he try again?"

The glint returned to Stronbert's eyes. "I should like to see him try. But no, I intend to handle things myself now, though if you and Peter are willing, I will keep up the watch."

"Certainly, sir. Peter has never minded much, it being daytime and all," Jeff said with a grin.

"Should you like to switch?"

"No, sir, there seems to be more activity at night." He met the older man's amused gaze gravely and the two rode back to town in silence.

Lady Gorham was considering the possibilities of a nap. She sat in the winter parlor, feeling the warmth of the sun make her drowsy. The melody Cassandra was playing in the music room, too, was inducive to a short rest, and Lady Gorham had finally determined that she would just lie down for a bit when the rattle of wheels on the carriage path aroused her. No one was expected and she could not see the front of the house from the winter parlor. Well, visitors would be more amusing than a nap in any case. The abbey had seemed lonely since the Coombses had left, she thought sadly.

The aged butler appeared at the door to announce, "The Dowager Marchioness of Stronbert and Miss Carnworth," much to Lady Gorham's amazement. She watched her friend enter with plumes waving on an admirable bonnet, an attractive gown gracing her figure, and a colorful parasol gripped in one hand, which she refused to give up to the butler. "Evelyn," she gasped, "you are quite fashionable!"

The old woman smirked with satisfaction and cast a conspiratorial glance at her companion. Miss Carnworth uttered a small "Harumph" but said nothing further. "We have come on a matter of some importance, Charlotte, and cannot stay long. May we have tea?"

Lady Gorham was used to her friend's ways and immediately rang. "There is no trouble at the court, I hope."

"At the court, no. Though I am beginning to wonder . . . Well, never mind that now. I have brought you a note from Nigel. I am sure he explains the situation admirably. Most unfortunate. Go ahead and read it. Pay no heed to us," Lady Stronbert said grandly as she seated herself gingerly on a chair with a vase-shaped back and spindly legs which she considered too fragile to sustain her ample self.

Lady Gorham read the letter slowly. Her frown gathered as she read of the fire and Alicia's straits, turned to a puzzled quirk when the suggestion for funds was advanced, and mellowed into a whimsical smile when Stronbert revealed his intentions. Lady Gorham could understand his reluctance to approach her obstinate friend but she hoped he would be successful when he did. She had spent enough time in Stronbert's presence to feel that it would be an admirable match. She was not so sure that Alicia would have him, though, after the life she had endured, even for the position and comfort he could offer her and Felicia. A sigh escaped her, and she became aware of her guests suddenly. "Most unfortunate. As if the poor woman had not enough to bear. I shall be pleased to become a partner if Alicia is agreeable. Set the tea tray by Miss Carnworth, please, Richards. You will not mind pouring for me, will you, dear?"

Miss Carnworth was delighted to assume the task and Lady Gorham excused herself to write a letter to her friend's son. In this she admitted that she would not be able to come by a substantial amount of capital very easily and agreed to the proposed arrangement. "I feel you should know," she wrote, "that Alicia has told me she does not intend to marry again. She is aware that it might make life easier in some respects, but her first marriage has soured her. Nonetheless I should like to see you successful in your suit, and I wish you luck." Lady Gorham proceeded to seal the letter carefully before she wrote a separate letter to Alicia and returned to the winter parlor.

CHAPTER EIGHTEEN

When Tackar left Sir John, the charming smile he had maintained during their interview faded from his face and he made all speed to his estate. Although he made no comment to Martin on the disastrous fate of his project, the valet had no doubt that things had gone awry, but carefully concealed his delight. His employer had obviously spent the night in his clothes, and from the pallor of his face it seemed likely that he had not slept overmuch, and that his recent wound was paining him.

"Bring me the brandy!" Tackar snapped as he sank into an overstuffed chair in his bed chamber, his dressing gown wrapped loosely about him.

"Right away, sir. Will you be wishing dinner in your room?" It was the closest Martin could come to commenting on his employer's disheveled condition.

Tackar froze him with a glare. "Certainly. I have no intention of dressing again for your amusement."

Left alone, he considered once again the expeditiousness of his capture and what it signified. During the uncomfortable night he had spent, it had occurred to him that he had been expected. Since he had divulged his plans to no one, including his valet and his brother, for fear of being in their power or suffering from their carelessness, he had realized that the giant who had taken him had been waiting for such an event. No particular event, just standing guard over Lady Coombs and her daughter. And he had no doubt that Lord Stronbert was behind it. Protecting his own preserves, no doubt.

What was most daunting about that view of the situation was that if Stronbert were involved, Tackar would not consider it beyond the marquis's power to pursue the matter of prosecuting him.

Staring glumly at the marquetry sunburst on the tallboy, Tackar acknowledged that he had no desire to spend a great portion of his life in jail, nor to wind up at the end of a rope. He rubbed his constricted throat tentatively. Certainly there could be no fear of that: He was a rich man, and rich men seldom met such an end. Nonetheless, he was in a very awkward position now and it made him angry to find himself in a situation not of his making, and rather beyond his control.

Matters had gone too far now. The possibility of Bow Street Runners was real indeed. The thought brought a cold sweat to his forehead and his native caution advised him that he would have to leave the country. Without a word he watched Martin place the decanter of brandy and a glass within his reach. When the valet again withdrew, he poured himself a generous portion and took a healthy gulp. As the liquid burned down his throat, he had a blinding flash of intelligence. Stronbert's intentions toward the beautiful widow were honorable! The realization was so amazingly logical and so exquisitely amusing to Tackar that he indulged in a bout of hysterical laughter. It provided such a wide scope for his devious brain that he neglected to fuel himself with further brandy. He would have to go abroad, and things were unsettled in France since the overthrow of the Bastille. Still, he had always enjoyed it there and he had no doubt that he would yet.

All the wild plans of revenge that his imagination had thrown up with regard to Stronbert, Lady Coombs, and her daughter were forgotten. Here was a superlative retaliation! Making mischief from France in the present instance would prove so much safer than in

England, and certainly just as effective. Rumors started from a distance gained such incredible veracity at the same time that they expanded so well. Tackar took up his glass again in high good humor.

After the fire, the days passed swiftly for Alicia. There was work for her to do and to supervise. She accepted Lady Gorham's offer of a partnership reluctantly, for she feared that her friend could ill afford to be so generous. But she did not wish to wound her by saying so, and it did seem the only possibility to save herself and Felicia from becoming dependent on her brother in the not very distant future. The fabrics from the second room of the shop had been aired thoroughly and were then offered at reduced prices. The unscarred fabrics from the front room would not give up the smoky smell and she had to discard them. The vicar told her, when she brought them to him apologetically, that there were those who needed the clothing badly enough that they would not mind the honest smell of smoke. The shop itself had been repaired, with the weak flooring replaced and new counters and shelving introduced where needed. The paint still smelled fresh; she had hesitantly acceded to Stronbert's suggestion that the outside trim be painted, too.

Her new stock was beginning to arrive. It had necessitated a trip to York, but Miss Carnworth had offered to accompany her, and Stronbert had insisted that they use a court carriage. Except for the expense of the endeavor, it was a most exciting day for her. York itself she had not seen for some time, and the choosing of the materials made her feel like a child in the confectioners. Miss Carnworth's acerbic comments and sensible advice had been bracing and welcome. Felicia had spent the day with the Maples, whom she frequently saw now, so her mother concentrated on accomplishing as much as she could during the day. It was growing dark when they arrived back in Tetterton, but Alicia could see the sign clearly. She had not thought at the time of her discussion with Stronbert of any reason he should ask her the new name of the shop. But the sign read: TETTERTON MERCERS, LINEN DRAPER AND HABERDASHER, ESTABLISHED 1790, A. COOMBS, PROP.

Alicia gave a gasp that was half-sob, half-giggle and pointed with a shaking finger for Miss Carnworth. That redoubtable lady merely commented, "Very proper. About time the Dean sign was removed."

"But I did not order it."

"Of course you did not. Nigel did. It is a present to you," she explained patiently.

"It somehow makes me very proud," Alicia confessed, "not just for me, but for everyone who helped to put the shop back together. I shall of course tell Lord Stronbert myself, but I hope you will just mention that I am . . . grateful and pleased."

"Of course, my dear. I am sure he will not be long in London."

"He has gone to London? I think he did not mention that he was planning a trip," Alicia said, curiously hurt.

"I gather he received a letter yesterday which necessitated the journey. No doubt he assumed I would tell you." Miss Carnworth's eyes held Alicia's for a moment before the latter's dropped.

"Yes, well, there is no reason he should tell me."

"We assume he will be back in time for Christmas," her companion said comfortably.

"I imagine the dowager marchioness would be rather put out with him if he were not," Alicia replied with a grin.

Alicia climbed out of the carriage and thanked Miss Carnworth for her help. Felicia greeted her cheerfully when she entered the cottage and chatted about her day with the Maple sisters. Her mother spoke of the purchases she had made, the items ordered which would arrive in a few days in time for the heaviest shopping of the year.

But Alicia could not shake the despondency she felt. There was no reason he should tell her that he was leaving for London. No reason that she should suddenly feel very lonely. She no longer feared Tackar; Stronbert had assured her that though Sir John had released him, the marquis had brought the matter to higher authorities and if Tackar set foot in England again, he would be arrested. When Stronbert had returned to the court after seeing Sir John, he had sent a man to keep watch near Tackar's estate. In due time the man had informed him that Tackar had returned and left again within the day, a carriage overflowing with luggage taking him to the coast where he had sailed for France. Although the channel was rough at that time of year, word was eventually received that there had (unfortunately) been no mishap to Tackar, who had duly arrived in Paris.

With the holidays approaching, the activity at the shop increased and it required all her time and attention to organize the new merchandise and wait on customers. Felicia overruled her objections and came to assist in the shop regularly for the period. And still the days went by and Lord Stronbert did not return. Alicia and her daughter received an invitation from the dowager to spend Christmas at the court, and they accepted. But there was no word of or from Stronbert, and Alicia could not shake the heaviness of her heart. She did not wish to examine her feelings. There was no sense in it. But she peeked each night at the enameled snuff box she had seen in York and ordered among others to be delivered to the shop. When it came, she took it to her room, reminding herself that if he could give her a sign for her shop, she could give him a simple snuff box by way of thanks for all his help. She kept it carefully wrapped in her drawer.

Felicia was concerned when she occasionally discovered her mother, thinking herself unnoticed, with a sad countenance and unhappy eyes. The girl herself was reasonably content, her friendship with the Maple sisters leading to others in the neighborhood. She missed Dorothy and Rowland, but she relied on Rowland's word that he would be back, and it could not be so very long now. If he did not return, well, then she would probably look like her mother did now. *Dear God,* she thought suddenly, *Mama is missing Lord Stronbert.* She became more attentive to her mother's moods and actions but there was no sign, no word. Perhaps she was wrong after all.

Stronbert left the court at the end of his patience with Tackar, and Stronbert was a very patient man. The letter he had received was from a friend in London informing him that various people, himself included, had received letters from Tackar in France containing damaging references to Stronbert and a Lady Coombs, the widow of Sir Frederick Coombs. The insinuation was that Tackar had made Lady Coombs his mistress years ago when Sir Frederick abandoned her. He had further suggested that this was why Sir Frederick had willed his property as he had. Not satisfied with that, Tackar had indicated that he had tired of the lady and dropped her, whereupon she had moved to a town near Stronbert Court and lured the marquis into her net.

Tackar did not hesitate at this juncture to point out that there was also a nubile young daughter involved in the current arrangement. For good measure he suggested that the marquis had viciously laid the blame on him for a fire set in the widow's shop in order to rid himself of Tackar, since Lady Coombs still pined for her former lover.

Lady Coombs was situated too far from London, geographically and mentally, to come in contact with these rumors, Stronbert knew, but he refused to allow them to circulate. In fact he refused to allow Tackar to live any longer if he had any say in the matter. He made the journey to London in record time to assess the damage done and by his very presence, allay the rumors as best he could. Then he set out for France, his friend George Bryant, who had written him, accompanying him. The channel crossing was reasonably good, and within four days they were in the capital. Stronbert insisted he must see Tackar immediately, but his friend grumbled, "It has been a wearying journey, Nigel, and it is late. Let us call on him first thing in the morning."

"You need not accompany me, George, though I will ask that you act my second in the affair. You are right; it is late. But I will be gone before you arise in the morning."

George yawned and muttered, "As you will, Nigel. Now leave me to get some sleep."

Stronbert woke early and breakfasted before hiring a hack to take him to the address Tackar had given his correspondents. The concierge responded immediately, his eyes expressing his excitement. "But no, monsieur, you have just missed M. Tackar. He has left for the Bois de Boulogne already." The man gave a knowing wink.

Stronbert regarded him curiously. "He has gone to fight a duel?"

"He was never up so early before," the man said slyly, "nor does he usually leave with a pistol case."

"Thank you," Stronbert said, passing him a coin. He remounted his hack and set off with all possible speed for the Bois de Boulogne. Trust Tackar to embroil himself within weeks of his arrival. Damn it, he did not want someone else killing the villain. He urged his mount faster. A light snow started to fall as he approached the wood and the neigh of a horse directed him to the scene of the activity. As he leapt from his horse his eyes fell on the tableau before him. Two men stood with their pistols aimed, awaiting the drop of the handkerchief. One was Tackar, the other was his nephew Rowland.

CHAPTER NINETEEN

Rowland and Dorothy had left Tetterton in rather downcast spirits, in spite of the fact that they were eager to see their mother recovered from her recent illness. The horrifying condition of Lady Coombs's shop had impressed a mental image on each of their minds which did not seem to diminish as the distance from the scene increased.

"We should have stayed to help," Dorothy protested for the third time as they reached the inn where they were to spend the night.

"Uncle Nigel will do all that is necessary, you may be sure. They would not have let us delay our departure," Rowland pointed out once again. But he grieved for the mother and daughter laboring under this new catastrophe. Perhaps Felicia would not even be there when he returned to the court. The thought was unbearable, and he thrust it from his mind, determined to take an optimistic view of the situation. Lady Gorham would lend her assistance; she was Lady Coombs's particular friend. And after the new year, when he would be free to return to the court, he would do all he could to lend his support to the two ladies.

Although he was depressed to think how little he could do, this decision had to satisfy him for the time being. Dorothy was aware of his restlessness on the journey, but he refused to allow her to draw him into any further useless recapitulation of the fire at the shop. Their arrival at their home near Bath allowed Rowland for a short while to dismiss his worries in the relief of seeing his mother fully recovered. But soon his restlessness grew, and his mother urged him to accept his friend Charles March's invitation to spend some time in London before Christmas.

"You really would not mind if I left again so soon?" he asked with a frown.

"No, my love, so long as you are back for the holidays. Dorothy is so pleased to be with me again that she will not leave my sight," Mrs. Clinton admitted with a chuckle. "Go to London and enjoy yourself. We will plan some amusements for the holidays so that you won't be bored then."

"Lord, Mother, I'm not bored," he protested. "I just feel . . . at loose ends right now."

Mrs. Clinton was well aware of his disquiet and probed gently for its source. "No doubt at the court there was always something to do. Did Nigel keep you forever occupied?"

"We saw a great deal of him, of course, and he let me drive his new phaeton several times, but you know what he is. He expected us to provide our own amusement for the most part and is not forever arranging insipid activities for his guests. He lets you know what there is to be done in the neighborhood and then lets you have at it."

"Dorothy spoke of a party he gave your last night there."

"Yes, that was famous," Rowland agreed enthusiastically, the thought of Felicia's lithe figure going through the steps of the dance clear in his mind.

"I understand one of the shops in town was burned that night. Dorothy seemed upset about it." Mrs. Clinton regarded him questioningly.

Rowland could be as bland as his uncle when he did not wish to reveal his emotions on a subject. "She must have told you that we had ridden often with Lady Coombs's daughter. It was distressing to leave them with such a disaster on their hands when we wished to help them." He turned to contemplate his father's portrait over the mantel. "You do not think Father would mind my going to London?"

"No, dear. He has much to catch up, after so many months of sitting in my pocket."

Her son laughed. "I hardly think he would put it that way, Mother."

With this encouragement, Rowland had set off for town the next day. His friend March had lodgings in Chapel Street and was in a position to show Rowland about London, introducing him in the clubs and acquainting him with several gaming houses. Fortunately there was nothing of the gambler in Rowland's make-up, but he enjoyed their outings and the people he met. He had not forgotten the name his uncle had given him, however, and after a few days in town he sent a message to Mrs. Frazier requesting her permission to call on her.

When her affirmative response came, he found that he was strangely loath to present himself. Those few previous adventures he had boasted of were true enough, but he felt inexperienced in the face of a real courtesan. And it did no good to tell himself that he was doing this for Felicia. Though he hoped that it was true, the absurdity of voicing such a thought, even in his own mind, appalled him. He bathed and dressed with infinite care, explaining nonchalantly to March, "I have an engagement tonight, old boy."

"Do you now? With whom?" March asked curiously.

"Friend of my uncle's," Rowland improvised. "No one you would know."

March regarded Rowland's attire sardonically but said only, "I dare say."

Rowland had decided to walk, as Mrs. Frazier's address was not far distant, but he was plagued with doubts on the way. Was it understood in her allowing him to present himself that they would . . . ? How was he to know how much to pay her? He could hardly expect her to post a bill of charges. The thought of asking such a question was daunting indeed. He very nearly turned back several times before reaching her home. Drawing a deep breath, he tapped on the door with his cane.

The servant who answered his knock ushered him into the hall of the small house and accepted his card. Rowland could hear the sound of laughing voices in a room down the hall, and as the servant proceeded in that direction he had a good mind to let himself out and escape from the place. How was he to walk into a room filled with people? Had Mrs. Frazier simply allowed him to attend some sort of soirée? After all, he had only asked if he might call. Well, how was one to ask if one might come and bed a woman? Surely no one was that crass!

A feeling of panic welled up in him as the servant returned. His chance to escape was fast disappearing.

"Mrs. Frazier asked that you await her in the yellow parlor, Mr. Clinton. She will be with you shortly." The man opened a door off the opposite side of the hall from where the gathering appeared to be in progress. With as much savoir-faire as he could manage, Rowland handed over his hat, gloves, and cane and entered the small, sparsely furnishd room. When the door closed behind him, he emitted a sigh and surveyed his surroundings. The draperies were of yellow damask, with the seat covers to match, and the furniture was in excellent taste, though there were not many pieces. There were two paintings on the walls, one of a race horse and one of a woman.

Rowland studied the latter, a woman of perhaps thirty years with raven-black hair and serious blue eyes. The face was heartshaped with a determined chin and a provocative smile. High cheekbones and a straight nose gave the sitter an almost classical look, but the impression was distorted by the sensuous lips.

Unaware that someone had entered the room, Rowland was startled when he heard a voice ask, "Mr. Clinton?"

He swung around to face the original of the portrait, though he judged her to be slightly older than she had been when she sat for the painting. "Ah . . . yes. Mrs. Frazier?"

The woman nodded and indicated that he should take a seat, regarding him gravely all the while. "I understand you are Lord Stronbert's nephew."

"Yes, ma'am. I . . . I did not realize you were entertaining. Perhaps I should not stay."

She smiled encouragingly, but her eyes continued to disconcert him. It was not that they did not share the smile with her lips, but that they managed to remain searching all the while. "I am not myself entertaining, Mr. Clinton. Mrs. Forrest, who shares the house with me, has some guests at present. There is no reason why you should not join the party if you wish."

"No, that is, I had hoped to . . . be alone with you."

"You might enjoy a glass of punch with the others," she suggested gently.

"Yes, but I think I would rather not. I have never been to such a gathering and I would not know how to conduct myself."

Her lips twitched slightly but she said reassuringly, "You would find it little different than any other social function, Mr. Clinton. A bit more relaxed and outspoken, perhaps, but not essentially unlike the evenings to which you are accustomed. I would like you to come as my guest."

"Very well," Rowland murmured.

Mrs. Frazier rose and Rowland leaped to his feet to open the door for her. It was but a step across the hall, and he was surprised to find that rather than the dozen people he had presumed to be there, they numbered only six, five of them men. Mrs. Frazier introduced him to each of them and handed him a glass of punch. He was not sure what he had expected, but certainly not what he found. Both Mrs. Frazier and Mrs. Forrest were dressed alluringly, to be sure, but there was no suggestion of the unseemly. The men were lounging about the room in easy conversation with each other and the two women. Rowland was asked by his nearest neighbor if he was interested in horseracing.

Oblivious to the passing time, he was drawn into various conversations with each person in the room. There was a freeness in the language to which he was not accustomed in the presence of women, but after a few glasses of the potent punch he drifted into a more relaxed frame of mind and speech himself. Mrs. Frazier glanced at him approvingly from time to time and eventually freed herself from the gentleman with whom she was speaking to come over to him.

"May I show you a piece of Sèvres I have just acquired, Mr. Clinton?"

"Why, certainly. I would be honored," Rowland agreed and followed her from the room.

She led him up a short flight of stairs, all the while discussing the merits of the fragile bowl. The door she opened led into a sitting room, with a dressing room and bed chamber beyond, all done in delicate shades of blue. "It is an extravagance of mine, the purchase of a few pieces which I cannot resist." Carefully she lifted the bowl from a rosewood pier table and offered it to him for inspection.

Rowland made the appropriate comments, but wondered whether he would be expected to return to the party below. Surprisingly, he had enjoyed himself enormously in the casual atmosphere, but the loose talk had stimulated him and the drink had freed him from the nervousness he had suffered when he entered the house. As he passed the bowl back to Mrs. Frazier, their eyes held and their hands touched.

"Will you not sit down, Mr. Clinton? We have had no opportunity for private conversation." Turning her back, she gently returned the Sèvres bowl to its place.

There were several chairs and a twin-back settee; Rowland chose the latter. After a tug on the bell cord,

Mrs. Frazier joined him on the seat, commenting, "I have rung for some brandy. Tell me about yourself, Mr. Clinton. Where do you live?"

"Near Bath with my parents and my sister. I haven't spent much time there recently, as I was at Oxford and then at my uncle's recently when my mother was ill. It's a handsome place, hundreds of acres and a stable full of prime blood."

A youthful maid entered and set down a tray with a decanter and two glasses. With a hasty curtsy she vanished again, and Mrs. Frazier leisurely poured out two glasses and handed him one. "Is your mother well now?"

"Yes, I have just come from there and she's blooming again." Rowland sipped at the brandy, unable to decide whether he was expected to make some move. The woman's lips were slightly parted, invitingly, and one hand lay close to his leg. Her eyes were as steady and grave as they were shown in the portrait, but a warm light glowed in them. Rowland picked up her hand and raised it to his lips, first kissing the back and then turning it over to kiss the palm lingeringly.

Mrs. Frazier set down her glass and Rowland did likewise, retaining his grasp on her hand. With his other arm he encircled her shoulders and drew her to him, never taking his eyes from hers. The response from her lips sent fire through his body and he pressed her to him eagerly. "I want you," he murmured.

Her grave eyes regarded him thoughtfully as she withdrew slightly from his embrace. "I choose whom I will have, Mr. Clinton, and I do not like to be handled . . . roughly."

"Good God, of course not!" he exclaimed, a flush rising to his cheeks. "I never meant to . . ."

"No, to be sure." She rose and offered him her hand to lead him into the bed chamber. "Savor your desire, sir; it will be satisfied."

Mutely Rowland watched as she untied his neckcloth and removed it. When he had been relieved of his coat and waistcoat, she began to unbutton his shirt. He leaned down and kissed the top of her head and she lifted her face to smile softly at him. Hesitantly he enclosed her in his arms, turning her face up to kiss her. Again the fire raced through his body but he released her and assisted in removing his shirt, breeches, and drawers before indicating her gown and asking, "May I?"

She had nothing on beneath the gown and he tentatively reached out to touch her, running his hands over the soft curves when she did not stop him. Again he kissed her and pressed her naked body to his, but he carefully controlled the fierce desire that washed over him.

"Come to bed," she whispered.

Rowland smelled the faint scent of lavender as he climbed between the sheets. A shock ran through him when she touched him, stirring him to yet higher desire. "Teach me what to do for *you*," he said gruffly.

The light in her eyes grew and her lips curved into a warm smile. "I thought I was not mistaken in you," she sighed as she took his hands and guided them to her body. "Very gently, here and here. No, not so low. Oh, yes." When he thought he could no longer restrain himself, she nodded and he experienced a release greater than he had ever known, his pleasure heightened further by her own.

Since Rowland had few commitments in town, and the grave-eyed Mrs. Frazier was willing to receive him, he spent more than a little time at her house. She was currently under no one's protection, and did not take offense at his curiosity or lack of knowledge. His fears of not knowing how, what, or when to pay were alleviated by her frankness on the subject and his own growing confidence.

One evening when he was about to leave for her house, Charles March stopped him, a worried frown wrinkling his forehead. "Rowland, m'father showed me a letter today. Well, I brought it with me. Understand, he does not believe a word of it, but I thought you should see it." Anxiously he delivered the paper into Rowland's outstretched hand. While his friend read the letter, March nervously swung his quizzing glass back and forth. "M'father knows your uncle, Rowland, and has the greatest respect for him. Knows Tackar, too, for that matter, and has always thought the fellow a cad. Not a word of truth in it, you see, but still it's a great pity."

Rowland had developed an angry flush as he read, and when he arrived at the insinuations about Felicia he choked. "I will call him out for this!"

"I say, Rowland, can't do that. Let your uncle handle it. He'll know just how to go about it. Sure to."

"There is nothing to know, Charles. Do you figure there are more of these?"

March eyed his friend warily, but confessed, "M'father said he knew of two other people who had received them. Probably more."

After noting the address from which Tackar wrote, Rowland returned the letter to March as though it burned his hands. "It's too late to leave tonight. I'll be off first thing in the morning. Thank you for having me, Charles."

"You can't go alone," Charles protested. "I'll come with you."

"I doubt your father would like that."

"Needn't know, Rowland. Don't see him all that often, you know."

Rowland rubbed a hand thoughtfully over his chin. "I should have someone with me in case. Very well, Charles, if you are sure you wish to come."

March was not at all sure he wished to dart off to France and possibly see his friend killed, but he was loyal and adventurous, so he replied firmly, "I shall be ready in the morning."

"Early," Rowland urged, and left his friend without another word.

As had become her habit, Mrs. Frazier had Rowland shown to her sitting room, where she set down her book on his arrival. One look at his face convinced her that he was under considerable stress. "What is it, Rowland?"

He had not considered what he would tell her, beyond that he could not stay with her that evening. The grave eyes invited his confidence and he soon found himself pouring out the whole story. "So you see, I must leave for France immediately."

"You would do better to let your uncle handle it."

"My uncle has a family, two children, and he has already faced Tackar. I will not let the villain continue to spread his lies, ma'am. To wantonly blacken Felicia's name in this way! As though he had not done enough harm to her already! I am no longer a child. This is my responsibility and I shall see that it is discharged."

Mrs. Frazier watched him jump to his feet and pace about the room. "You have parents and a sister. And what of Felicia herself?"

"What good am I to her unless I act when she is presented with danger? How am I to hold up my head if I do not destroy such a man, who with a careless stroke of his pen could ruin her life?"

"She would not have you put your life in danger, Rowland. You are no good to her dead," she said gently.

"And I am no good to her alive if I do not go," he answered simply. The grave eyes continued to regard him mournfully. "I must do it, ma'am. I have no choice." Rowland raised her hand to his lips and murmured, "Thank you for being so good to me."

"Godspeed, Rowland."

The journey, endured impatiently by Rowland, had been more successful than his confrontation with Francis Tackar. Tackar had refused to meet him.

Astonished, Rowland had stared at him for some

time. "What the devil do you mean, you won't meet me?"

"I cannot face every hotheaded young cub who takes offense at something I say," Tackar retorted.

"You have insulted my friends Lady Coombs and her daughter, as well as vilifying my uncle's character. Your malicious lies are spewed forth in an attempt to ruin them all and I will not allow it to continue." Rowland coldly surveyed his opponent and drew his gloves restlessly through his hands.

"You had best go home to your mother," Tackar laughed. "She will be worried about you."

Rowland struck him across the face with his glove. "You will meet me tomorrow morning or I will horsewhip you, Tackar."

His eyes narrowed to glinting pinpoints, Tackar rasped, "Very well, Clinton. Have your second wait on mine this evening to arrange the details."

Charles March had accomplished this mission and now he stood, heavyhearted, awaiting the signal. He had noticed the arrival of a lone rider, and for a moment had feared, and hoped, that it was the authorities come to put a stop to the duel. After dismounting, Stronbert stood perfectly still, not daring to utter a word that might distract his nephew's attention.

CHAPTER TWENTY

Rowland stood pale and still. The white signal fluttered as it was dropped and in the soft quiet of the falling snow, two pistols roared simultaneously. Stronbert watched helplessly as his nephew fell and started running to him. He saw immediately that the ball which had struck him was embedded in the thigh, and breathed a sigh of relief. There should be a doctor, he thought, and looked around to see a man bent over Tackar, who was sprawled on the ground. The black-coated figure, who carried the bag of his trade, shook his head briefly and turned toward Stronbert.

Rowland, who had lain unconscious until now, opened his eyes and asked of no one in particular, "Did I kill him?"

"Yes, Rowland," Stronbert replied, "but I had rather you allowed me to do it."

Rowland's pain-filled eyes focused on his uncle and a slight grin twisted his mouth. "You had your chance, Uncle Nigel. It was my turn."

When the ball had been removed from his thigh, Rowland and his second were taken to Stronbert's lodgings. George Bryant spoke to Stronbert exasperatedly, "Lord, Nigel, I have not eaten yet and you're bringing wounded bodies to me."

"I would like to introduce you to my nephew, Rowland Clinton, and his friend, Charles March. Rowland has just dueled Tackar."

"And?"

"Tackar is dead."

"Excellent. Now I hope I may enjoy my breakfast in peace," George grumbled. "When do we return?"

"When Rowland can travel comfortably."

"I should rather leave immediately, Uncle Nigel. My parents are expecting me for Christmas." Rowland spoke from the depths of the sofa where his uncle had placed him, his voice calm but his eyes tortured with pain and wretchedness.

Stronbert rested a hand on Rowland's shoulder understandingly. "Then we will arrange to leave as soon as George has had his lengthy breakfast. If you are comfortable, Rowland, I have an errand I should like to accomplish."

The return journey was of necessity slow. Rowland had a fever the first night and his uncle sat with him listening to the disjointed phrases which tumbled from the young man's lips. Toward morning he was calmer and opened his eyes to find Stronbert pouring out a cup of coffee. "Have you been here all night?"

"Yes. Are you feeling better?"

"There is less pain," Rowland said carefully.

"From the wound." Stronbert poured a second cup of coffee and handed it to his nephew. "You did what you had to, Rowland. Do not torture yourself. I would have done the same."

"But I didn't know how I would feel! A man is dead by my hand, Uncle Nigel—a rogue, a scoundrel, but still a man. How am I to live with that?" He drew a shaking hand over his eyes.

Stronbert sighed. "It will be difficult. I thought about it when I took Tackar to Dr. Carmichael. Had he died, for all that he deserved it, I knew it would be a burden to carry with me. Remember that I would have done it if you had not, Rowland. And he aimed to kill you, I could see it in his face. I am grateful for snow," he said simply, "for I believe only that distorted his vision enough to spare you."

Sipping thoughtfully at his coffee Rowland made no reply, but he determined to speak no more of the matter. No useful purpose would be served by lamenting his actions, and in many ways he did not regret them. If it took more courage to live with the outcome than it had to face Tackar, he would have to find that strength. "Do you suppose they have those exquisite rolls here?"

Stronbert had watched the struggle in his nephew's face, and now he smiled. "I would not be at all surprised."

Although there were frequent stops on the journey to relieve the agony of the jolting carriage, it was just over a week before Stronbert restored Rowland to his family. No mention was made of the duel; Rowland had sustained his injury in a driving accident.

"Really, Nigel," Stronbert's sister protested, when she had him alone, "I had thought I could trust you to take care of Rowland when he was with you."

"He is quite old enough to take care of himself, Mary."

"Well, he does not seem to have been doing so," she muttered.

"With the care you will lavish on him he will be set right within the week."

His sister smiled reluctantly. "Will you stay for Christmas, Nigel? There is hardly time for you to get home."

"Thank you, my dear, but I must go. I shall look forward to seeing Rowland early in the new year. If you are up to the journey then, perhaps you will come, too, Mary."

"I shall think on it. I have not seen Mother for some time."

"Good. Now I must leave."

"But you just arrived," she said helplessly.

"I know. But I have important business at the court. Try to come, Mary." His eyes were gravely intent.

"I will," she said, accepting that it was important to him.

"Thank you. Happy Christmas."

Stronbert did not arrive at Tetterton until late on the afternoon of Christmas Eve. He came first to Lady Coombs's shop, noting that the sign he had caused to be erected was in place. Mr. Allerton was leaving the shop at the time, and his employer was alone and ready to lock up as she left.

He stepped into the shop quietly and watched her reaction as she looked up at the ringing of the bell. She did not attempt to hide the pleasure it gave her to see him but approached with outstretched hand. He took it firmly in his and held it a moment before saying ruefully, "I have been so wrapped up in my concerns, Lady Coombs, that I have not had a moment to think of gifts for my household. I pray you will indulge me by keeping the shop open a while longer."

"It is the least I can do for you, sir. Did you see the sign? I am so pleased with it, and I thank you for your thoughtfulness. Come, shall we start with Miss Helen?" Alicia led him about the shop, with occasional suggestions for the dowager and his son, for Miss Carnworth, and the general. It took the better part of an hour to conclude the transactions, but Stronbert was well pleased with the results.

"My mother has invited you to the court, has she not?" he asked as he prepared to depart.

"Yes, she is sending the carriage for us."

"Good. I will walk you to the cottage."

Alicia pulled her green pelisse over her dress against the bitter cold of the December evening. "Felicia is doing some last-minute sewing, I think, in preparation for tomorrow. She keeps hiding what she is working on, so it must be a surprise."

"How is she getting on? Does she see much of the Maple girls?"

"Yes, almost daily, and there are others in the neighborhood who have come to accept her and invite her to their homes. I am well pleased for her."

Stronbert paused at the threshold of the cottage and Alicia invited him to step in for a moment, but he replied, "I have not been to the court yet, and I can only imagine that my absence is bitterly lamented. I shall see you tomorrow."

When the carriage came for the two women the following day, the world was an icy wonder. Icicles hung from the gables and coated the trees down to the smallest sparkling twig. The carriage horses were hung with bells in the spirit of the day and the sweet music rang along the lane, causing Felicia to run to the window. The stomping horses with their breath visible as white puffs about them came to a halt before the cottage, and the footman jumped down to escort the ladies cautiously over the frozen, slippery ground. The ride to the court was beautiful, provided with its own music, and the women arrived pink-cheeked and cheerful. Helen rushed into the hall to greet them, and Matthew followed more sedately.

"I have something for you," Helen whispered to Felicia, as she put her arm through the older girl's.

"Do you? Then it is fortunate that I remembered your package," Felicia murmured. "Shall you have it now?"

"No, for Papa expects us to bring you to the gold parlor now. What is it?"

"You must wait to see."

Stronbert stood at the door of the room and wished them a happy Christmas before taking them to his mother. The dowager remarked that Lady Coombs's gown was surely the most beautiful she had seen in some time and Alicia smiled and answered, "Felicia made it as a present for me." The dowager nodded and allowed them to pass on to greet the other members of the party. When Felicia and the children had finished their tea, they were allowed to leave the adults and follow their own pursuits. This led them to the schoolroom where Helen had carefully deposited Felicia's present.

It was a lovely white fur muff on which Helen had spent hours of careful work embroidering Felicia's initials. The older girl's delight was everything Helen could have asked for. She had in turn received a very grown-up shawl that Felicia had made for her, and Matthew was delighted with his traveling chess set. "I have something for your papa, too," Felicia said shyly, "and for Miss Carnworth, as they have been so good to me."

"Wait here and I shall bring them to you," Helen urged. "They must be finished with tea by now. And if they are not, they will surely tell me." She returned a while later with Stronbert, Miss Carnworth, and Alicia, who had been pressed to join the festivities. Matthew had been showing Felicia about the schoolroom, explaining what he was studying and that he was to go to Eton the next fall. "But Papa says I need not stay if I do not like it," he admitted.

His father, coming in to hear the end of this, regarded him fondly and agreed gravely, "Yes, that is the bargain we have made."

Felicia hesitantly joined the adults and offered Miss Carnworth a package containing a lacy white mob cap, and Stronbert one containing a stick pin. "You have both been so very kind to me," she murmured.

Miss Carnworth, for all her gruff ways, was moved by the girl's gift and impulsively hugged her to her sparse bosom. "What a dear child you are!"

When he had thanked her, Stronbert's eyes twinkled as he said, "Your present is marked with your name, Felicia, but you shall have to find it."

"A treasure hunt!" Helen squealed enthusiastically. "May I take you around to look?"

"I shall certainly need help," Felicia confessed. "Will you not give us a hint?"

"No, not yet. If you cannot find it after a bit, I will perhaps take you to it." Stronbert turned to Alicia with a smile. "I should like to show you about the house; you have seen very little of it. Shall we follow the youngsters?"

They trailed along behind the children at a more moderate pace while Stronbert indicated the various rooms and the history of the building. When the second floor had been covered, and the first, and finally the ground floor without Felicia's gift having been discovered, the children waited for their father to catch up with them. "Have we missed it, Papa?" Matthew asked curiously.

"No."

"But we have been all over the house."

"True."

"Then it is not in the house?"

"No."

"Oh, Papa, that is too bad of you," Helen pouted. "We shall never find it outside."

"Yes, you shall, for I shall take you there now. Put on warm wraps."

Alicia looked inquiringly at Stronbert and he nodded. "Yes, you shall come, too, if you will."

It was to the stables that he led them, and Felicia's countenance grew excited and anxious at once. She was almost afraid to enter, and Stronbert took her hand and led her to Dancer's box, where the little mare had a red bow in her mane and a sign on the door read "For Felicia." Tears streamed down her cheeks and she impulsively hugged Stronbert and placed a timid kiss on his cheek, before opening the door of the box and repeating the procedure.

"It is too much," Alicia whispered, stricken.

Stronbert held her eyes with his and replied, "No, it is not enough after what she has been through. Please do not deny me the pleasure of giving her the mare."

"I know you mean well, Lord Stronbert, but what would people think?"

"Do you really care?"

"No, but for Felicia's sake . . ."

"Then have her keep it here for the time being, or better yet simply say nothing and people will assume that she borrows it as she did when Rowland and Dorothy were here."

Felicia had become aware of the low-voiced discussion outside the box. She had not heard the matter under consideration, but her questioning glance at her mother informed her that there was a problem. "What is it, Mama?" When Alicia did not reply, her daughter transferred her gaze to Stronbert, whose countenance she could not read. Her hand had remained on the mare, which nuzzled her then, and she gasped in disappointment as she understood. "I am not to be allowed to keep the mare."

There was a silence and Helen and Matthew stood uncomfortably watching the other three. Alicia wanted to explain to her daughter, but she could not seem to find the right words. Stronbert finally spoke. "Your mother and I need to discuss the matter further, Felicia. Perhaps we can find a solution."

Felicia's lips trembled but she nodded and, with a final pat to the mare, determinedly walked out of the loose box and closed the door. The group returned to the house in considerably worse spirits than they had departed, but there were only a few minutes before dinner and the matter of Dancer was not raised.

Alicia was seated to Stronbert's right at the meal and she felt very hard-pressed to keep up her share of the conversation. The general, on her right, did not seem to notice her silence, for he was never at a loss for words himself. Alicia found it difficult to swallow the magnificent procession of dishes which arrived at the table and felt a real gratitude to the dowager when she rose to lead the ladies to the drawing room. The young people, who had been permitted to dine with their elders for this special occasion, immediately sought out several games for their own amusement, since Helen and Matthew were determined to see Felicia smile again.

Alicia had seldom felt less like singing and playing the harpsichord, but she obligingly performed her share of the entertainment. The Christmas songs soothed her for a while, but she found her concentration wandering when she was offered a hand at whist. After a while she found Stronbert at her shoulder and heard him suggest that Miss Carnworth take her place for a while. She rose obediently and followed him across the room away from the others.

"No one will rest easy until this problem is settled," he commented calmly. "I wish you will allow me to drive home with you so that we may discuss it at leisure."

Alicia bit her lip unhappily. "Perhaps that would be wise."

"Shall I call for the carriage now?"

"Yes, if you will. Felicia and I will make our farewells."

CHAPTER TWENTY-ONE

There was no discussion in the carriage of the mare. Stronbert instructed the coachman to await him at the Feather and Flask and followed the women into the cottage. In the hall Alicia hugged her daughter and said she would try to do what was best. Felicia nodded sadly and shook hands with Stronbert before unhappily climbing the stair. There was no fire in the drawing room, as Mavis had gone home to spend the day with her family. Stronbert lit the candles and got a blaze established on the hearth. Alicia watched him silently.

When he had completed his tasks he turned to find her still standing in the doorway. "Come and sit down, Lady Coombs. I have a great deal to talk about with you."

"We must decide the question of the mare," Alicia said woodenly as she seated herself.

"We will arrive at Dancer eventually," he conceded. "There are several more pressing matters to discuss."

Astonished, Alicia said stubbornly, "I cannot imagine what. It would have been wisest if you had consulted me first about the horse."

"I can see that now. I did not mean to cause you distress, my . . . ma'am." He rubbed a hand across his forehead and said gently, "I do not know if I should burden you with what I am about to tell you, but I feel you would resent it if I did not. And you might come by the information some other way," he said ruefully.

"Then you must tell me."

"I went to London because I had a letter from a friend informing me that Tackar was in France spewing forth epistles which defamed your character . . . and your daughter's . . . and mine."

Alicia felt suddenly sick at heart. "Tell me exactly what he said."

Instead Stronbert drew a letter from his pocket and placed it carefully in her lap. Alicia numbly read the sheet full of innuendoes and lies. In disgust she rose to throw it on the fire. "No," Stronbert cautioned her, "I have need of it."

"What for?"

"We shall discuss that another time. Right now I want to explain to you what happened when I went to London and then to Paris." He proceeded to do so in a level, diffident voice that hypnotized her.

"Rowland killed him?" she finally asked, aghast.

"I had no way of knowing that Tackar's rumors had reached him. In fact, I did not really think of him at all in connection with the affair. But he is devoted to Felicia and took matters in his own hands."

"But he might have been killed!"

"You must not think of that now. He was not. You shall have to decide whether you wish to tell Felicia about this or not."

"Dear God, all you do is force me to make decisions all day," she wailed.

"That is not the last of them," he drawled, a grin lightly touching the corners of his lips. "I have a present for you and you shall have to decide whether to accept it or not."

"Well, if it is a horse or if it is valuable, I shall not," she retorted emphatically.

Stronbert drew a small jeweler's box from his pocket and set it on the table between them. Alicia stared at it, horrified.

"I thought you said you had no time to do any shopping," she accused him.

"I did not feel it necessary to mention that while my friend George ate his breakfast and Rowland rested, I made use of the free hour to visit a jeweler in Paris. I had promised myself that I would not do so until Tackar could no longer bother you, and that was the first opportunity I had." He indicated that she should open the box.

"I cannot."

Stronbert reached down and opened the box to exhibit a sparkling emerald surrounded by diamonds. He did not attempt to remove it from the box or to hand it to her. "It is a betrothal ring," he explained unnecessarily. "I wish to marry you."

"But why?" There was a quiver in Alicia's voice and she could not meet his eyes.

Stronbert did not speak until she finally, hesitantly, lifted her eyes. "Because I want to take care of you and Felicia. I can offer you the security and position you deserve. I feel sure the children would be pleased if I married you; they are genuinely fond of you and your daughter. But mostly, my dear, because I love you."

Alicia regarded him with fascination—the handsome, dependable man she loved and needed to make her life complete. She made a half-gesture of extending her hand to him, but let it drop back into her lap. Marriage demanded more than she could give. She would be expected to be more than a companion and substitute mother to his children; she would be expected to be a dutiful wife in bed. An uncontrollable shudder ran through her, and she bowed her head. "I cannot be a wife again," she said miserably.

Since this was no more than Stronbert had expected, he asked gently, "You cannot return my regard?"

"It is not that!" she declared fiercely. "I am very fond of you. I can see that you would give me and Felicia all we could ever hope for out of life. And I can see that I should marry you if only for Felicia's sake. But it would not be fair to you, my lord, because I could not fulfill my . . . share of the bargain."

Stronbert watched Alicia bend her head, her face flushed and sad. "I had thought of that. Let me suggest something to you. I have already a son and daughter and need not produce any further children for the sake of the succession or for my own personal satisfaction. In fact, in marrying you I would gain another child I am fond of already. I am willing, although not eager, to make a compromise. If you do not feel you could accept the consummation of our marriage and the subsequent physical responsibilities, I will undertake to make no such demands on you."

Alicia could not believe she was hearing him correctly. But then his voice continued in the even lazy tone, "However, in exchange for this concession, I would expect your full acceptance of my . . . activities elsewhere. I would be discreet, of course, and no embarrassment would attach to you from them. I had rather not live a celibate life, you understand."

"You cannot be serious," she blurted, shocked.

"Well, but I am. Ordinarily I would consider marriage bound me to faithfulness, but under such circumstances . . ."

Inexcusably Alicia felt very angry. He was telling her that every time he left for York, or London, or anywhere, she might expect that he would be with another woman. Sir Frederick had spent all his time with another woman, and she had, except for the shame of it, been relieved that he had. Why then should she balk at such an offer? Surely she could not ask for more—a home, a man she loved, security for her daughter, and an undisputed social position. She wanted to slap him.

Stronbert witnessed the flash in her eyes and concealed his satisfaction. He rose, leaving the jeweler's box on the table, and suggested mildly, "Perhaps I should give you time to think on the matter. I realize marriage is an important step and you will want to consider the various aspects of it. May I call tomorrow evening to discuss it further?"

Alicia valiantly swallowed the anger, that mysterious, unjustified emotion she should not be experiencing at this time, and said through taut lips, "Yes, please, I should like some time to decide." She had risen with him and now tentatively touched the box on the table. "You must keep the ring for now."

"As you wish," he agreed and snapped it shut before replacing it in his pocket. Alicia's eyes remained for a moment on the spot where it had disappeared. "I think we should let the matter of the mare alone until we have spoken again," he continued, as he stepped into the hall.

"Yes, of course," she replied numbly. Then she remembered the little enameled snuff box in her reticule and, without a word, disappeared back into the drawing room to retrieve it. She presented it to him shyly in the palm of her hand. "Happy Christmas."

She was flooded by the warmth of the very special smile he bestowed on her occasionally when he was particularly pleased with her. Would she ever receive it again if she refused him? Mechanically she bid him good evening and watched him walk down the steps to stroll around to the Feather and Flask. Wearily she attended to the fire, put out the candles, and climbed the stair to her room. Felicia was waiting there, nervously attempting to school her countenance to acceptance of her mother's decision on the mare.

Alicia found it difficult to return her mind to what had begun to seem to her a very small problem in light of the other. She could not ignore the expectant face, however, and said, "Felicia love, we did not come to a decision on Dancer, but agreed to settle it tomorrow night. I am sure something can be worked out, so do not despair."

Felicia did not consider this an altogether satisfactory conclusion to her long wait, but she could see that her mother was tired and did not wish to discuss the matter further. So she hugged her and whispered, "Happy Christmas, Mama," and left her mother to her thoughts. Alicia lay awake for some time trying to analyze the turbulence of her emotions and finally fell asleep exhausted.

Stronbert left the court at mid-morning the next day to ride alone to Tosley Hall. Sir John was reluctant to have him admitted, but thought it prudent to do so. His eye began to twitch again, and he was coldly formal when Stronbert entered. "May I be of service to you, Lord Stronbert?"

"Yes, I think you can," Stronbert replied easily. "I believe I told you when last we met that I would expect you to answer to me for any further harm Tackar caused Lady Coombs."

Sir John's ruddy countenance paled. "Surely he has not caused her any more problems! I had heard the man was in France." He dropped into a chair.

Stronbert, assuming that since Sir John had seated himself he should do the same, carelessly draped himself in the chair opposite. He reached into his pocket and withdrew a letter which he handed to the squire, saying, "This and similar letters were received by several people in London before Tackar's death."

"His death! Surely you did not kill him!"

"No, I did not kill him, but he is dead all the same. Read the letter."

As Sir John perused the letter the twitching of his eye and face intensified. "Disgusting," he said faintly, thrusting it from him.

Stronbert replaced the letter into his pocket and said slowly, "There is not a word of truth in it, and yet the man has managed to damage several reputations. Those who knew Tackar for what he was will ignore the libelous accusations, but there are others who will spread them. I do not wish to see Lady Coombs's and her daughter's reputations so scandalously abused. And I think perhaps you should do your utmost to see that they are not."

"I? What can I do to allay such gossip?"

"Well, you know, I think a few well-placed letters from your wife of indignant denial might not come amiss. Few would disbelieve her considering her lack of fondness, shall we say, for the ladies."

"She would never write such letters."

"I dare say she would not, on her own. I expect you to see that she does."

"And why should I do such a thing?" Sir John blustered.

"As I said before," Stronbert explained patiently, "I hold you to account for the damage Tackar has done since you carelessly released him."

"He could have written the same from a jail," Sir John protested.

"Do you really have a desire to nitpick with me, Sir John? Do you feel no sense of responsibility for this latest outrage? If so, I will trouble you no further." Stronbert rose.

"No, stay," the older man said faintly, his hands twisting before him on the desk. His voice came low and agonized. "I do hold myself responsible. I have met Lady Coombs and her daughter and admire their perseverance in face of the disasters that have befallen them. I cringe when I hear my wife speak of them with contempt. But I long ago abdicated my duty to hold sway in my household. My wife and son rule me instead of the reverse, and I have allowed it so that I might have some peace."

Stronbert felt a reluctant pity for the ineffectual man, married to a shrewish woman and sire to a pompous but negligible son. "Then leave it, Sir John. Lady Coombs is not likely to let it overset her, and those who matter will not be swayed by the malicious words of a dishonorable man." He turned to leave.

"I will not leave it!" the voice behind him declared,

stronger in its determination. "The letters will be written as you suggested. I will see to it."

Stronbert studied the careworn face carefully. The eye was no longer twitching and an air of resolution permeated the man's bearing. He offered his hand to Sir John. "Thank you. I would appreciate it, Sir John."

"It will be done," the reply came flatly, as the two men shook hands, "today."

CHAPTER TWENTY-TWO

Alicia spent the day in indecision. There could surely be no reason to refuse Stronbert when he offered her everything she could ask for. Certainly she owed it to her daughter to accept him. Felicia should have the kind of life she would enjoy at the court. And Alicia had only vowed not to marry again because of her fear of intimacy with a man. Stronbert was offering her release from that fear. Could she trust him to honor his promise? Yes, of course she could. That was not the problem. If he said he would not touch her, he would not. She was well aware that many husbands had outside affairs, mistresses. The thought of someone using her body as Sir Frederick had made her shudder and recoil. She did not wish to be put in such a situation again, where she was powerless to refuse. Not for any amount of money, not even for her daughter's sake. She would have submitted to Tackar when he held Felicia, but she would have suffered a personal degradation that she did not think she could have overcome.

And Stronbert was offering her freedom from all that. She had only to share him with whomever he chose to bed, whenever he chose to do so. There would not be the shame Sir Frederick had cast upon her by deserting her. Then why did she feel this anger every time she considered the proposal? Stronbert had indicated that it was not his choice of arrangements, merely one he would be willing to offer. It was really extraordinarily accommodating of him, and she still wished to smack him for suggesting it.

Alicia sat through her evening meal vaguely aware of Felicia's chatter but unable to respond with any real attention. She was unable to eat much, nervous at the prospect of facing Stronbert very soon. What was she to tell him?

The women sat in the drawing room doing needlepoint and occasionally exchanging a remark, when there was a tap at the door. Alicia started with dismay. She had still not decided how to answer him.

Stronbert stood in the drawing room, speaking with Felicia. After a while Alicia heard him say, "If you should not mind, Felicia, I would like to speak with your mother privately for a while," and the girl nodded and left the room, quietly closing the door after her. Alicia heard her ascend the stairs and shut herself in her room. Stronbert went to lean against the mantelpiece, his eyes on Alicia, who stood frozen where she had risen.

"You have not reached a decision?"

"No. No. I have thought of little else."

"Tell me where the problem lies, and perhaps we can settle the matter."

"I do not know," she said helplessly. "You are being so . . . reasonable."

"Would you rather that I were not?" he asked, a trace of amusement in his voice.

Alicia could not answer him. She did not know what she wanted any longer. Stronbert held out his hand to her and said firmly, "Come here, Alicia." It was a voice that admitted no disobedience, gentle yet commanding. She walked over to him and hesitantly extended her hand to his waiting one.

"Shall I tell you why you cannot decide?" he asked softly.

"Yes, please," she murmured.

"Because you are a woman and for all you have been abused and mistreated by men, you respond to me as a man. You are afraid of me, of what I could do to you, that I might hurt you. But you are not afraid enough to agree to allow me to go my own way. Something tells you that you may change your mind and that perhaps you would suffer worse knowing that I am with someone else, and you would not be able to bring yourself to tell me so. To tell me that you are willing to be my wife, truly, with all it entails."

Alicia blushed painfully. "That cannot be so. I vowed after that night, the night Tackar was here, that I would kill a man before I would let him touch me."

"Did you? How bloodthirsty of you." His tone was light, but he put a hand on her head and pressed it against his shoulder comfortingly. "I have talked with your brother."

"Stephen? When did you see Stephen?"

"I went to him after that night. I knew I would not get your permission to protect you then, and so I sought his. I could not bear to think of your coming to any further harm. I hope you can forgive me for speaking with Stephen without your permission."

Alicia's eyes were wide with astonishment. "Then that man, Jeff, really was there to protect me? I thought I must be overwrought even to imagine such a thing. What else did you discuss with Stephen?" she asked suspiciously.

"I shall tell you," Stronbert replied, picking her up in his arms, "when we are seated comfortably." She made a little squeal of protest, but subsided stiffly in his arms as he sat down with her in his lap on the sofa. "Be still, Alicia. I told Stephen that I intended to marry you if you would have me, and that I wanted to see you were protected since he was so far away. He granted my request." Stronbert paused for a moment unsure how to approach the rest of what he had to tell her. He unconsciously stroked her hair. "I also pressed him for information on your fear of men. He told me what he could." He felt Alicia's body stiffen against him, but he continued to stroke her hair. "He told me that you threatened to kill Sir Frederick if he touched you again, after Felicia was born."

"That is true," she whispered.

"And did he?" There was no answer and he asked again, "Please tell me, Alicia, did he?"

"No."

"I am glad. Now I want to explain something to you, my love. Not all men, in fact very few, are like your husband and Tackar. Most men learn to control their desire for a woman, be she his wife or not. You have had some very damaging experiences, and you were very young at the time you wed. Oh, Lord, I sound so patronizing. Would you look at me, love?"

Alicia raised her head from where it was pressed defensively against his shoulder. When he spoke again, her eyes were on him. "All I really want to say, Alicia, is that I would never hurt you. Do you know that you can receive pleasure from your body?" She nodded mutely. "But you have never done so with a man?" Again a silent answer, the shake of her head.

His lips brushed her forehead, touched her eyes. He felt her stiffen automatically in his arms. "Do not be afraid, my love. I will not hurt you." Lightly he kissed her unresponsive lips. When nothing further happened, after a while she opened the eyes she had closed and regarded him gravely. "I can tell that you want me," she said accusingly.

He laughed and shifted her slightly from his lap to his leg. "Of course I want you, goose. You are a very desirable woman. But I am not going to take you." He felt her body relax slightly at the words. "I want you to kiss me, Alicia."

She gazed at him incredulously. "I cannot."

"Yes, you can. Give me your hand." She produced it from where it was tucked against his shoulder. He gently kissed the fingertips and then, holding it lightly, drew it over his forehead, brows, and along his chin before laying the fingers against his lips. "You see, they are not the least bit dangerous. Kiss me, Alicia."

She swallowed nervously and bracing herself against his chest, pecked softly and quickly at his lips. He made no move, his expression blank. Alicia leaned back and said defiantly, "There, I did it."

"I thought we were agreed you were a woman," he commented dryly. "Just so might you kiss your brother."

Stung, she leaned forward and kissed him again. "Better," he commented, "we have now risen to the level of your daughter."

Alicia let out a little gurgle of laughter. With her fingers she traced the lines of his face, exploring the curves and depressions. And then she put her arms about his neck and kissed him. Eventually she drew back, embarrassed, and found he was smiling the special smile that made her insides flutter. "I love you," she whispered. "I have never loved a man before." He pulled her to him, the feel of her firm breasts against his chest, and kissed her until she was breathless. He released her then, curious to see how she would respond. Her eyes and face were softened with desire and he sighed contentedly. "I think, my love, that you should marry me, and be my wife."

"Yes," she agreed. "I think that would be wise. But, Nigel, I cannot be sure that when the time comes I can . . ."

"I understand. I promise you I will be patient. You will need time to learn to trust me."

"What am I to do about the shop?" she asked anxiously.

"I intend to keep you far too busy to involve yourself with the shop. Perhaps Mr. Allerton would agree to managing it for you. Shall you mind?"

"Not so very much. I enjoy some of the work, but there have been so many problems, and I shall not miss them. I . . . I would not embarrass you by continuing to involve myself there, of course. Have you thought what people will say to your marrying a shopkeeper, Nigel?"

"I could not care less, Alicia. You know that it has never bothered me."

"Yes, and it is very strange of you," she retorted.

"There is one thing more I must tell you, Alicia." He held her in his arms lightly now and said somewhat awkwardly, "You and I are partners in the shop."

Alicia regarded him with astonishment. "What do you mean?"

"When the fire made it necessary for you to take Lady Gorham as a partner, I had written her offering to provide the financial support if she would lend her name to the project. I feared she would not have the necessary funds to help you just then." He eyed her dubiously. "I did not do it to deceive you, but because I wanted to help and felt responsible since I had undertaken your protection."

"Indeed!" Alicia replied indignantly. "You knew I would not accept your help and you tricked me." She rose from his lap to stand above him, her eyes glaring. "I am surprised that Lady Gorham consented to such a suggestion."

Stronbert smiled reluctantly and drawled, "She was aware of my intentions toward you."

"You seem to have made no secret of them with anyone but me!" she retorted.

"Not so. I told only your brother and Lady Gorham because it was necessary."

"And what if I had not agreed to marry you?"

Stronbert had allowed her to glare down at him all this while, but he rose now and stood facing her. "It would not have affected my actions in any way, Alicia. I could not leave unprotected the woman I love, whether she would have me or not. And if you had not agreed to marry me, then I would not have told you of my arrangement with Lady Gorham. I consider my money well invested. I will not hold you to marry me if you do not wish it."

Alicia's defiance evaporated as quickly as it had risen. "I thought I could manage by myself," she said sadly. "You have shown me that I did not."

"Had it not been for Tackar you would have achieved all you set out to do," he responded calmly as he lifted her chin with a gentle finger. "Will you marry me, Alicia?"

"Yes," she replied simply and responded warmly to his kiss.

"In that case I see no reason why Felicia should not have the mare," he suggested quizzingly.

"Felicia! How could I have forgotten that she was waiting for an answer," she gasped guiltily. "I must tell her right away." She turned toward the door but stopped when Stronbert spoke.

"I wish you will let me give you your ring first," he said ruefully.

Alicia grinned as she shyly held out her hand to him. He took it firmly and placed the ring on it. She was moved by his tender expression and stood on tiptoe to kiss him.

"You are making good progress, my dear," he laughed.

Alicia flushed and said, "Shall I bring Felicia down?"

"Yes, I should like to talk to her."

Alicia nodded and disappeared from the room. She knocked softly on her daughter's door and was bid to enter. Felicia turned an anxious face to her as she had the night before. "Have you decided, Mama?"

"Yes, dear, you are to keep Dancer."

The girl flung her arms about her mother. "Thank you, oh, thank you."

"I have something else to tell you, love, which is very important."

Felicia drew her mother over to sit beside her on the bed. "Not more trouble?"

"No, dear, quite the reverse. Lord Stronbert has asked me to marry him and I have agreed."

Felicia smiled mischievously. "I was sure he would. Are you happy, Mama?"

"Very. I am excessively fond of his lordship. He would like you to come down."

Felicia agreed with alacrity and descended the stairs far more quickly than her mother. Stronbert held out his hands to her and she took them readily. "I am so glad," she said.

"Thank you, Felicia. It is important that we have your blessing. I look forward to welcoming you to the court as my newest daughter. Do you think you will like living there?"

Alicia smiled as she heard her daughter answer fervently, "With all my heart. Do Helen and Matthew know?"

"Not yet, but I am sure they will have no objections."

"Your mother might," Alicia suggested softly.

"No," he said thoughtfully, "I think she will be pleased, my dear. But you will both learn, if you have not already, that she can be . . . difficult at times. I find her eccentricities amusing for the most part, but others find them embarrassing," he said gravely, a twinkle lighting his eyes.

"She has been very accepting of us," Alicia replied, "but it has occurred to me that you had something to do with that."

"My mother likes both of you, but she was on her high ropes at first. I did no more than urge reasonable behavior."

Felicia laughed. "I think she's a dear."

Stronbert released her hands and asked the women to sit with him a moment. "I am hopeful that my sister Mary will come in January, and I should like to be married while she is here."

"It will not be a year since Sir Frederick's death," Alicia commented diffidently.

"Would you mind?"

"No," the two women answered together.

"Shall we say in a month's time then?" he asked, observing Alicia closely.

She swallowed nervously but agreed. "I shall have

to write to Stephen and Jane. I would like them to be here."

"Of course. And Lady Gorham." Stronbert proceeded to enumerate the guests it would be necessary for him to invite. Alicia and her daughter had no one to add, and the matter was arranged quickly. "I would like to send you both to York with Miss Carnworth so that you may choose any items which are not available to you here." At Alicia's sign of protest he continued calmly, "You are to be a marchioness, Alicia, and it will require a suitable wardrobe. The same applies to Felicia. I hope you will both feel comfortable to come completely out of mourning now. I have the most active desire to see you both in some bright, cheerful colors."

Felicia sighed gustily. "I can scarcely wait. I have had my eye on that jonquil muslin ever since it arrived and I have been in a fret that someone else would buy it."

"As you wish, L . . Nigel. But I do not like to impose on Miss Carnworth. Felicia and I can manage in York," Alicia suggested.

"I would not dare deny her the treat," he laughed. He felt confident that Miss Carnworth would not only enjoy it, but would insist that an adequate shopping was done on his behalf. "Felicia, I will bring Dancer to you tomorrow and arrange to have her stabled at the Feather and Flask, if that is agreeable."

"Perfectly, sir."

"And you shall have to decide what you are to call me when I marry your mother. I am agreeable to almost anything but my title. Now, if I might just have another word with your mother alone . . ." Felicia leaped to her feet and bid them good night. Stronbert turned then to Alicia and said, "If you feel I am rushing you . . ."

"N-no. I am sure a month will be sufficient time to prepare my wardrobe." Alicia stared at her hands uncertainly.

Stronbert took her hands and said gently, "It is not your wardrobe which concerns me, my love. Rest assured you shall have all the time you need, married or not."

"Thank you, Nigel. I feel very stupid."

"Please do not. I want your companionship, Alicia, more than anything else. We will work things out together. There will be plenty of time." He kissed her brow and left her.

Alicia gazed down at the new ring on her finger and hoped she could indeed be a wife again. He had aroused a desire in her which her body wanted satisfied. But she was not so sure that her mind would cooperate. Perhaps she should have insisted that the wedding not take place until her mourning period was over. That would have given her an additional two months. No, she thought exasperatedly, two months would not help her. Better to wed him and face the situation straight on. Other than that she was very happy.

CHAPTER TWENTY-THREE

The month hardly seemed long enough for the preparations after all. There were two trips to York and several to the dressmaker. The arrangements for the shop had to be made; Mr. Allerton agreed to manage the shop and find an assistant who would work with him. Alicia and her daughter went many times to the court, but the first time after the betrothal was the most difficult for them. They feared that some of the residents might be resentful or scornful, but they were welcomed warmly by the dowager, excitedly by the children, and kindly by the others in the household. Felicia was taken off to see the apartment which would be hers, with its separate dressing room and enormous bedroom. Helen returned shyly then to lead Alicia to the room which had been Helen's mother's.

"I am pleased that you are to marry Papa," she said softly. She gazed about the room sadly for a moment and admitted, "I have not been here since my mama died."

"I can understand that," Alicia replied. "I am sorry that I did not know your mother. You must miss her dreadfully."

The little girl burst into tears and sank onto the floor. Alicia sat down beside her and stroked her hair gently. "You must not think that my coming here in any way diminishes her memory, my dear. You will always have that——you and Matthew and your papa. But I think your papa is lonely and I am lonely, too. Together we may form a different family, with you and

Matthew and Felicia, so that we need not be so lonely any longer. After a while, when we know each other better, things will be easier for all of us. At first I will be a little lost here, you know, for all of you have been here so long and I will be new. Felicia is young and she will adapt more readily, I daresay, but I am so set in my ways that . . ."

Helen looked up curiously, the tears streaming down her cheeks. "You mean you are a little afraid to come here?"

Alicia laughed. "Yes, I guess that is what I mean."

"But we all want you to come. Papa told us he would not be happy without you," she confessed, as she wiped the tear stains away with the handkerchief Alicia offered her.

"And, you see, I would not be happy without him. But I will need help to become familiar with your ways here. I am not sure I even know everyone's name," she admitted shamefacedly.

"Oh, I shall help you, ma'am, I promise. And Matthew will, too. You have not been in the towers yet. They are our secret place, when we want to be alone. You may use them if you like," the girl offered generously.

Alicia hugged her and thanked her for her thoughtfulness. When they left the room they were holding hands and chatting about the court and how easy it would be for someone new there to become lost. Stronbert met them in the hall and invited them to go riding with him, and over his daughter's head he bestowed on Alicia the smile she always longed to produce from him.

When Stronbert's sister arrived, she had her husband and Dorothy and Rowland with her. Felicia's days were filled with the brother and sister and her endeavors to assist with her mother's wardrobe. Alicia had not told her daughter of Rowland's encounter with Tackar, though she had mentioned that Tackar was dead. Rowland appeared to have matured in the short while since he had left. He was more serious and yet more confident; he reminded Alicia somewhat of Stronbert.

Mary Clinton was not aware that her son had fought a duel. She would have been terrified. But she had come to meet her brother's fiancée and she was well pleased with Alicia. Mary did not miss the significance of the relationship between Rowland and Felicia, and she made a special effort to become acquainted with the young woman. It puzzled her that Felicia was on such easy terms with Rowland and yet held a reserve about him as well. Their banter was playful and serious by turn, and Mary found them each gazing fondly at the other when they thought they would not be observed. But there was a formality in their actions, almost a quality of pantomime, when Rowland handed Felicia up on her horse or Felicia handed him a book.

"It is almost as though they were afraid to touch each other," Mary mused to Stronbert one day. "I had not thought our society so prudish."

"You are by far too observant," Stronbert remarked dryly.

"What is that supposed to mean?"

"Nothing much. They will have to work it out on their own, Mary."

She regarded him suspiciously but said nothing further. It was her own opinion that they would need some talking to, but she had no intention of speaking with either of them. Let the girl's mother speak with her, and Mr. Clinton with Rowland. She would reserve her motherly advice for her daughter when the time came.

Lady Gorham arrived with Cassandra the same day Stephen Newton arrived with his family. All of the guests were staying at the court, which could easily handle them, though the numbers for tea became so great that the younger people escaped the daily duty unremonstrated. Alicia found it necessary to spend whole days at the court to assist with the guests and plans for the wedding. She began to look rather peaked as the wedding day approached.

Stronbert had suggested that they honeymoon at his estate near Ambleside and Alicia had agreed. It would require perhaps fifteen hours of driving and Stronbert had arranged that they spend the first night at the Griffin in Leeds. The remainder of their journey could be made the following day, or they could travel more slowly as they chose. Stronbert began to seriously doubt that Alicia would be up to making the journey in two days and sent a messenger to bespeak a room at the Royal in Kirkby Lonsdale.

"You are trying to do too much, my dear," he cautioned Alicia two days before the wedding. "Let my mother and Miss Carnworth handle more. Mr. Allerton seems to be managing very well with the shop. Your sister-in-law and my sister are anxious to help here, too. I cannot like to see you look so pale."

"I am frightened," Alicia whispered.

"Of me? Alicia, I would not have it so for the world. If you wish to cry off, you must not hesitate. It would be embarrassing for only a little while; life with me would be permanent." The pain in his eyes was evident even as he offered her a chance to draw back.

She raised a hand to touch his cheek. "Oh, no, never think I do not wish to marry you, Nigel. But I keep thinking of the inn, that first night. It will be so strange with no one about that I know but you."

"Should you like to take Mavis with you?" He was beginning to understand her anxieties.

"Yes, if I may." Alicia sounded discouraged.

"Alicia, look at me. I will not bed you that night or any night until you are ready. Do you understand me?"

"Yes," she said in a choked voice. "But what if I am never ready?"

"Is that what you are afraid of?"

"I don't know," she whispered.

Stronbert put his arms about her and held her to him, undemanding. He made no attempt to kiss her, just held her until his strength seemed to invade her. "I have promised you I will be patient."

"Yes," she mumbled against his coat, "but I am afraid that if I make you wait too long you will go . . . elsewhere."

"I see. Well, that is not like to happen, my love. I do not want to say I will wait for a month, or for a year, or for five years, because then you would feel it necessary to make some effort, possibly against your better judgment, before the time was out. I don't want you to make an effort, Alicia. When you are ready to give yourself to me, you will know. I should never have taunted you with such a bogey. I did it only to make you angry," he admitted.

She regarded him in confusion. "Why did you wish to make me angry?"

"Because I knew your pride would not allow such a situation, especially after Sir Frederick. But I thought it was the only way I could convince you to consider marrying again. When I first had the idea I thought to discard it. I should have."

"No," she replied thoughtfully, "you were right. It rankled all day when I thought of it. For the first time I considered the possibility of being your wife, truly. But now I am frightened again, with the wedding so close."

"We can postpone it, my love. You may have all the time you wish."

Alicia shook her head. "No, that would be pointless. I feel better now. But not at the inn . . ."

Stronbert laughed. "Even the best of inns are not conducive to privacy. Rest easy, my dear, I have ordered separate rooms for us."

Alicia relaxed somewhat after their discussion and was able to enjoy the ball the night before their wedding. Her brother, who had been concerned for her, felt relieved. Lady Gorham nodded her beturbaned head when Stronbert led Alicia out for the first dance. The dowager sighed, and Stronbert's children watched from the gallery with whimsical smiles. In the morning, though, Alicia felt nervous and found the sanctuary of her room did not preserve her from the well-meaning attentions of the dowager and Lady Gorham. Even Felicia did not calm her as she usually would. There was a light tap at the door after these visitations and Alicia wearily bade the caller to enter. Helen thrust her head around the door and said, "I have seen them all come and go. Do you wish to be alone for a while?"

"No, no, come in, dear," Alicia urged, holding fast to her quickly disappearing equanimity.

Helen giggled. "That was not what I meant. Shall I take you to the tower?"

Alicia's eyes sparkled with a conspiratorial glow. "I would like it of all things. Can we get there unnoticed?"

Helen nodded and led her through a bewildering maze of corridors to what looked like a heavily barred door. This was mere trimming, for the girl lifted a small latch and pushed it open. "That just puts off the adults," she said breezily. They climbed a circular stone stair until they reached a small room where there were cushions on the floor and one could look through the windows to the countryside about.

"How lovely!" Alicia exclaimed.

"I am glad you like it. Can you find your way back?"

"I think so. Do you not wish to stay?"

"You need to be alone for a moment. If Papa looks for you, I will tell him where you are, but no one else. And I will not tell him unless it is urgent," she declared stoutly.

"You are very wise, Helen. Thank you." Alicia smiled as the girl disappeared down the stairs. She sat in the tower for an hour, concentrating on the scenery. It was peaceful to see if she could follow the lanes with her eyes, and to wonder where they went. When her composure was restored, she returned, though not without losing her way several times, to her room.

Mavis smiled and began to dress her in her wedding gown. When Felicia came to help, her mother was in better spirits and they discussed the amount of time Alicia would be away when her daughter would be parted from her. They had never been apart before, but both seemed perfectly happy with the novel experience.

The wedding was brief but impressive. Alicia did not falter in her responses, but kept her eyes on Stronbert's, which were reassuring and loving. The wedding feast seemed to last for ages, but finally Alicia escaped to change to her traveling clothes. She had a chance to speak with each of those who were special to her before being bundled, almost impatiently, into the traveling chaise by her daughter and Lady Gorham, who exclaimed, "Be off. Half the fun is discussing the wedding once you are gone."

Alicia laughed and waved as they drove off. When she returned her gaze to her husband, she found him regarding her questioningly. "What is it, Nigel?"

"Where did you get to this morning? Helen said she knew, but she would not tell me."

"Ah, then it must not have been urgent," Alicia retorted. "She promised she would tell only you, and then only if it was urgent."

"Were you pestered to death?"

"I just needed a few moments to myself. Helen took me to the room in the tower."

"She is a thoughtful child, and she is fond of you." Stronbert extended a hand to her and Alicia took it. They sat thus through the drive to Leeds, sometimes speaking and frequently enjoying a companionable silence. Mavis had left earlier with the other servants and luggage and was there to meet Alicia when she was shown to her room.

Stronbert ordered supper in his room and Alicia joined him there. "We make an early start in the morning, so it is off to bed with you," he ordered when they had finished. "We can decide during the day whether to stay at Kirkby Lonsdale or proceed to the estate." He walked with her to her room and opened the door for her. "Sleep well, my love."

Alicia lifted her lips for his kiss, but he merely brushed her forehead with his and pressed her hands. She felt slightly disappointed but smiled at him and closed the door softly. The day had been too exhausting for her to spend much time thinking. Soon after her head met the pillow she was asleep.

Mavis woke her in the morning. "Milord says you are to breakfast in the parlor, ma'am, if you will. There be a nice fire burning there and his lordship, not wishing to delay for a private parlor."

Alicia joined Stronbert in the cheerful wainscoted dining parlor which was already bustling with trade; the house was a coaching inn. The passengers were being called to take their places and Alicia watched through the window as the cloths were whipped off the horses and they clattered out of the courtyard. Those who remained were discussing the hunt they were headed for while they put away enormous quantities of buttered toast and muffins, kidneys and poached eggs, steak and rashers. Alicia smiled shyly at Stronbert and denied any desire for the pigeon pie, ham, or cold boiled beef displayed in the glazed cupboard with cheeses and pastries. "Just coffee and a muffin, please."

"Did you sleep well?" Stronbert asked as he beckoned the waiter.

"Yes. And you?" Alicia felt herself blush at the insignificant question.

"Admirably," he responded with a grin.

Stronbert produced a traveling chess set during the morning's drive (Matthew insisted that you would be eager for a game) and they decided after luncheon that they would spend the night in Kirkby Lonsdale after all. It was still light when they reached the Royal, and Stronbert suggested a ride before their meal. Alicia had been given Muse as a wedding present by her husband, and both their horses had been brought with them. The ride along the river was exhilarating after the hours cooped up in the carriage. Alicia returned to the inn pink-cheeked, her eyes sparkling. Again there was supper in Stronbert's room, but this time he did not send her off to bed immediately.

He was lounging in a chair near the window and Alicia nervously paced about the room, glancing at him from time to time. His eyes were nearly closed, and she thought he was paying no attention to her.

"Are you tired, Nigel?" she asked with some asperity.

"No." He did not open his eyes.

Hesitantly she approached him and stood before him, her eyes on his face. Without opening his eyes he beckoned her to sit on his lap. When she hesitated he spoke slowly. "You have my promise, Alicia."

She flushed and nestled onto his lap, where his arms slipped about her gently, and nothing further happened. "I had thought," she whispered, "that you might wish to kiss me."

"I do." His eyes were still closed, and he made no move to do so.

Exasperated, Alicia slid her arms about his neck and kissed him. There was nothing wrong with his response. His arms tightened about her and his lips met hers eagerly. His hands held her sides, ran under her arms and near her breasts, but they made no move to touch her further. Alicia withdrew from his kiss, breathing quickly, and snuggled her head on his shoulder, her face against his neck. She was attempting to recover her calm, but the hands at her sides began a sensuous stroking, never touching her breasts but nearly so. Even through the layers of the riding habit she felt his touch quicken her pulses again until she ached for him to touch her. His hands fell still after a few minutes. She looked at him questioningly but his eyes, drat the fellow! were still closed.

Alicia shifted slightly in his lap in the hopes that he would open them. He did not. She nestled closer to him and his hands began their sensuous stroking again at her sides. When her longing for him to touch her reached an unbearable point, she murmured incoherently, but the hands remained where they were. She eyed him suspiciously, but his face was unreadable, his eyes closed. Frightened by her boldness and her desire she took each of his hands in one of hers and moved them timidly to her breasts. There they gently continued to stroke her until the mounting excitement in her body found release and she gasped with astonishment and pleasure. He held her to him for a while, then finally opened his eyes and rose to set her on her feet. "It is time you were in bed, my love," he said gently and led her to her room, where he again kissed her forehead and turned away as she entered. He did not hear her shaken whisper of, "Thank you, Nigel."

They reached the estate in early afternoon the next day. There was a small manor house of aging stone with a gabled porch that rested on a small plot entirely surrounded by trees. They spent the afternoon exploring the house and the neighborhood. After their evening meal Alicia tried her hand at the aged spinet in the drawing room. She felt awkward about ascending to bed that night and attempted to draw out the evening with playing and singing. Eventually Stronbert closed her music and held out his hand to her. She took it nervously and followed him to the bedrooms. She had been given one which connected with his. At her door he said, "Have Mavis get you ready for bed. I shall join you shortly." She nodded mutely and did as she was bid. When she lay in the bed, a candle still burning on the table beside her, she heard a light tap on the door and bade him, in a quaking voice, to enter. He smiled at her reassuringly as she watched his progress across the room. Her attempt to return the smile was ludicrously pathetic, but he made no notice. She watched horrified as he took off his dressing gown and laid it over a chair. He was wearing a nightshirt. As he pulled back the cover to join her in bed she mumbled, "Nigel, I . . ."

"Hush. Do not make me repeat myself, Alicia," he said patiently. "I have promised that I will not rush you, nor will I. Tonight is no different than last night. You must learn to trust me, love. I can see no possibility of your overcoming your fears if we have no contact whatsoever, if you stay in one room and I in another. Just lie by me and relax." He patted the bed beside him, since she had shrunk unconsciously to the other side as he entered.

Alicia wiggled over until she barely touched him and lay rigid. She took the opportunity to study the ceiling of her bedroom. Stronbert smiled at her unobserving face and blew out the candle. He talked to her for a while of the estate and the people he had met in the neighborhood; he did not come there often, for he had a good man to run the place. She asked a question now and then, her voice tense and high pitched, much as she tried to control it. When there had been silence for some time, he leaned over and kissed her lips. "Good night, Alicia. Sleep well."

She lay by him then in the dark feeling foolish and afraid. He turned his back and pressed lightly against her side. When he made no further move, she rolled onto her side away from him, but touching him lightly. He fell asleep, and she could tell, and she became inexplicably angry. It was all very well for him to be patient, she thought, but he need not be such a saint about it. He might have held me for a minute, like last night. No, perhaps in bed that would not have been wise. She became aware of the light nightdress she wore, and the nightshirt which covered his naked body. She blushed in the dark and concentrated on falling asleep.

For a long time she stared at the tall wardrobe which now contained her clothes. Then she pleated the sheets with her fingers and thumped her pillow into obedience.

She changed her position again so that she was lying on her back. Restless that way, she turned on her other side, toward her husband, and eased herself against him. She listened carefully for any change in his breathing, but could detect none. Comfortable at last, she fell asleep against him.

Sometime during the night Alicia became aware of a subtle change in her body. The contact with her husband had warmed and comforted her, but it had done more. She realized that her nightdress had ridden up, as had his nightshirt, and that her bare skin was in contact with his from the waist down. For a moment she lay very still listening to his breathing; he appeared to be asleep. She laid a hand tentatively on his hip, felt the warm skin beneath her fingers. At the same time she became conscious of her breasts against his back through the two layers of material. She longed for his touch on them, and pressed herself tighter against him. The hand on his hip was firmly enclosed by one of his and she gave a gasp of fright.

Alicia lay rigid for a few moments, but gradually relaxed as his hand merely stroked hers. He brought it to his lips and kissed it, a finger at a time, his thumb continuing to stroke the palm. Gradually he shifted onto his back so that he could look at her. Alicia's eyes were wide and regarded him gravely. He lifted himself onto an elbow and bent to kiss her. At first she made no response and he started to lie back, but she brought his head to her again and kissed him eagerly. His hands returned to the spot under her arms, near her breasts, and he began the sensuous stroking. Her murmur again had no effect on the placement of his hands and she once again moved them to her breasts.

Nigel did not stroke her then but, holding her eyes with his, lifted his hands to untie the bow at her neck. Her faint gasp of protest he responded to by kissing her forehead and turning over on his back, not touching her. Alicia could have cried with vexation. Slowly she wriggled out of the nightdress and pushed it onto the floor. He turned to her again and she could see his smile even in the dark room. "You are laughing at me," she whispered fiercely.

"Never," he replied, covering her lips with his. His hands found the soft skin of her breasts and a shiver ran through her, but it was of anticipation and not of fright. His hands explored her body then, as she clung to him. Slowly, patiently he excited and reassured her until she no longer cared that she was vulnerable. The knowledge that he loved her and would never hurt her now became something that she could feel as well as believe. And when his warm brown eyes regarded her inquiringly, she nodded and murmured, "I love you, Nigel." He was well rewarded for his patience; her response was everything either of them could have hoped.

Alicia felt her cheeks wet with the tears of relief and joy. Nigel kissed them away and held her close to him. "Will it always be like that?" she asked wonderingly.

"No," he admitted. "But sometimes. I hope often. You are a very sensuous woman, my love."

"Do you mind?"

Nigel laughed until his body shook against hers. "No, dear, I am very pleased."

"I think I may still be afraid sometimes," she confessed.

"Yes, for a while, but that will pass." He let her go for a minute then and reached over to strike a flint and light the candle. She shyly pulled the cover about her, as he pulled his nightshirt over his head and tossed it to the floor. He shook his head when he saw her clutching the cover and gently removed it from her fingers. "Do not deny me the pleasure of seeing you, Alicia. I know it is difficult, but better now when you have experienced the pleasure your body has to offer than in the morning when it will be but a memory."

Alicia blushed under his gaze but did not turn her head away. He tickled her feet and she reciprocated by tickling him under his arms. Their match soon degenerated into a pillow fight and when Alicia lay back exhausted, she was aware that she had in the course of it been exposed to his naked body. "How could you know that would be even harder?" she whispered.

"It just is," he replied evenly. He put out the candle then and lay next to her in bed. "When you feel comfortable about . . . everything, I hope you will speak with Felicia. Rowland wishes to marry her, you know, and if she can see that you have left your bad experiences behind, she may be amenable. I think she cares for him."

"Yes, I am sure she does. You would approve of such a match?"

"Certainly, but it has nothing to do with me. My sister already suspects what is going forward and she seems well pleased. He is a good lad, Alicia."

"I know," she mumbled sleepily. "He reminds me of you."

Nigel laughed and kissed her. "Go to sleep, love. I have plans for you tomorrow."

CHAPTER TWENTY-FOUR

"Would you mind if I join the hunt tomorrow, love?" Nigel asked a week later as they lay in bed. "It's likely to be the last of the season and I seem to have been too occupied this winter to participate. I won't go if you'd rather I did not."

Alicia regarded him fondly. "Poor dear, you have spent the whole of the season too immersed in my problems to have any fun."

"I have had a great deal of fun," he retorted, touching her nose. "Would you like to come?"

"No, thank you, but I hope you will go. I have a stack of letters to answer, and I never seem to find the time when you are with me."

With a sigh he murmured, "And here I thought you treasured every moment we shared."

"I must accustom myself to a few moments from your side," she declared virtuously.

"But not until morning," he laughed as he gathered her into his arms.

Alicia awoke for the first time since they had arrived at the estate to find him gone from the bed, and puzzled for a moment over his disappearance. When she remembered that he was to join the hunt that morning, she arose leisurely and rang for Mavis. "I shall have tea and toast here, Mavis, please and if you will, build up the fire. I think I shall write my letters at the escritoire." The snow was falling outside and she moved to the window where she caught a distant glimpse of scarlet coats through a break in the trees. Thinking that she would take a walk later in the snowy landscape, she picked up Felicia's letter and reread it. Strange to be away from her, she mused, but she is growing up. The time will come . . . Well, there was no need to think of that now.

When she had spent an hour diligently scribbling answers to the half dozen letters before her, she was interrupted by a knock at the door.

"Begging your pardon, ma'am," Mavis said, "but a Mr. and Mrs. Gray have come to call. The housekeeper says they are acquainted with his lordship and are neighbors."

"Very well, Mavis. Have them put in the front parlor and I shall be with them directly."

As she entered the room, Alicia surveyed the middle-aged couple with interest. They had not had many callers and she was curious about their neighbors. The woman was tall and angular, in contrast to her short and stocky husband. There was a look of long-suffering about Mrs. Gray's eyes which was not entirely dissipated by her courteous smile.

"I hope we do not intrude, Lady Stronbert. It is so seldom that Lord Stronbert visits Ambleside and we wished to offer our felicitations on your marriage."

"That is kind of you, Mrs. Gray. Unfortunately my husband is out this morning, but I hope you will have tea with me."

Mr. Gray entered the conversation with boisterous alacrity. "Very thoughtful of you, my lady! Just the thing on a cold day! Quite a chilly ride over here, you know. Our estate is some five miles to the north, don't you see? Didn't think to have hot bricks for such a short journey, but it would not have been amiss, eh, Mrs. Gray?"

His wife murmured her assent as Alicia pulled the bell cord. "I trust you find yourself comfortable here.

Our weather is so lovely in the summer that it seems a pity for you to visit here first when it's so miserable out."

"Oh, I enjoy the snow," Alicia assured her before turning to advise the footman that they would have a tea tray. "I have not traveled much and I find the area lovely."

"That it is!" boomed Mr. Gray. "No spot in all England to match it for my money!" No one could summon up more than a mumbled assent, so he proceeded, "I understand you come from Scarborough-way, Lady Stronbert."

Surprised, Alicia agreed that she had lived there many years.

"And you've a charming daughter from your previous marriage?"

Although Alicia tried to tell herself that there was no cause for it, she experienced a stab of alarm. How did this man know so much about her? His wife wore a disapproving expression, but he paid no heed to it. "Yes, I have a daughter Felicia who is sixteen."

"Yes, indeed. Mrs. Gray and I have not been blessed with children, and we regret it, I assure you. No one to carry on the name, and all that. A great comfort, children. And I imagine you especially are aware of that."

This time Alicia did not attempt to ignore the alarm that gripped her. The man was purposely alluding to Sir Frederick's desertion of her, and she had no doubt that he would manage to inquire into her shop next if she did not immediately turn the conversation. Very clearly she saw the words Tackar had penned to any number of people in England before his death, and she could easily believe that Mr. Gray had seen or heard of them. How could she have been so stupid as to believe that Nigel's efforts to erase the rumor would be entirely effective? Somehow it had not mattered in Tetterton, and at the court. But outside her narrow boundaries people could still believe, and spread, the gossip.

She pointedly turned to Mrs. Gray, who had suffered through her husband's remarks uneasily. "My husband has joined the hunt this morning. He asked me if I should like to go, but I had some letters to write, and I have never hunted myself. Are there ladies in the neighborhood who do?"

Apparently Mr. Gray thought himself better equipped to answer than his wife. "Not many. The occasional hoyden joins the field, but the ladies are frowned on. Can't keep up, and if they do they are forever overriding the hounds."

A footman appeared with a silver tray laden with the tea apparatus and a plate of biscuits. Relieved, Alicia began to pour out for her guests as she offered some casual remarks on the merits of Gunpowder and Pekoe over Congou and Souchong.

"I have the greatest apprehension, myself, of green tea, Lady Stronbert. A slow poison, I assure you, and bound to destroy the nerves. Of course, each to his own, but I will not have it in my home." Mrs. Gray seemed as eager as Alicia to keep their discourse on the most mundane level, and though Mr. Gray not infrequently attempted to enter the conversation with such remarks as "What a blessing your poor daughter should now have the marquis as her guardian!" or "It will be a relief for you to live out of town, without all the noise and shops about, after being in that market town, Lady Stronbert," he was consistently ignored.

Refusing a second cup of tea, Mrs. Gray rose and said firmly, "We must be leaving, Mr. Gray. I hope you will convey our best wishes to your husband, Lady Stronbert."

Alicia assured her that she would; she felt sorry for the woman, who obviously cringed at her husband's rude conduct. Eager to see the two of them from the house, Alicia incautiously offered Mr. Gray her hand in parting. He grasped it tightly in his pudgy hand and squeezed it familiarly, at the same time offering a knowing wink. Since Mrs. Gray had preceded him and was out of earshot, Alicia quelled him with a cold stare and said softly, "We will not see you again, sir. You would do well not to believe every malicious bit of gossip to come your way. It does you no credit, and my husband less."

An angry flush rose to his cheeks, but he made no reply as he stomped after his wife. Alicia watched the door close behind them before she seated herself once more on the sofa. Her head had begun to pound and she knew that she should lie down on her bed, but she had to think about what this meant—to her, to Nigel, to Felicia. Of course, few were as ill-mannered as Mr. Gray; she was unlikely to be confronted with such a blatant display if she remained at the court. And Nigel, well, she could not imagine anyone having the nerve to pull their tricks with him. He was above reproach in her eyes, and she did not doubt that anyone who met him would feel the same. But Felicia, what weapons had she to fight such slander? Sooner or later she would be faced with a wider world than Tetterton, and could Alicia protect her in such a world?

This was not the time to worry over such problems —not on her honeymoon. By the time Felicia was old enough to venture beyond her new home perhaps sufficient time would have passed to eradicate any lingering rumor. It would not be fair to burden Nigel with the problem. When she thought of all the efforts he had made on her behalf in the last few months, she was ashamed to even contemplate mentioning the matter. Ridiculous to be so upset by Mr. Gray—uncouth and disagreeable as he was. What she needed was to clear her head, and a brisk walk outdoors was the perfect remedy.

Nigel rode up to find her tramping through the snow in a fur-trimmed scarlet mantle, her cheeks rosy from the cold. She turned eagerly at the sound of hoofbeats and smiled up at him. "I thought you would be longer. Did you have a successful morning?"

He swung himself down from his horse and kissed her cheek. "Not bad. There's too much woodland for really good sport."

"But did you get the fox?" she asked anxiously.

"Lord, no!" he laughed. "With all these woods for cover? A few of the men tried to tell me they sometimes do run one to ground, but I think it is only a glorious fantasy. Have you been worrying about the poor fox?" he quizzed her, laughter twinkling in his eyes.

"Actually I had not thought of it at all until you rode up. Foxes do a great deal of damage to the farms, no doubt, but it seems grossly unfair for a pack of hounds and dozens of riders to chase one poor little fellow."

"So it does, my love, but the real sport is in the ride—over the hedgerows and fences."

Alicia shook the snow from the hem of her mantle as she said, "We had some callers this morning, a Mr. and Mrs. Gray."

"I remember them," he replied with a slight frown. "Not a particularly endearing couple, as I recall. I hope they did not bore you."

"They did not stay long. You must be famished. Shall I order a luncheon?"

Although he detected a slight undercurrent of disquiet in her, Nigel dismissed the thought when she smiled up at him, pink-cheeked and bright-eyed. "If you will, Alicia. I won't be a moment in the stables."

Determined to forget the morning's less agreeable incident, Alicia chatted cheerfully over their meal. While her husband discussed estate matters with his agent, she finished several more letters, and rode out with him late in the afternoon. Still unable to shake her worries, she found it difficult to sustain a conversation at dinner and Nigel asked gently, "Are you missing Felicia, my love?"

"Why, no . . . well, perhaps a bit. Her letter was delightful and it is rather lowering to think that she goes on perfectly well without me." Alicia assumed a mock distress, which did not entirely satisfy her husband, but he made no comment.

Instead of asking her to play for him, he suggested that he read to her. "I found Cowper's *Winter Evening* in the library. We have all six books of *The Task* at the court, but this is the only one I could find here. Certainly the most appropriate, in any case."

Charmed by the exquisite description and the wealth of kindliness that flowed through the work, Alicia relaxed in the shelter of his arm, and watched the snow falling beyond the windows, until she fell asleep. For some time Nigel gazed down at the lovely face, with the long eyelashes fringing her cheeks and the lips soft in repose. Then he lifted her in his arms, and she snuggled sleepily against him while he carried her to her room.

Mavis was waiting there but he said, "I'll see to her. She will call you in the morning." Alone, he placed her on the bed and undressed her like a child, awkwardly shifting each arm and leg as she murmured unintelligibly. At last he managed to slip the nightdress over her and tuck her under the covers before he went to his dressing room. When he returned and slipped carefully into her bed he was surprised to find her awake.

She had had a nightmare. Once again she had been seated at her dining table in Tetterton with Francis Tackar seated opposite. The bonnet was no longer lying on the table, but she was seated naked before his gaze as he crunched fiercely at the partridge bones. He kept singing, "The bonnet, the bonnet, bring on the bonnet," and Mr. Gray had appeared with the bonnet perched precariously on his head. From beneath the floppy brim he had ogled Alicia and protested, "*I* have the bonnet now. She is mine to do with as I wish. Don't be so greedy; you can have the other one. A child needs a guardian. That's it, you shall be her guardian. Children should be a comfort; she will be a comfort to you. *This* one is mine." And he had reached out his pudgy hand to fondle her.

Confused, and with her brain still fogged by the dream, Alicia shrank away from Nigel as he climbed in beside her. An uncontrollable shiver shook her body.

"Are you cold, love? Shall I build up the fire?" he asked gently.

"No. No, I am fine." She blinked nervously at him as he took her hand.

"You're as cold as ice! Let me warm you." When he held her to him he was aware of her rigidity and he stroked her hair to calm her. Although she warmed from his contact, she did not relax in his arms. "Are you upset, Alicia?"

Still in the grip of the fear from her dream, she shook her head, more to reassure herself than in answer to him. "I am ready," she whispered.

"For what?"

"To oblige you."

Nigel took her by the shoulders and held her away from him. "Don't you *ever* do that again! Never, do you hear, Alicia?"

"Do what?" she asked on a sob. "What have I done?" Bewildered, and hurt by his anger, she could not restrain the tears that crept down her cheeks.

"Forgive me, love, for startling you." He cradled her in his arms and rocked her until the tears dried. "Do you think I cannot tell when you are frightened, Alicia? Am I so demanding that you must offer yourself to me when you don't want to?"

"I wanted to please you," she choked.

"You would better please me by telling me what has upset you, my love."

"I had a dream . . . about Mr. Tackar and Mr. Gray."

"Gray? Just what happened here this morning, Alicia?"

Haltingly she repeated the remarks Mr. Gray had made. "It does not sound like much, I know, but I could tell that he had his information from those odious letters. He made my skin crawl, Nigel. I do not mind so much for myself, but Felicia. She will have to face people one day who will believe those lies."

"And did you think to hide away at the court, Alicia?" he asked seriously. "I have done what I could to banish the gossip, but it will be necessary for you to be seen to set matters straight."

"I don't care what they say about me, Nigel."

"Well, I do." The unbending steel was in his voice, though his hand continued to stroke her hair. "It is my intention to have you and Felicia presented at a drawing room this spring."

"You never said so! Nigel, I have never even been to London. Really, there is no need."

"It is important to me, Alicia. I have my own name to protect as well as yours. You must not forget my children. What scandal attaches to my name is inherited by them."

"Then of course we shall go. I am ashamed that I did not think beyond myself." A flush rose to her cheeks, but she met his eyes earnestly. "I would do anything in my power to help you and the children. For so long there has just been Felicia, and I am not accustomed to my new family as yet. You will have to remind me when I am selfish. I don't mean to be."

"Dear Lord, Alicia, I would that you knew *how* to be selfish!" He rumpled the auburn hair affectionately. "You must not think of going to London as purely a trial. There are delights to be found there that you could have nowhere else, and the sooner you are accepted there the more you will enjoy them. Not for the world would I hide you away at the court when I know what pleasure you will find in the sights and the shops, the balls and the theater."

"Felicia will be seventeen in March; that is young for her to come out."

"Under the circumstances it is necessary, and I believe she won't mind. Do you feel easier now, love?"

"Yes, Nigel, but I am exhausted," she replied tartly.

"Just so," he murmured with a grin. "Good night, my dear."

CHAPTER TWENTY-FIVE

"I am too old to be jauntering off to London, Nigel," his mother claimed pathetically. "The life here is perfectly suited to me at my advanced years. What need have you for me to accompany you and Alicia to town? I would be *de trop*."

He regarded his mother's woeful countenance with fond exasperation. "We are going to bring Felicia out, Mother. You will know precisely how to go about it. You cannot expect Alicia to fathom the workings of London society. She has never been there."

"The girl is young; I see no reason why you should not wait until next year when Alicia will have had a chance to familiarize herself with the pattern."

Nigel drew his chair closer to hers and commanded her attention with his penetrating gaze. "I need your help, Mother. No one but you can provide quite the same protection for my wife and her daughter."

"Protection? Whatever are you talking about, Nigel?"

"I suppose you will need to know the whole story if you are to come with us, but I have no intention of telling you unless you plan to do so."

Her curiosity piqued, the dowager grumbled, "If you do indeed need my assistance, I will of course accommodate you." Her eyes widened as he related the events of the past few months, with some information on Alicia's history before she arrived in Tetterton. The light of battle grew in her eyes, and she proclaimed,

"The poor dear! I had no idea. You might have told me."

"No, but I tell you now because you will need to know what we face. Alicia is especially concerned for her daughter. I want no snubs or smirks to mar her visit. It will mean a very careful selection of guests at first, until the truth is established. I rely on you for that, Mother."

"You may safely do so," the dowager replied enthusiastically, already turning over in her mind the most propitious plan of attack. Her new daughter-in-law had accepted the management of the house from the dowager with unusual consideration and frequent applications for advice, but the old woman could not deceive herself that her assistance was great. Alicia was not unfamiliar with the running of a house, although Katterly Grange could not compare in size or complexity with the court. But here was something the dowager alone could accomplish, and she was grateful for the opportunity. "Leave everything to me, Nigel. No breath of scandal shall attach to our name or that of your wife and Felicia, I promise you."

In London the dowager had started her program with a dinner followed by cards, an evening which was notable for its quiet elegance. Amongst the guests were to be found nodding matriarchs of her own age, a larger number of couples of her son's, and a sprinkling of younger people. These last included one of the Maple girls, as well as Charles March and his sister. Nigel had had no objection to Rowland's coming to town with them, as he was still at the court when the marquis and Alicia returned from their honeymoon. The young man's attentions to Felicia continued steadily if less conspicuously in town.

"Let her spread her wings a bit, Rowland," Nigel had urged. "She will look to you for support when she needs it, and appreciate your being there, but this is a time for her to make her own place in society, to find new friends."

Rowland did not protest at this pronouncement as he might have done several months previously. Although he knew his own mind, and had for some time, he agreed that Felicia should enjoy the freedom of learning hers. The bond between them had strengthened, but he could not be sure that she did not view him as a brother since he had made no advance toward her after the attempted rape. He was content for the time being to be around when she needed him.

As Charles March approached him during the card party, Rowland smiled ruefully. "I hope I told you how much I appreciated your coming to France with me. The journey home was a bit hazy."

"I'm just glad you were around to make the journey home," his friend retorted, "and, yes, you thanked me, as did your uncle." His gaze wandered to where Felicia sat with his sister. "She doesn't know anything about the duel or the letters?"

"No. I trust you will do what you can to see she is not bothered by any whisper of that gossip."

"Glad to do what I can, Rowland. Are you still seeing that friend of your uncle's?"

"No, I do not intend to resume the connection."

"Mind introducing me to her?" March asked with an impudent grin.

Rowland laughed. "I'll take it under consideration. She's a very gentle lady, Charles."

"I can be a very gentle man, Rowland," his friend retorted.

"Then you shall have an introduction." Rowland noticed that Felicia had turned her gaze to him, and he smiled in return. "Shall we join your sister and Miss Coombs?"

The court dresses chosen by Alicia and her daughter were flattering, but unwieldy. The night before their presentation Felicia practiced walking gracefully and curtsying in the hooped skirt. "Will that do, Mama?"

"Yes, love, even the queen will be enchanted," her mother assured her, laughter dancing in her eyes.

"How can you jest with me? I have never been so nervous. What if I trip or am tongue-tied? I would disgrace you and Nigel."

"Never think it. You would not be the first, in any case. Have you not been attending to the dowager's tales of disaster at presentations?"

"Yes, and I can picture myself committing every *faux pas* she has mentioned," Felicia groaned.

"But you won't, love. Remember that I am in the same position. Think instead of your ball; that should cheer you."

"I cannot see why! The dowager has spent hours instructing me in how I should behave, and I know I shall not remember the half of it. Every moment I am not with Samantha Maple or Lucy March she seeks me out and bombards me with etiquette."

"You are not alone." Her mother gave a lamentable sigh. "She finds my education as lacking as your own. I have no doubt she means well, but I find myself at the theater unable to attend to the performance because her voice is echoing in my ear, 'And never mention Methodism to Lady Rumtouch or you will not be quit of her for an hour.' I am sure I have never met Lady Rumtouch and could well live my life without the pleasure!"

Felicia giggled. "She's probably the one who fell asleep at the Maples' on Tuesday—and snored."

"No, no, I feel sure that was Lady Lowther. Seriously, love, do you not look forward to the ball?"

"Oh, yes. Several gentlemen have already asked me to save a set for them. I am to open the ball with Nigel, of course, but Rowland has insisted that I be his partner for the second set." Her eyes glowed with happiness as she curtsied to an imaginary partner and accepted his arm, her head held high. Suddenly she stopped and asked, "Is it pleasant to be kissed, Mama?"

"Very, my dear, so long as you like the man who is kissing you. I have meant to speak with you again about men. When we talked before, I had nothing but bad experiences to speak from. It is otherwise now, Felicia. Intimacy can be a truly joyous expression of love, and I hope you will not fear it. If your husband is understanding and considerate, you need feel no embarrassment or uncertainty, but rather a marvelous physical release and spiritual joining."

"I am so happy for you, Mama," Felicia said simply as she hugged her mother. "All the men here treat me just as they ought, you know, and I have come to believe that there are few like Mr. Tackar. I would not want just anyone to . . . to kiss me, but I am not so frightened at the thought anymore."

"You may always come to me with your fears, Felicia. It is not unnatural to be nervous of what you have not experienced." Alicia kissed her daughter's forehead and asked, "Shall I have Mavis come to you now?"

The ballroom occupied the entire rear portion of the second floor, and it was aglitter with candlelight and the scent of the spring flowers that adorned every possible niche. The dowager surveyed the room and its occupants with satisfaction, her pleasure heightened by her son's words of praise earlier in the evening. Alicia, too, had hugged the older woman and exclaimed, "It is truly magnificent! How can I thank you, ma'am?"

"By calling me Evelyn," she had responded abruptly, "and remembering what I have told you."

"I shall do my best, Evelyn." Alicia was aware of the affection that the dowager held for her under her typically gruff manner. "You have made our stay a pleasure, and I had feared it. I am grateful to you."

The dowager waved aside her thanks with an awkward gesture. "The vast numbers tonight make it impossible to assure you complete protection from that wretched rumor, my dear. Keep a sharp eye for any discomfort to your daughter."

Alicia was reminded of her words as she watched her daughter going down the set on the arm of a young man she had only met that evening. Felicia's countenance, which had been glowing a moment earlier, was now set rigidly, and she stumbled slightly in the steps. Alarmed, Alicia cast her eyes about the room for Nigel and with relief saw him approaching the set from one direction, and Rowland from another. A glance was exchanged between the two before they reached her daughter. Without the least commotion, and almost before she was aware of the change, the young man was leaving the floor with Nigel, and Rowland had taken his place in the set. The dance floor was crowded and the dancing spirited; no notice seemed to be taken of the incident. Alicia found the dowager's eyes on her and watched the older woman's nod of satisfaction.

When Nigel appeared at her side, she turned to him questioningly. "The Honorable Thomas Morgan has been called away rather suddenly," he remarked dryly. "I do not think he will approach your daughter again."

"Do you know what he said to her?"

"No, but it could not have been much considering their surroundings. She will receive a note of apology from him tomorrow."

"I hope it does not spoil her evening. She was feeling much more easy about men when we talked the other day. Your mother has arranged our entertainments so carefully that no previous cloud has darkened them, but she warned me that she could not warrant that tonight would be as secure with this press of people." She turned to observe Felicia, who smiled confidently up at Rowland as he led her toward them. By the time they arrived they were bickering good-naturedly.

"Rowland says it does not count as a dance, so

that he should still be allowed one other this evening," Felicia explained.

"And Felicia claims that the dowager instructed her that she must not stand up with anyone more than twice in the evening, so that I have used up my quota," he returned mournfully.

Their laughing appeal to Alicia calmed her fears and she said judiciously, "I think, as you did not enter the dance with him, that he may have his second dance, but I would advise that it be later in the evening."

"There. You see, Felicia? Not the least need to question my judgment," Rowland admonished her with a grin.

Felicia regarded him almost shyly. "Then in future I shan't, sir."

As he watched the young people move away, Nigel remarked, "She is growing up, my love."

"I know, and it is suddenly happening too fast." Her gaze rested proudly on her daughter. "Your mother must be pleased with her tonight; all her lessons have been well applied. Thank you for acting so quickly, Nigel, for she seems to have disregarded the incident."

"I doubt either of you will be much troubled in the future, Alicia. Are you glad we came to London?" he asked teasingly.

"You know I am, wretched fellow, but I look forward to returning to the court, too. After all this bustle I will enjoy settling into a normal life with you and the children."

"And Rowland, and my mother, and Miss Carnworth, and the general, and . . ."

CHAPTER TWENTY-SIX

The brilliant June sunlight streamed through the windows of the folly, a gothic jumble of bricks in a state of organized decay. Felicia surveyed the distant buildings of the court fondly, then turned to Rowland with a mischievous smile. "Mama is not to be a shopowner any longer, you know. Mr. Dean, bless his soul, left his estate to Mr. Allerton, who is to purchase it from Mama."

"Thank God," Rowland replied fervently, his eyes dancing in the light. "Now it will not be necessary for me to marry the daughter of a shopowner."

Felicia regarded him wonderingly as he took her unresisting hand. His eyes became serious as he asked, "You will marry me, will you not, Felicia?"

"I . . . I should like to, Rowland, for I cannot bear to think of a life without you. But I am only turned seventeen and Mama will think I am too young."

"We will wait a year, if they wish it. Uncle Nigel does not seem to mind that I have moved into the court more or less permanently."

"He is the most accommodating man. Do you know he has invited my oldest cousin to come here with an eye to teaching him the management of his estate near Ambleside?"

"Felicia, you are straying from the subject," Rowland pointed out gently. "Will you . . . can you marry me next year?"

"Yes," she said softly, "of course I can."

"I know what happened last autumn." His eyes held

hers as she involuntarily tried to withdraw her hand from his clasp. "No, there is no need for you to be afraid of me, ever, Felicia."

"I am not afraid, Rowland, I am ashamed," she murmured as she turned her head away.

"There is even less reason for that. Will you come with me to speak with your mother and my uncle?"

She nodded mutely and allowed him to assist her onto Dancer. Her hopes, her dreams, were being fulfilled, but the June day somehow did not seem as bright as it had. The young man riding beside her, familiar as he had become, was after all a stranger, who had for months known of her humiliation and not revealed his knowledge. It would have been horrid if he had, of course; she could not have borne that. But all his consideration was based on his knowledge. She reviewed in her mind the countless times he had avoided touching her, asked her permission to hand her onto her mount. How could she not have realized that he knew?

Alicia and Nigel were seated companionably in the summer parlor discussing the visit of her nephew. They had appropriated the room for their own use, a desire which was respected by the residents of the court. As it was unusual for anyone to seek admission to their sanctuary, Nigel raised his brows curiously at the tap on the door, but called, "Come."

The young people who entered displayed none of the radiance that might have been expected in a newly engaged couple. Felicia smiled hesitantly at her mother, but her overall demeanor was worried, while Rowland sought his uncle's eyes anxiously. "I have asked Felicia to marry me, sir, and she has accepted." He turned to Alicia and said gravely, "We hope to have your approval, ma'am, and are prepared to wait a year if you think it necessary."

The news was no real surprise to Alicia, but her daughter's expression certainly was. She had expected that unbounded joy would accompany such an announcement, for, although Felicia did not speak of her feelings toward Rowland, ever since the ball she had chosen his company over that of every other young man who had sought her favor. And Felicia's acceptance of Rowland's touch had become quite routine and unconscious, or so her mother had thought. Concerned, Alicia turned to Nigel for direction, and he appeared as troubled as she.

"Sit down, if you will," he suggested calmly, with a reassuring smile to his wife. "Perhaps we could get to the source of this unalleviated gloom. I myself remember feeling quite elated when your mother agreed to marry me, Felicia."

The girl lowered her eyes and spoke softly, her hands folded anxiously in her lap. "He knows about what happened . . . in the autumn."

"Yes, I told him, my dear, to forestall his upsetting you in any way inadvertently. I am sure he told no one else," Nigel offered, and there was a quick, confirming nod from his nephew.

"But I didn't know that he knew," she protested, with a pleading look at her mother. "Can't you see, Mama? He has treated me differently, and I did not even know!"

Rowland gave a helpless gesture and addressed Alicia earnestly. "I cannot see what difference that makes, for I could not have done otherwise."

"I was equally upset when I learned that your uncle was my partner in the shop," Alicia informed him ruefully as she took her daughter's hand. "Felicia, love, Rowland's protection of you would not have been of any use if he had not been able to disguise his knowledge. I agreed to Nigel telling him at the time so that you might not be overset by any innocent exchange. You must not feel deceived, for Rowland heeded the advice out of his very real concern for you."

While Felicia brightened somewhat under her mother's persuasion, Rowland grew more restive. At length he said abruptly, "I brought Felicia to you for a different reason, actually. I cannot leave her in ignorance any longer of . . . what happened in Paris." His eyes entreated his uncle for support.

"No, I suppose not," Nigel said thoughtfully.

Rowland paced the length of the room, aware of Felicia's gaze on him. He returned to take her hands as he crouched in front of her. "I wanted you to be with your mother when I told you, my love. If you cannot bring yourself to marry me, I will understand, but I could not just pretend that it never happened."

He seemed unable to proceed and Alicia, with a weighty sigh, murmured, "She is but a child, Nigel."

"No, love, she must become a woman now, for she is contemplating marriage."

Felicia followed their remarks curiously and studied Rowland with alarm. "What is it that I should know, Rowland, that everyone else knows?"

"After Mr. Tackar tried to burn the shop, he went to Paris. Letters from him were received by a number of people in London, in which he told lies about you and your mother and my uncle. I could not allow such a matter to pass; it would have been unthinkable." His voice pleaded with her to understand. "And so I went there and I fought a duel with him. It was a matter of honor, Felicia. I went intending to kill him, and I did."

She stared at him incredulously. "I always thought Nigel must have killed him. He was away at that time."

Alicia interposed. "Nigel met Tackar the day after he was at our cottage, and Tackar was seriously wounded. But Nigel did go to Paris to meet him again, only to find that Rowland had preceded him."

"I see," Felicia said softly.

"My outrage and my anger carried me through the duel," Rowland admitted. "Afterward I felt wretched —not the wound, you understand, but that I had killed a man. You must not think that I take it lightly,

Felicia, for I have never done anything so dreadful in my life. It is all very well to say that he did not deserve to live, which is true. It is another matter to have killed him myself."

Into the silence which followed Rowland's remarks, his uncle spoke. "By law he would have been guilty of a capital crime, had he been prosecuted. Tackar was familiar with a gentleman's code of honor, and chose not to abide by it. Doubtless the honorable course it not always the easiest to follow, Rowland, but under the circumstances, as I told you at the time, you had no choice."

"I could have aimed to wound him."

"Which would have served no purpose at all," his uncle replied firmly. "You do not put your life in jeopardy with such a scoundrel to no end. You could as easily have been killed."

Felicia's face paled at the thought and she clutched at Rowland's hand. "I would not have let you do it! Not because you killed him. I can feel no remorse for him, awful as that may sound. He deserved to die, and though I know it is hard for you to reconcile yourself to killing him, I am not horrified that you have done so. But you should not have taken such a chance to protect my name. My mother has taught me that I can hold my head high no matter what others say of me."

"Such a pity that men cannot see it that way," Alicia added pungently, with a grimace at Nigel. "They must be forever charging at windmills in defense of our honor." She shook her head but continued sadly, "Unfortunately there is some justification of their attitude. A ruined reputation can prove the end of a young woman who has no means to refute it. Nigel and Rowland quite effectively managed to do so in this case, Felicia, and I hope you will not think unkindly of Rowland for doing what he felt he must."

"No, of course not," the girl replied softly. She

raised a hand to touch Rowland's face tenderly. "I am proud that you thought enough of me to undertake such a dreadful task, my love."

When Rowland bent forward to kiss her, Nigel grasped his wife's hand and hurriedly drew her from the room. They wandered hand in hand to the solarium where they gazed over the lush lawns and flower borders.

"I suppose he had to tell her," Alicia said wistfully.

"Yes, love, he did. In his eyes she had the right to refuse him for his actions. You must let her become a woman, Alicia. With the strength you have given her, she can help him share his burden." Nigel pulled her to him, to the astonished amusement of the gardener working in the flower beds, and kissed her gently.

"I have protected her since she was a baby," Alicia sighed.

"It is time you let Rowland do so, my dear."

"Yes, I promise I shall." She looked up to see his very special smile and asked, "You will help me?"

"Yes, love, I will help you."